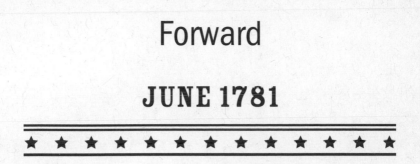

Forward

JUNE 1781

★ ★ ★ ★ ★ ★ ★ ★ ★ ★ ★ ★ ★ ★ ★

After six long years battling for independence, America's spirit was at an all-time low. There had been few patriot victories against the powerful British forces. George Washington and the ragtag Continental Army, along with French General Rochambeau and his troops, were camped outside of New York in Dobbs Ferry, hoping for one last chance to defeat redcoat General Clinton and gain control of the north. British General Cornwallis and the notorious Colonel Banastre Tarleton were rampaging through the southern colonies, burning crops, stealing livestock, destroying towns, and smashing any patriot resistance they met. Desertion was rampant, the Continental Congress bankrupt, and the dollar was worthless. America needed a miracle, and time was running out.

1

ROANOKE RIVER, VIRGINIA

★ ★ ★ ★ ★ ★ ★ ★ ★ ★ ★ ★ ★ ★ ★

William! No!" screamed his mother, Martha, as William broke out of her grasp. He leaped from the porch of their farmhouse and ran toward his brother, who stood surrounded by redcoats on horseback over by the freshly plowed field at the edge of the woods. "Dear God! William!"

Still dressed in her yellow dress and white bonnet, her arms covered in flour, she bent down to help her burly husband, Benjamin Tuck, who lay still after being shot in the leg by a soldier of the British procurement troops. Bo, the old family bloodhound, howled from the end of his rope, which was tied to the front stoop.

"Asher!" cried William. He raced along the wooden fence that held the family livestock, past two British supply wagons. Four black men, dressed in shirts with the words "We Are Free" written in red paint across their fronts, had begun to slaughter the Tucks' hogs and chickens and load the carcasses. Former slaves promised their freedom by the

British, they went about their bloody business with axes and clubs.

William ran as fast as his legs could carry him across the field, past the bodies of three British soldiers and Asher's fallen friend, a fellow member of the Virginia militia. The battle had been short and deadly. What had begun as an argument had ended in an explosion of muskets. Asher, a crack shot with his Virginia rifle, had killed two of the twenty British soldiers who had come to take the family livestock for General Cornwallis's army as he rampaged through the southern colonies.

A British captain stood pointing an accusing finger at Asher. The brass buttons on the officer's red uniform coat gleamed in the sunlight. The black feather cockade of his dragoon helmet pointed straight up into the blue of the hot June sky.

Suddenly, the captain slapped Asher across the face with his glove, knocking his tricorn to the ground. He barked an order, and ten redcoats quickly dismounted and began to drag Asher to the nearby woods. Hopelessly outnumbered, Asher did not resist but stood proud and defiant as the soldiers tied him to a tree.

"Form up!" ordered the captain. He then marched arrogantly over to his men as they lined up to form a firing squad. The soldiers began to check and load their muskets.

"I, Captain Barrington Scroope, humble servant of His Majesty, King George III, do hereby sentence you to death for crimes against the Crown." Scroope drew his saber. "May God have mercy on your soul."

"No!" choked William, tears streaming down his cheeks.

"William! Stay back!" called Asher.

"Make ready!" commanded Scroope as he raised his sword above his head. In perfect unison, the ten soldiers brought their Brown Bess muskets up into position and pulled back the cocks.

"Present!" The redcoats took aim. Captain Scroope waited, as if relishing his power.

William sprinted, his feet flying over the ground.

Seeing William running toward his brother, Scroope cocked his head slightly and smiled with false pity—the saber scar that ran down the left side of his mouth turned it into a ghoulish grin.

"Asher!" cried William desperately, racing to get to his brother's side. As he reached the firing squad, one of the redcoats swiftly turned and smashed his musket into the side of William's head. William fell to the ground as blinding pain shot through his body. Blood began to pour from his scalp and drip into his eyes, and his ears rang as he tried to find Asher.

"Fire!" Scroope sliced the air with his sword. Asher turned his gaze from his younger brother and faced his death. The crash of ten muskets ripped the air and tore the heart right out of William Tuck.

★ ★ ★

William lay in his bed, staring numbly at the shadows on the ceiling caused by the lantern flickering in the humid night air. He briefly closed his eyes. He suppressed the urge to cry out as the vision of Captain Scroope's scarred, sneering face appeared before him. William gingerly touched the bandage on is head. The blow from the British musket throbbed terribly. He listened to the quiet. His mother's weeping had died down to a whimper. The sound of shovels digging the earth had stopped earlier in the evening. Throughout the day, visitors had come. Nearby farmers who'd heard the gunfire had dropped over to check on his family and express their sympathies. Two coffins had been hastily constructed from the wooden planks of the old henhouse, one for Asher and one for his friend. His father and mother had collapsed in grief at the sight of their son, lifeless and handsome, bloodied from his execution. The neighbors washed him and dressed him in his best shirt. William combed his brother's long brown locks before helping to lower the coffin into the ground. The minister from the little church down the road said his prayer of peace after Asher was buried and the body of his friend taken away in a wagon by his family. Two of the neighbors, war veterans, had remained behind to tend to his father's wound. They cut out the lead ball, sealing the flesh with a hot knife—promises had been made by all before they'd returned to their own farms. They would see to it that the Tucks would survive, though nothing was left after this terrible day. The redcoats had taken everything. Their livestock had been butchered and loaded up, the family horse and the two milk cows tied to the wagon and led away. For good measure, Captain Scroope had punished the Tucks for the

The

SECRET
MISSION
of William Tuck

Eric
Pierpoint

sourcebooks
jabberwocky

Published by Sourcebooks Jabberwocky, an imprint of Sourcebooks, Inc.
P.O. Box 4410, Naperville, Illinois 60567-4410
(630) 961-3900
Fax: (630) 961-2168
www.sourcebooks.com

Library of Congress Cataloging-in-Publication Data
Pierpoint, Eric
  The secret mission of William Tuck / Eric Pierpoint.
    pages cm
  Summary: "After seeing his brother murdered by the British, William leaves home to join the Patriot effort. While on a mission to deliver a secret message, William meets Rebecca, posing as a boy. Together they embark on a cross-colony journey through a secret network of Patriot spies that leads them on a quest to find General Washington himself"-- Provided by publisher.
  (13 : alk. paper) 1. United States--History--1775-1783, Revolution--Juvenile fiction. [1. United States--History--1775-1783, Revolution--Fiction. 2. Spies--Fiction.] I. Title.
  PZ7.P6148Se 2015
  [Fic]--dc23
                                                    2015009887

Source of Production: Versa Press, East Peoria, Illinois, USA
Date of Production: July 2015
Run Number: 5004385

Printed and bound in United States of America.
VP 10 9 8 7 6 5 4 3 2 1

This book is dedicated to all the inspiring, courageous, smart young students I've had the privilege of meeting during my classroom visits and the wonderful teachers and librarians who lead them.

And to my mother, Patricia Pierpoint, who has given me a lifetime of love and encouragement. No matter how old you get, you're still your mom's kid.

loss of his own men by burning all the crops. Only some dried pork in the smokehouse remained.

William studied the room around him. Some of Asher's clothes hung on a peg next to the bed. His extra pair of shoes rested beneath. Asher was always very tidy. William held his breath and listened for his brother's voice, his hearty laugh. There was only silence. No longer would he hear of Asher's tales of glory, of heroic deeds done by the men of the Virginia militia. Asher was William's true hero and a growing legend in the Virginia farming community along the Roanoke River. A marksman, his nineteen-year-old brother had fought alongside "Old Waggoner," the brilliant and daring General Daniel Morgan, at the Battle of Cowpens. He had braved the cavalry assault of the cruel and despised Colonel Banastre Tarleton, one of the most feared British commanders, who'd run roughshod through Virginia and the Carolinas. Men like Asher had handed Tarleton his worst defeat that cold January day in North Carolina and, in just one hour of battle, had lifted the spirits of a tired revolution—a revolution that was now six years old. In all the terrible times of the war, the struggles to break from Great Britain, and the stranglehold King George III had on America, there had been few victories. Cowpens was one of them.

"Asher Tuck, the hero of Cowpens," whispered William. And what of himself? Compared to his brother, he was nothing special, he thought. Just a sandy-haired, brown-eyed boy of twelve years, lean and strong from working the farm. He was no one of consequence. And Asher? He'd fought and died today. For what? He shook away the questions.

William slowly sat up on the bed as Bo, the bloodhound, came in for some attention. He leaned over and held the old dog's sad face in his hands and stroked the floppy ears. William reached down for one of Asher's shoes. He pulled out the stocking inside and rolled it up his foot. Then he tried on the shoe, but it was too big. He placed it next to the other one and picked up the jackknife that lay on the stump that rested between the two rope beds. He ached as he pulled out the blade; Asher had promised to give it to William for his thirteenth birthday, which was six months away. Asher had always been doing things for William. William longed to do something in return. But his brother was gone. There was nothing.

Asher's red-and-blue drum sat on the end of William's bed and reached straight into his heart. Drumming was what they'd done most together, and it brought them the greatest joy. The lantern light flickered across the golden eagle painted on the side. It was the drum Asher had used in battle when as a young boy he ran away to join the Continental Army. It was a position of great responsibility. Once he had learned all the drum calls, Asher had beat them to signal men and armies into formations and battles for two years under the orders of Generals Morgan and Lafayette and others in the colonies of Virginia, Pennsylvania, and the Carolinas. After he'd returned from battle, he'd taught William every call. They had practiced whenever they could when they weren't plowing the fields or tending to the many other chores on the hundred-acre farm. For hours, they would drill with musket and drum, then race along the Indian path to the river and dive into its cool waters. Finally, when Asher was old enough to fight in the Virginia militia, he had taken up his back-country rifle and given the drum to William.

William picked up the drum. The right talon of the golden eagle clutched a flag with the word *Freedom* stamped upon it.

"Freedom," he said quietly to himself. It was the word his brother was always saying. He could almost hear Asher's voice.

It's everything, William. It's the right of every man.

He turned the drum around. The eagle's other talon gripped a musket. He stared at the eagle as he rubbed his fingers across the stretched skin of the drum. The great bird's dark, fierce eyes beckoned to him. Reaching for the drumsticks, he softly, so as not to wake his parents, tapped General, the command given to the army to strike the tents and prepare to march.

"Advance," he said quietly as he tapped out the call. "Retreat." *Tap-tap-tap. Tap-tap-tap.* Sorrow turned to resolve as his hands softly flew over the drum. Suddenly he stopped. A feeling began to grow inside him. He stared at the drumsticks in his strong, calloused hands. He felt strength of purpose flow through him. It seemed to fill the dark holes of despair. Quietly, he lay the drum and sticks down, reached for his breeches, and pulled them on over his undergarment. He picked up Asher's stockings and rolled them carefully up his calves, buckled on his shoes, and then buttoned his breeches around his knees. He paused a moment to quiet the throbbing of his head and then gingerly put on his home-spun hunting shirt and deerskin vest. As he pocketed Asher's jackknife, he noticed the blank, white parchment next to the quill pen on the little wooden desk by the door. He could feel the pounding of his heart as he sat down to write a letter to his parents. His eyes began to fill with tears, for he knew the words were sure to hurt them. But still he wrote.

Dear Mother and Father,

I am sorry. When you wake, I will be gone. Though I have no rifle to fire at the Enemy, the beat of my Drum shall be heard through all the Land and people may call my name as they do Asher's someday.

Your loving Son,
William

"I'm sorry, Mother," William whispered as the tears began to flow. He blotted the drops that had fallen on the parchment with his sleeve and placed the letter and pen in the center of the table. Pulling back his long sandy hair, he then tied it with a strip of leather. He grabbed his tricorn, eased it over the bloody bandage on his head, and then he picked up his drum and went outside. He set his drum down carefully on the porch, so as not to wake his parents. Reaching for the lantern, he made his way to the smokehouse. He stuffed several pieces of pork into his leather pouch, grabbed a large bone, and crept to where Bo lay on the porch, his tail wagging. The old dog gave him a questioning look as William set the bone down. Bo seemed to know something was up for he ignored it and gave a quiet whine.

"I'm sorry, Bo, not this time. You stay here," said William as he slipped the rope over the dog's head and tied the other end to the porch post. He sat down beside the bloodhound. "You take care of Mother and Father, hear?" He held out his hand and Bo gave it a lick. He took the big dog's head in his hands and inhaled his scent one final time, so he could remember. His throat thickened as he felt the ache of leaving. He offered the bone again. "I'll be back, I promise." That seemed to satisfy Bo, who chomped on the bone, holding it between his paws.

William picked up his drum and headed out into the field. He had no real plan, but as it was known that the French General Lafayette was fighting in Virginia to harass General Cornwallis's rear guard and curb the destruction caused by Banastre Tarleton and the traitor General Benedict Arnold, he would head that way and maybe catch up with the army or militia. Bo suddenly gave a deep bark from the porch. William took one last look back at his home and doubled his pace, fearing his parents would wake up. He shook his head against the doubt that was starting to build and listened to his shoes as they brushed over the tall grass in the bloodied field. Quietly, he began to beat the call to march on the skin of his drum with his fingers. He would follow that beat past the farms of the Roanoke River, past the ghosts of fallen patriots, and past the lonely wail of Bo, who called again for his friend in the moonlight.

2

SWAMPS AND DRAGOONS

★ ★ ★ ★ ★ ★ ★ ★ ★ ★ ★ ★ ★ ★

William hurried along the pig trail, through the stinking sludge of the swamp. Virginia was full of swamps. The light was fading fast, and hungry mosquitoes were torturing him for good measure. His drum bounced a steady beat against his chest. It had been over two weeks since he had left home. For days during his trek, he had relied on the kindness of farmers for food and any news of battle. The rumor was General Lafayette and his army had been seen south of Richmond. The ferryman at the James River told him to head east to the Post Road and turn north, but William decided to save time and try a shortcut through the bog. So singular was his aim to find the Continental Army that he pushed on using the pig trails through the woods. It paid off. The rattle of muskets firing in the distance had stopped him briefly. Now they were silent, so he doubled his speed.

He ran along the trail as fast as his tired legs would carry him. Rain began to fall in the forest. At first, it sifted gently through the trees. Then it started pounding all around him, the big drops smacking the branches and splashing into his eyes. The roar of the rain through the trees was deafening. But then his ears detected a different sound—the jangling of metal. Soon hoofbeats thundered through the bog just twenty yards to his left. Cavalry dragoons! But were they friend or foe, patriot or British? Would he find a helping hand or the cold steel point of a sword? William tucked himself behind a large tree. Sap-soaked torches lit the darkening swamp. Swords rang out in front of him, just yards away on the trail. The flash of a blue uniform streaked past. Then more. Dozens of patriot soldiers of the Virginia Light Horse, the first Regiment of Continental Light Dragoons, swept by him with hissing, spitting torches. William ran straight through the bog after them. He yelled as loud as he could. Suddenly, he crashed face-first into the swamp and got a mouthful of mud. Coughing and sputtering, he struggled to right himself.

"Stop!" he called. He was floundering around in an effort to pry himself out of the bog when his leg slipped on a submerged branch. He could feel something cut deep into his leg. He tried to drag himself from the swamp but was being pulled under by the sucking slime. He was clinging desperately to his drum to keep his head above the muck when a rope hit him flush in the face.

"Well, young man, you seem to be in a bit of a mess," said a voice. William looked up and saw a soldier on horseback, dressed in the blue jacket and red collar of an American dragoon. His brass helmet that sported a white feather cockade framed his ruddy, torch-lit face. The cavalryman leaned down toward William and grinned, as if amused at his plight. Other dragoons began to appear around him. William gripped the rope for dear life. The soldier tied the rope to a brass ring on his saddle and slowly began to back his horse up and pull him out of the swamp.

"Wait!" William let go of his drum and reached down to free his leg.

"Hold on, lad!" the cavalryman gave his horse a yank.

"My leg!" cried William. Then he broke loose from whatever it was that had held him under the surface. Pain shot up his leg as the dragoon pulled him out of the bog. Blood gushed from a wound in his calf. Both his shoes were missing, sucked into the smelly mud. He reached down and tried to stop the bleeding.

"Sergeant Dobbs!" called the soldier.

"Yes, Captain Frazer!" bellowed a voice. A grizzled older dragoon rode up from the rear of the troops.

"Assign two men to take the dead and wounded back to camp. Tend to the boy here and get him to the surgeon in the morning. Have his leg looked after. The rest, move out!" The captain spurred his horse and dashed up the muddy pig trail. Fifty other blue-uniformed dragoons fell in line and rode after him.

"Yes, Captain." Dobbs turned in his saddle and barked an order. "You heard him. Williams! You and Moberg get these boys back to camp. Organize a burial detail. I want them in the ground before dawn!"

"Yes, Sergeant!" Two soldiers rode up and began to separate the horses carrying several dead soldiers from those that would carry the half-dozen wounded men.

"Leave me Davidson's horse," said Dobbs as he pointed to a dead body tied to a horse. "He won't need it."

The two men cut the body loose and put it atop a corpse on another horse, tying the dead soldier's hands and feet to the saddle with leather straps. Williams and Moberg mounted and then led the horses at a slower pace up the pig trail, the wounded soldiers in front and the dead behind. The pouring rain began to dissipate to a drizzle.

"Bloody nursemaid, I am," cursed the sergeant as he dismounted and looped the reins of his horse to a low branch. After securing the other horse, he knelt down with his torch and looked at William's leg. "That's a nasty one. Just what in blazes are you doing out here, lad?" He took a cloth out of his saddlebag and wrapped it around the wound.

"Looking for the army." William tried to stand, but exhausted from his ordeal, he suddenly fell against the man, dirtying his uniform.

"Well, you've found it. Camp is just a few miles ahead." The sergeant gave a sniff and brushed off the mud. "Lord, you stink! We'll give you a wash off in that creek before you get on this horse. It belonged to a good man, and I'll not be putting you on him smelling like that."

"What happened to him?"

"We had a tough one today against some of Tarleton's boys. He didn't make it."

"I'm going to be a drummer," said William.

Dobbs helped him to the stream on the other side of the trail, and they wiped the sludge from his clothes and hat. After cleaning him up as best they could, Hobbs went to the dead man's horse and began to adjust the stirrups for William.

William limped over to retrieve his drum, which rested on the edge of the bog. He looked around for his drumsticks, but he knew they'd most likely been sucked into the swamp.

"Here," said the sergeant, reaching for the drum. William handed it to him, and the dragoon tied it to his saddlebags. Then he gripped low on William's good leg and helped him onto the horse. "How many of the drum calls do you know, lad?"

"All of them," said William as he settled painfully into the saddle.

★ ★ ★

After a night spent in Dobbs's tent, William sat in the field hospital in just his breeches, waiting his turn with the field surgeon. His right leg was still oozing blood. He held a filthy cloth against the wound. The rest of his clothes were drying outside in the steamy morning sun. A Virginia militiaman lay moaning on the cot beside him. The field doctor unwrapped the bloody bandage from the man's head. Then he leaned over and gave the soldier a long drink of rum. The man took it gratefully, coughing as the liquid went down.

"The musket ball didn't go all the way in, but I've got to

get that swelling down now," said the doctor as he took a swallow of rum for himself. "Are you ready?"

The soldier nodded weakly, unable to speak.

"Master Tuck, make yourself useful and pick up that bite stick," said the surgeon, turning to William. He nodded toward a stiff, six-inch length of leather that lay on the table with his instruments. Careful not to touch the already-bloodied instruments, William picked up the bite stick and held it out for the doctor.

"Put it between his teeth." William placed the stick in the soldier's mouth, and the poor man clamped his teeth on it, trying to bite the pain away.

The surgeon wiped the soldier's wound. "This looks bad. All this blood and fluid has got to drain. Boy, hand me the trephine."

William glanced around at all the saws, pliers, and bottles on the table. "Which one is the trephine?"

"It's the one with the handle and the round blades."

"This one?" William held up a corkscrew-like instrument.

"That's it." The doctor took the trephine. "You might want to take a drink of that rum as well. Brace yourself. This could get ugly."

William reached for the bottle, raised it to his lips, and took a drink. He sputtered and coughed as the liquid burned down his throat and into his stomach. Embarrassed, he quickly set the bottle down next to the instruments.

"First drink?" The surgeon smirked.

William nodded his head, gasping from the fiery alcohol.

Suddenly, the militiaman stiffened. His whole body seemed to rise off the cot as the surgeon began to turn the trephine, drilling a hole in the side of the man's head. The soldier moaned and shook as the doctor twisted the instrument farther into his skull.

"Hand me that bowl, Master Tuck."

Horrified, William couldn't move.

"Master Tuck!"

William tore his eyes from the grisly scene. He reached for a wooden bowl that sat near the instruments and extended it to the doctor. The soldier began to kick his legs violently. The doctor grabbed the bowl and tried to set it under the man's head, but it was too much to both drill and contain him.

"Grab his legs!" the doctor ordered. William wrapped his arms around the patient's thrashing legs, but it became impossible to hang on.

Just then, Sergeant Dobbs entered the tent. When he saw what was happening, he pulled William away, knelt down, and seized the shaking soldier in a bear hug until he stopped kicking. William took the bowl from the surgeon and placed it under the dripping wound, gagging as he tried to force down the contents of his rising gorge. For several minutes the only sound in the tent was the ragged breath of the stricken man. Finally, the militiaman went limp. A long sigh escaped his lips. The surgeon placed his ear to his chest. He then put his fingers to the soldier's neck. Sadly, he shook his head.

"Lost him." The doctor rose from the cot and stretched his

back. He pulled the trephine from the soldier's skull, wiped it on his shirt, and placed it on the table.

"Not your fault," assured Sergeant Dobbs. "A musket ball in your head, chances are your life won't be worth—"

"A Continental dollar. I know." The surgeon bent down, picked up a blanket from the ground, and covered the body. The man's boots peeked out from under it. "Now that leg of yours, Master Tuck. We might have to cut it off."

"Cut it off?" William gasped.

"Looks bad. Very deep," said the doctor, winking at Dobbs.

William clamped his hand over his mouth and limped outside. What there was in his stomach came up. As he retched, he heard the laughter from inside the tent.

"Get back in here, lad. Not to worry," Dobbs said, having a good time at William's expense.

"Come in and sit down. I'll fix you up quick." The surgeon poked his head from the tent and waved William inside.

William sheepishly limped back into the tent. The doctor reached for a dirty rag and motioned for William to sit.

"Just a little gallows humor. Goes a long way these days." The surgeon chuckled as he wiped off the blood and then wrapped a clean cloth around the wound. "There, good as new. It'll heal pretty quickly, but you may scar. It might match the one on that thick skull of yours." The doctor ruffled William's hair good-naturedly. William rubbed the scab that had formed on his head where the redcoat had smashed him with his gun.

Sergeant Dobb's leaned over and studied the dead soldier's boots. He glanced at William's bare feet.

"They might be a bit large, but try these on." He removed the boots and handed them to William. "Get some rest. We may have a job for you this afternoon."

"What job?" asked William as he pulled on the boots. They were too big, but he would make do.

"Drum!" bellowed Dobbs as he headed out of the surgeon's tent. "It's the bloody Fourth of July!"

★ ★ ★

Boom! A loud blast shook William from his dreams. Thinking they were under attack, he sat up on the dirt floor and crawled on his belly to the opening in Dobbs's tent. He drew back the tent flap and saw ranks of patriot soldiers marching along the edge of the woods. Cannons at the far end of camp fired in celebration. William had never heard such a sound. He grabbed his drum and headed outside. French and American soldiers were lining up in formation in front of the hundreds of tents. In minutes, several thousand men, dressed in many different combinations of uniforms and colors, stood at attention. The French troops were the best dressed, in splendid white with black four-cornered hats and long coats in different shades of blue. They were well armed, and their new muskets and gleaming bayonets sparkled in the sun. The blue coats of the Continental Army had cuffs and collars of different colors, depending on where the soldier was from. The best-uniformed men stood closest to the road, muskets in the Shoulder Firelock position. Raggedy Virginia militiamen, in their hunting shirts and pieced-together garb, stood proudly behind them. *Boom!* The troops sang and yelled, "Huzzah! Huzzah!" after each blast. The day of independence—it had been just five years since brave men in America had declared their separation from England with their signatures.

William, dressed in clean clothes and the dead soldier's boots, half limped, half ran along the rows of soldiers to find the command post of General Marquis de Lafayette. His drum, which had been meticulously cleaned by the dragoons, bounced on his chest. A new set of drumsticks were shoved into his pocket next to his knife. The thunder of the cannon blasts was deafening. Two lines of mounted dragoons suddenly raced past him. William felt the sting of flying dirt and rocks as he lurched out of the way. He went down to one knee and threw his arm up to protect his face.

"Well? You said you wanted to drum!" bellowed a voice.

William looked up to see the smiling face of Sergeant Dobbs. The soldier reined his stomping horse, drawing it into a tight circle. He pointed to a Fife and Drum Corps that flanked a large tent on a low hill a hundred yards away. "Find your place with those boys at the command tent!" He then spurred his horse and galloped ahead to his company of dragoons.

William was so excited he hardly felt his wounds as he scrambled to reach the drummers and fifers. Boys around his age—they looked to be ranging from about ten to sixteen—stood ramrod straight, playing a spirited tune, as Dobbs and the Virginia dragoons kicked their horses into formation on either side of the command post. William caught the eye of a short, red-haired boy. As the young boy beat his drum, he gave William a nod and shifted to the side. William moved beside him. For an instant, he hesitated, awestruck at the sight of so many soldiers in formation, cheering, firing their muskets. He took a breath and raised his drumsticks. Then, as if he was born to it, he began to beat his drum for his country for the very first time.

Suddenly, the flap of the command tent flew open and out strutted the young General Marquis de Lafayette. Assigned by General Washington to patrol Virginia and the southern colonies, he looked more the privileged upper-class gentleman than a military man. Next to him was the infamous "Mad" Anthony Wayne, an older, fierce brigadier general of the Continental Army known for his audacious war tactics. William couldn't take his eyes off the French general in his crisp, white uniform with the long, blue coat with red cuffs and black hat. Mad Anthony clasped Lafayette's hand as they passed through the Fife and Drum Corps—the American general knew well that without the French Army, America's hope for independence would be lost. The two men paused for a moment in front of the cheering soldiers. General Lafayette drew his saber and held it in the air. Orders for silence echoed in the camp.

"Men!" called Lafayette. "We have been given word that General Cornwallis and his army have left Williamsburg and will be crossing the James River. If we march, we may meet him and deliver a blow he will not soon forget!" He paused to let the news sink in. Murmurs from the troops built to a rumble. "Are you with me?"

"Huzzah!" cried the troops, and a tremendous roar filled the camp. Muskets exploded. The two generals turned back to the tent. General Lafayette paused by William and nodded. William straightened up and stood at attention.

"Beat General, my boy!"

"Yes, sir!" said William. He clicked his drumsticks together three times, and he and the other drummers beat the call to arms as the roar of the cannons shook the valley.

3

THE BATTLE OF
GREEN SPRING

★ ★ ★ ★ ★ ★ ★ ★ ★ ★ ★ ★ ★ ★

William limped into battle behind the troops, sweating in the merciless July sun as he beat the call to March. Musket fire cracked, and smoke drifted across the battleground on the Green Spring Plantation. It was terrifying and thrilling. American spies had ridden into camp late the night before with the news that Cornwallis had moved across the James River, with most of his enormous army and supplies already with him. William continued drumming as Mad Anthony Wayne and nine hundred soldiers of the Continental Army headed up the four-hundred-yard field in formation toward the swamps, pounding the rear of the redcoat army.

William looked back to see General Lafayette scouring the field with his telescope. Four thousand of his men stood at attention behind him. Up ahead to his left, sharpshooting Virginia riflemen carved up the enemy from the trees. Wayne shouted an order, and soldiers began to swing two cannons into place. Once the big guns were loaded, they let loose with grapeshot, and the British soldiers were forced back toward the swamps near the river. Many began to break rank and run for cover. General Wayne and his troops cheered as they overwhelmed a British cannon that stood in the field. The battle would soon be over.

Then the world turned upside down. William froze as smoke from British muskets poured from the woods on either side of him. With frightening precision, thousands of British soldiers marched from the trees on the left in solid lines. Mercenary German troops, the Hessians, emerged and fired upon the Americans from the other side. Their first volley mowed down dozens of Wayne's men. Suddenly, the black-helmeted Colonel Banastre Tarleton and several hundred of his green-uniformed British dragoons bolted on horseback from the trees and raced to prevent the patriots from retreating to Lafayette's position.

"It's a trap!" cried William. He raised his drumsticks, but without orders, he didn't know what to do.

The call to beat Retreat thundered from Lafayette's army. But Wayne was engaged in heavy fighting and had no way of hearing. William steeled himself and ran forward, beating Retreat as the musket balls whistled and buzzed through the air. The British pulled several cannons from the woods and quickly wheeled them into place. The roar of the heavy guns and the blast of grapeshot ripped through the Continental Army.

"Oh dear Lord!" William gasped as he stumbled to his

knees. Terrified, he rose and raced ahead, beating his drum as loud as he could.

The terrible shrieks of flying metal and wounded men, the clash of swords, and the crack of pistols made it nearly impossible to hear William's drum. General Lafayette and four thousand troops began marching forward in an organized wave of blue-clad soldiers, but they were still a quarter mile away. The British would soon annihilate General Wayne, and then General Cornwallis and his superior force of nine thousand men would turn on Lafayette. The vice was closing.

As William reached the front line, Wayne's formation was broken. The Americans, lost in the panic, fled toward the advancing French general still hundreds of yards away. But General Wayne would not have it. He came tearing up to William on his horse, saber in his hand.

"Beat March!" he commanded. "Bayonets! Advance!"

William followed orders and beat March. General Wayne rode among the men, shouting encouragement and orders. Tarleton's dragoons began to cut through the troops with their swords. Then a great cry went up. Sergeant Dobbs and two hundred mounted dragoons flashed up from the rear and attacked Tarleton and his men, drawing them away from Mad Anthony Wayne's troops. In seconds, Wayne's soldiers regrouped, and with bayonets fixed to their muskets, they turned and charged back toward Cornwallis's army. Surprised, the British began to withdraw to the edge of the woods, where they stopped and regrouped. The two armies fought hand to hand. Bayonets flashed in the sun. Muskets were swung like axes.

Buoyed by their superior numbers, the redcoats beat back the patriots, who began to break ranks. The British cannons shot their deadly lead into the retreating troops. William stood his ground and drummed like a madman as Lafayette and his troops marched closer. Suddenly, Mad Anthony rode from the smoke of battle, swinging his saber, his men behind him in full retreat.

"Retreat!" shouted the general as he galloped past William.

William turned and ran, beating Retreat as hundreds of fleeing soldiers raced past him. It was almost impossible to see, so thick was the smoke. A great volley from the muskets of the British sent the air ripping apart. The earth heaved as a cannonball exploded in front of William. He tripped over the body of a dead American and crashed to the ground, smashing his drum into his chest. The wind completely knocked out of him, he lay there, staring into the dead soldier's wide-open eyes as he tried to suck the air back into his lungs. The world was coming apart all around him. He looked up to see bombs, fuses lit, tumbling from the sky, bursting in the air and on the ground, smashing and tearing the ranks of the retreating patriots.

Cut off from Lafayette, William grabbed his drum and ran desperately for the woods, through the choking smoke. A huge explosion just to the side of him took out two men. The shrapnel from the bombs buzzed past. William felt a searing pain in his left shoulder. A thin inch-long piece of lead stuck out of his hunting shirt, embedded in his flesh. Blood began to spread from his wound. Just feet from the woods, he staggered and reached for the piece of metal. He touched it. It was white-hot and burned his fingers. As he brought his fingers to his lips, a cannonball smashed into the earth just ten feet away and lay stuck, half-buried. But this was no ordinary cannonball. It was another bomb. It had a fuse, which sparked and spit. William turned to run, but it was too late. The bomb blew. The last thing William registered was being blasted into the air. Then everything went black.

★ ★ ★

He thought he must be dead. Or dying. He could not move or breathe. He could not see. He felt the pulse of his blood in his ears. The faint sound of a moan slipped into his consciousness. It was the cry of the dying. Was a moan all that was left of him? His whole young life had come to this, and it was to end in his very first battle. There would be no stories about him, he thought. No one would speak his name like they did Asher's. He had been useless. People would never even know how he had been his very best in battle—that he had been brave.

The moan grew louder. The ringing in William's ears began to ease. He tried to raise his arms but only managed to lift them a few inches. Slowly, painfully, he reached for his chest as if trying to find his heart. His hands found the jagged remains of his drum. Gradually, his vision began to clear.

He looked around in what appeared to be growing morning light. Wisps of smoke still drifted along the battlefield. Birds were beginning to sing. Their music sounded different from anything he had heard, and yet it must have been the same. He looked down at his chest. Covering it was twisted, blackened metal. His hunting shirt and vest were ripped open, and blood trickled slowly down his arm and chest. He raised his head. A sharp pain swept over him as he touched his wounded shoulder.

"Help," called a voice softly.

William tilted his head toward the sound, straining to see where it was coming from. He tried to speak, but could only manage a gasp.

"Help me," the voice called again—from the trees near the swamp about twenty feet away, he could tell now.

William's senses were returning. He reached into his pocket for his jackknife. His hands shook as he opened the blade. Propping himself up on his left elbow, he cut the strap that held what was left of his drum. Only the word *Freedom*, still clutched in a piece of the eagle's talon, remained intact. The rest was blown to bits. The drum was gone, but it had saved his life. He put the knife and the shard of metal in his pocket, then sat up and took an inventory of his body. Blood trickled from several small cuts on the left side of his face. He wiped the blood away as best he could and moved his limbs, wincing from the pain. His fingers found tiny slivers of shrapnel, along with the larger one, embedded in his left arm and shoulder, but somehow his life had been spared. William looked out on the battlefield. The Continental Army was nowhere to be seen. Some dead patriot soldiers still lay on the ground. About a hundred yards away, a number of British troops were caring for the last of their wounded and dead. Another groan came from the trees.

William slowly rose and staggered toward the woods. The dawn light led him to the edge of the swamp. Lying in the moss was a wounded man. Part of his right arm had been blown off and his legs were terribly mangled. With all the blood he'd lost, it was amazing he was still alive.

The injured man slowly looked up and beckoned weakly to him with his good arm. William went to him and knelt by his side. He reached for the man's canteen. The strap was tangled beneath his body. He quickly took out his jackknife and cut the leather strap. He gave the man a drink and then drank himself.

"Help me, boy," pleaded the man.

"Don't move," said William as he tied the canteen strap around the man's arm to try to stop the bleeding.

"Hurricanes at sea, I have braved. The likes you've never seen before, I'll wager. Battled rum pirates and malaria." The man laughed to himself. His breath was uneven. Suddenly, he was overcome with a coughing fit. Gasping, he waited for the pain to subside until he could speak again. "This wasn't even my fight. My luck, a cannonball drops in my lap. Won't be much use now, after this war. A one-armed watchmaker."

"You're a watchmaker, not a soldier?" asked William. The

man didn't seem to be making much sense. William cut a strip off the bottom of his hunting shirt and wrapped it carefully around his own bleeding left arm.

"Known to be a maker of the finest watches years ago. But for the cause, I became a messenger, a courier," the wounded man whispered. "I have urgent word. Get General Lafayette. Tell him the Watchman is here. He will know."

"I think Lafayette's army is gone," said William. "The Americans too. They've taken the wounded. I saw only British soldiers left in the field…"

"Then listen to me!" The dying man reached for him and spoke into William's ear. "Don't let the redcoats take me. Do you understand? The revolution depends on it!"

William rose and went to the tree line. The soldiers were working their way closer, checking the field for wounded. He ran back to the messenger.

"Redcoats!" whispered William urgently. "They're getting closer. They'll find us any minute."

The courier struggled to reach the leather pouch that rested by his side. "Boy, look in my pouch. You will find a letter."

William reached into the man's pouch and pulled out an envelope. He turned it over in his hands. There was a wax seal in place. Suddenly, the man gripped his arm, causing William to wince in pain. It appeared to take every effort for the man to speak.

"Take this letter. Do not let the British get it."

"I won't," said William as he put the paper in his pocket.

"In Williamsburg, there is a tavern. The Raleigh." The

man's words came in a horse whisper. His body began to tremble.

"Yes?" William drew closer, straining to hear.

"Ask the innkeeper. Find Lafayette's man. Get the letter to him. Say it is from Admiral de Grasse himself. The French fleet."

"Lafayette's man?" asked William. Behind him, British voices could be heard. They were getting closer, just twenty yards from the trees. "Who is he?"

"James."

"James?" he asked urgently. "James who?"

"Armistead." The man drew his shaking hand to a silver chain around his neck. He pulled a beautifully intricate gold watch from beneath his torn vest and held it up for William to see. "Take this. Tell him the Watchman sent you."

"I will." William lifted the chain over the courier's head.

"You must...find him. Time is everything." The courier searched William's eyes. He reached for his hand and squeezed it weakly. "The cause depends...on...it."

William held the courier's hand as the man took his last breath. He said a silent prayer, placing the hand gently on the Watchman's chest. William held up the beautiful watch, studied the exquisite casing, the bold face. As he drew it around his neck, he felt the weight of the Watchman's words. Voices at the tree line pulled his attention away from the dead man. Painfully, he rose and jogged deeper into the woods, careful not to get caught in the mud of the swamp. His mind raced. Questions about the message from the French fleet bombarded him as he ran, limping, through the trees. He had a mission. He had to get to Williamsburg. And he had to find Lafayette's man.

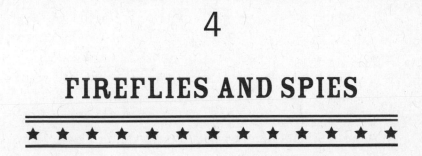

4

FIREFLIES AND SPIES

★ ★ ★ ★ ★ ★ ★ ★ ★ ★ ★ ★ ★ ★ ★

William, still bleeding from the shrapnel, ran from shadow to shadow along the lantern-lit streets of Williamsburg. He was exhausted and his shoulder throbbed painfully. Blisters from the loose boots of the dead soldier were forming on his feet. It was just now getting dark. It had taken the entire day to journey the fifteen miles from the battlefield. Several times, he spotted British soldiers on horseback, procurement patrols scouring the countryside for supplies. He hid in the thick woods along the road whenever he heard the sounds of anyone coming, watching and waiting as the redcoats rode past.

The clip-clop of horses rang out on cobblestone streets, shattering the quiet. William squeezed through a hole in the fence that bordered the church on Duke of Gloucester Street. He held his breath as a carriage went by. No soldiers. He waited until it was out of sight, then eased back through the fence and continued his search for the Raleigh Tavern. He crossed the street to a field of grass many yards long that led to the large Governor's Palace on his left. It was strangely dark, like most of the town's houses and businesses. He took a look at the still-ticking gold watch, squinting to see the time in the growing dark. It was just before nine o'clock. As he headed across the grassy field, he noticed a small structure near a few of the only trees left standing in the town. It was a gunsmith. A large rain barrel stood next to the shop. He climbed over the fence and crept to the rain barrel. Taking off his ripped shirt and vest, he began to wash off the blood. The cool water felt good on his battered body. He unwrapped the makeshift bandage, rinsed it in the barrel, and then redressed his shoulder. Painfully, he put his hunting shirt and vest back on and ran his hands through his hair, trying to neaten it. Then he jammed on his hat and headed toward the wooden walkway that went along the storefronts of the many shops on Duke of Gloucester Street. Trying as best he could not to arouse any suspicion, he slowed and began to walk casually, looking into the buildings. Most were boarded up or closed. He passed the courthouse and noticed an armory to his right. There were women's shops, a wig maker, a jewelry store, and even a post office. Many of the houses were large and well kept. Some were in need of repair. They graced the abandoned streets like lonely sentinels of a better time.

Moments later, he stopped. Just across the street rested the Raleigh Tavern. The large white wooden inn was open. Light flickered in the windows. An old gentleman dressed in a long coat emerged from the door and leaned on a walking stick. He staggered a few steps, swaying on his feet, before he adjusted his hat and shuffled down the street. Violin music drifted through the open door. William took a deep breath and crossed the street.

He entered the Raleigh Tavern to a smoke-filled room. It seemed a grand place compared to the little one-room country inn back home. A dozen men and a few women sat at wooden tables, eating or drinking. A flute player joined in with the violinist and they filled the tavern with a sweet, sad tune. All the tables were full in the main dining room. He looked around and spotted an open door that led to another section of the tavern just past a liquor bar where a man in a white apron served drinks to three thirsty travelers. He went through the door into a gaming room. Four men were playing cards around a table. Several others were throwing dice. William spotted one small table by itself, so he pulled up a wooden chair beside it, grateful to be able to sit and rest. Out of the corner of his eye, he noticed a lone man with long sideburns sitting by himself, drinking beer from a tall glass. His watchful eyes flicked back and forth as he studied the card players.

The discussion around the card table was growing loud as a plump waitress in a white bib and bonnet moved toward them with a bottle of wine. She gave William a sideways glance as she brushed past him.

"I tell you, I know what I'm saying! More wine, Alice!" shouted a tall, thin man as he took the bottle from the waitress. He looked like the drink was getting the best of him. "We'll all be better off once the Tories are given the boot!"

"You say that, Walter, but look around and tell me things weren't better under Governor Dunmore." A heavyset gentleman in a curled white wig set his cards on the table and picked up a tin. His ample jowls gave him the appearance of a frog. He pulled the top off the tin and took a pinch of snuff between his thumb and finger. "I myself had fifty slaves. Now I'm down to ten. We used to have a good tobacco crop every year. Not anymore." He shrugged his shoulders and sniffed the spicy snuff up his nose. "The war and the embargo have ruined us all."

"We all know where you stand, Mr. Talbert." Walter swayed to his feet and poured himself another drink. "Loyal to the King, you are! You'd tax us all and send it off to merry old England! Better off, you say? Why, the Stamp Act alone was enough to bleed us all dry. Tax paper? Even tax the bloomin' cards in your fat hands or the dice Mr. Morse is throwing there? Right, sir?"

"You dare call me a loyalist!" protested the rotund Mr. Talbert.

"Take these dice from my hands, Talbert, and I myself will see to it you're tarred and feathered!" From the gaming table across the room, old Mr. Morse, his white wig askew, picked up the dice in his thin hands and shook them at the card players. Then he laughed and danced a little jig. "They're running hot!"

"I'm no loyalist!" boomed Mr. Talbert. "I should run you through for that comment, you sod. Would you like a taste of my sword?"

"Don't tempt me, Tory!" Walter grabbed the hilt of his sword, struggling to pull it out of his scabbard.

"All right, gents." The waitress caressed Walter's cheek with the back of her hand. "Have a seat now, Mr. Billings, or you can have some of this!" Then she whacked him on the back of the head, the others having a good laugh at their friend's expense. The drunken Walter Billings sat with a thump and begrudgingly picked up his cards. The waitress sauntered over to William, taking in the cut on his head and the bloodstains on his shirt.

"I don't know who you are or where you came from, young man, but we don't serve beggars at the Raleigh Tavern." She began to wipe down the table, making it clear he was not welcome.

"I'm no beggar, mum." William tried to assure the woman. His stomach was growling and he felt light-headed. He hadn't eaten since the morning of the battle with the British and he needed food. "I could do with a meal."

"I doubt you have any money." She looked him over carefully.

"I do. Enough for a pot of stew." William pulled out several paper bills. He fanned them on the table.

"Ha!" cried the waitress. She scooped up the dollars and held them up for all to see. "Take a look, gents! This young man here wants supper! Now, can he get even a piece of old bread with this paper?" She turned back to William and tossed the bills on the table. "They're worthless. We take coin only."

"Alice," scoffed Lord Talbert. "Mr. Billings here can wipe his backside with it! That's all a Continental is worth!"

"It will be worth plenty someday!" challenged Mr. Billings. "Mark my words. I was here in this very room when Thomas Jefferson, Patrick Henry—"

"George Washington and George Mason!" countered Lord Talbert sarcastically as he ran his hand down his white-powdered wig. "In the Apollo Room! Do we have to hear this again and again, Walter?"

"Convened the Burgesses in spite of your Governor Dunmore closing down the House, the bloody tyrant!" Billings swigged the last of his wine and poured himself another glass.

"What's your name, young man?" asked Alice as she turned her attention back to William.

"William Tuck, mum."

"Well, William Tuck, unless you have hard coin to pay the price of a meal, you'll need to take yourself out of here." Alice stood strong, hands on her hips. "Get along now." She grabbed William's vest, attempting to extract him from his chair.

"I wish to see the innkeeper." William didn't budge. He grabbed the corners of the table and held on. The message from the Watchman was burning a hole in his pocket. If what the courier said was true, there was no way he was going to leave the Raleigh Tavern without fulfilling the dying man's last wish. "I'll not move from here until I speak with him."

"Fine." Alice pursed her lips. "We'll just see what Master

Southall has to say, then." She let go of William's vest and spun on her heel in search of the innkeeper.

William's hands shook. His shoulder ached. He felt so exhausted that all he wanted to do was lay his head on a soft pillow. He could still hear the musket fire and the cannon blasts from the day before.

"State your business, young man." William snapped himself alert. A man, the one behind the liquor bar, faced him.

"I was told to find the innkeeper." He thought he would get to the point quickly.

"That would be me," said the man. "James Southall's the name. What is it you want?"

"I'm looking for a man." William looked around the room. All the customers seemed to be involved in their cards or dice—except for the one mysterious fellow who still sat by himself, sipping his beer. Something about the man bothered William. "I was told you knew him."

Mr. Southall shook his head impatiently. "Young fellow, does this man have a name?"

"James. Armistead," William whispered.

"Never heard of him." Something in his eyes revealed a different answer.

"There was a battle. In Green Spring."

"Yes. Word of it came last night," Mr. Southall said with a wave of his hand. "Now, move along." He reached for William's collar to urge him from his chair.

"This messenger, a patriot. He gave me this before he died." William pulled the chain from his neck and brought out the gold watch. The innkeeper quickly yanked him to his feet. "Please, sir. I must find James Armistead!"

"Battle of Green Spring!" bellowed Lord Talbert. "Yes. The latest failure of your Mad General Wayne, no doubt, Walter?"

"You were there, boy?" Walter asked as he stood from the table, sloshing his wine.

"Yes, sir," William answered as he dropped the watch back down his shirt. "I was a drummer."

"So you saw what happened?" asked Lord Talbert, the red cheeks of his frog-like face fairly glowed beneath his white wig. "The idiot Wayne got his men slaughtered."

"It was a trap," William explained. "General Wayne ordered his men to charge the redcoats with bayonets. He was against thousands of them."

"There!" exclaimed Talbert. "Mad as a hatter!"

"It saved the men, sir!" William took a step toward the frog-like gentleman. "He drove the British back into the woods and then escaped!"

"Ah! See there, you Tory bastard!" challenged Walter Billings. "Wayne is a genius!"

"The messenger called himself the Watchman, sir," William said as he struggled in the grasp of Mr. Southall. "He died in my arms. He said to find—"

"Out, now!" the innkeeper grabbed William and began to march him toward the front door. "I'll not have the likes of a lying little urchin begging and working up my customers."

"Please, sir!" William struggled in the man's grasp. "I only want to find Mr. Armistead…"

There was no convincing the stubborn Mr. Southall. William felt shame as he was being dragged through the tavern. The customers all eyed him with pity or disgust. The red-faced innkeeper opened the front door and tossed William forcefully into the street. Then the man went back inside, slamming the door to the inn. William hit the ground hard, wincing from his battle wounds. After a minute, he got up and brushed himself off. He looked around the deserted street, wondering what to do. He felt like crying, but he was too exhausted and hungry. He limped along the walkway to the side of the Raleigh Tavern and leaned on the fence next to the garden. He had to at least find shelter, a place to rest for the night. He turned away from the tavern and headed down a side street, his hands in his pockets, feeling the weight of the Watchman's message.

Suddenly, a muscular arm clamped around his chest from behind and lifted him off his feet. He tried to cry out, but a hand tore off his hat and stuffed it over his mouth. The vice-like grip made it impossible to move. He struggled mightily in the arms of his captor, but it was useless. The immense man crushed William to his chest as he began to jog, almost lurch, through the shadowy streets. William freed his right arm and pounded on his captor's chest with his fist. He lashed out with his boots as he was carried along past the fenced houses, toward the dark woods in the distance. He tried with all his strength to break free, but the man was so powerful, nothing William did had any effect.

"Easy there, young fellow," whispered a deep voice.

William felt his breath nearly cut off and he started to choke. The man loosened his grip so William could breathe. Finally he stopped on a winding path near a creek and gently lowered William to the ground, sticking the hat back on his head. William turned toward the man. The rising moon revealed a wide, dark face.

"Name's Joshua Smith." His growing smile gave him an air of boyish innocence. "My master, Mr. Southall, says to take you to James Armistead. You all right?"

William nodded and rubbed his aching shoulder, studying the man in the moonlight. The slave motioned for him to follow, and together they walked along the path until it came to a wooden bridge that stretched across a tinkling creek. Just the other side was a wooden shed next to a barn half hidden in the woods. The black man carefully checked the surroundings and ushered him inside the barn. He gestured to William to sit on a stack of hay, and then he struck a match and lit a lantern that was nailed onto the wall of the barn. The light revealed the giant man to have a large hump on his back, behind his huge right arm. His left arm was much smaller and shorter. That side of his face drooped in a sad smile. He seemed sweet as a child but very powerful at the same time.

A gray mare, head in a feed bucket, stood in a stall. Next to the mare was a big brown horse with a black mane chewing on a clump of hay. It raised its head as if studying William. William looked around and noticed the tools of a blacksmith: hammers, pliers, and an anvil. Some iron chains hung from the wooden wall, a pitchfork leaned against a stack of hay in the corner. A doorway led to the inside of the shed at the side of the barn. In the shed, a lit candle flickered atop a small wooden desk.

"Now, you wait here. Master Southall says for me to fetch you some stew." The slave limped out of the barn. William grabbed the pitchfork and went to the entrance, peering carefully outside to check the surroundings. He tried to wrap his mind around the situation. First he'd been thrown out of the tavern, only to be dragged into a barn and offered food. It didn't make sense.

William held the pitchfork pointed in front of him as he slowly stepped from the barn. He made his way past a small corral near the creek. The snap of branches drew his attention to a clearing that led to a path into the thick woods. Carefully, he inched toward the sound.

"Boy?" a man's voice softly called. "Come closer."

William held his breath. With the pitchfork in his hands, he carefully approached the voice. He strained to look through the darkness. Fireflies swirled in the night, dancing in some ancient rhythm. Then he saw the face looming through the blinking lights of the insects. A black man, dressed in dark breeches, a white shirt, and a vest slowly walked toward him.

"James Armistead, Master Tuck," he said as he stuck out his hand. "I understand you're looking for me."

★ ★ ★

William sat on a barrel as he finished the last of his stew. He drank deeply from a tankard of cool cider, relishing the sweet and sour taste. He was beginning to feel human again. He handed the bowl to Joshua, who stood in the doorway.

"Mr. Southall says you can rest up here for the night."

"Thank you, Joshua." William handed the slave the cup, stifling a belch. "Tell him I am grateful for his hospitality."

"I will," said Joshua, taking the cup. "I'll come for you in the morning."

As Joshua headed out of the barn, William turned his attention to Armistead.

"It's the Watchman's all right," said James Armistead as he examined the gold watch. He handed it back to William and opened the envelope that contained the Watchman's letter. William pulled a barrel closer to the table and sat down as Armistead studied the letter in the light of the candle. The man had a certain dignity about him. He looked to be about thirty years old, with an intelligent, handsome face.

"It's an old code." Armistead leafed through a small code-book and muttered to himself, every now and then releasing a grunt of recognition.

"Well, Master Tuck. You've had quite a time of it," Armistead said as he studied the message. "Mr. Southall was right to get you out of there quickly. What you say in a tavern can get you killed if the wrong folks get wind of it. You can't trust anyone. There are spies everywhere."

"What's in the letter?"

"Well, I know it's from Admiral de Grasse and the French

fleet," said Armistead, scratching his head. He held the letter over a candle. "The message is in lemon juice. Heat makes the writing appear. See here?"

William looked over and saw writing begin to form between the lines of the ink text.

"The original letter contains some unimportant news about shipments of tobacco. The writing in lemon juice you see appearing is perhaps the real message. It talks mostly about supplies, sending a few of his ships from the islands up to New England to resupply George Washington and Rochambeau in New York. I would have thought the Watchman would have bigger news. Still, it might be of some use to Lord Cornwallis."

"Cornwallis!" William was shocked. "The Watchman said you were General Lafayette's man!"

"I am what is called a double agent, Master Tuck," said Armistead coolly as he continued to study the message. "But I'm loyal to Generals Washington and Lafayette." He smiled at William's puzzled expression. "I am also a slave belonging to William Armistead and a patriot. Put simply, I am a spy, an expert at misinformation."

"Misinformation?" asked a bewildered William.

"Taking information, changing it, planting it so the British will get it and head off in the wrong direction," he explained. "Even harmless messages like this one have value."

"The Watchman said it could change the war," William said, wondering if he had been through all the trials of the day for nothing.

"We'll see." Armistead reached over, took three small bottles from a cupboard, and set them on the desk. He then uncorked one bottle and brushed a liquid on the corners of the paper. He was suddenly agitated. "Dear Lord, something is going to happen!"

"What is it?" asked William.

"Not just something! Look here!"

William leaned closer. Another message began to appear in the corners and the margins. It was handwritten and also in code.

"It's like…"

"Magic?" Armistead peered at the forming message. "Invisible ink. A double message."

William stared wide-eyed at the appearing code.

"But it's not right. It can't be. All my information is wrong, otherwise…" James Armistead studied the message. "It says Cornwallis is going north to join General Clinton's army in New York to fight Washington and Rochambeau. Admiral de Grasse says he is taking the French fleet there to support General Washington. If they do that, the British will have them right where they want them. The war will be lost."

"My brother, Asher, always said that is what Washington wants—to win in New York."

"Yes, but Cornwallis is going south. I'd stake my life on it." Armistead shook his head and continued to pore over the message. He turned it over and over in his hands, checking his codebook. "If he crosses the James River, he could head either north or south, New York or down to Portsmouth, possibly back around to Yorktown," mused the spy.

"He did cross the river after he tricked General Lafayette into battle," offered William. "I was there at Green Spring. His whole army went over to the opposite side."

"Master Tuck." Armistead turned his head slowly and stared at William. "What did you just say?"

"Cornwallis crossed the river?" William asked.

"To the opposite side." A smile began to appear on Armistead's lips. He turned the message over and, with a steady hand, painted the paper. "Yes! The message is triple coded. Take a look at this."

"Triple coded?" William looked over the spy's shoulder. Numbers began to appear in the top right hand corner. "Numbers. I see numbers."

"What you see, Master Tuck, is a country being born." Armistead grabbed a small pamphlet from his vest, fanned it until he came to the blank last page, and spread it on the desk. "Make yourself useful. Go across the bridge. You'll find a garden on the other side of the road. Bring me a lemon from the tree."

"A lemon?" William hesitated, startled by the request.

"You'll see. The faster I get a courier to take this to Henry Townsend, the sooner it will get to George Washington," said Armistead. William hesitated for a moment. "Lemon, lad! Go!"

William, sore as he was, bolted out of the barn and crossed the bridge. He jogged along the path until he came to the road. Just on the other side was a garden with a fence around it. Leaning over the top rail was a branch of a lemon tree. As he picked the lemon, he heard the sound of horses. In the dim light of the moon, he could just make out British soldiers patrolling the street on horseback. He raced back to the barn.

"Redcoats!" he whispered urgently, handing the lemon to Armistead. "Just outside on the road!"

"Quickly then!" He sliced the lemon with a knife, squeezing the juice into a cup. William watched, fascinated, as Armistead worked. The spy dipped a quill pen into the cup and began writing furiously on the inside blank page of the pamphlet. The clear juice soaked quickly into the paper. When he finished, he blew on the paper to dry it until there was no mark of any kind. Then he uncorked one of the bottles, dipped a different quill tip into the bottle and began to write more invisible codes on the pamphlet. Satisfied, he tucked the pamphlet into his vest pocket. He then began to brush another liquid over the third secret code of the Watchman's original message. Suddenly they heard the sound of boots pounding across the bridge. William caught Armistead's eye.

"Put these into the cupboard," Armistead said as he handed William the bottles.

William opened the cupboard and stashed the bottles inside and then quickly closed the door. Armistead blew on the Watchman's message, set it on the desk, and smiled as he sat back in his chair. "Perfect."

With a loud crash, the door burst open and several

redcoats, armed with Brown Bess muskets, stormed into the barn. Behind them entered black-plumed Captain Barrington Scroope. William backed into the corner.

"You're right on time, gentlemen." Armistead stood and calmly faced the redcoats.

The man from the Raleigh Tavern, the lone watchful traveler with the long sideburns, stepped between the redcoats and advanced on Armistead.

"I'll take that, Mr. Armistead." The man crooked a finger at the Watchman's letter.

"From the Watchman himself, Mr. Shaw. The boy here found it," said Armistead as he gave him the letter. "Lord Cornwallis will want to see this as soon as possible. The information is beyond what I imagined. It might be the end of their revolution."

"How so, Mr. Armistead?" Captain Scroope walked up and snatched the letter from Shaw's hand and studied it.

"It could mean the absolute destruction of the French fleet and Washington's army in the north." James Armistead let the words drop slowly.

"How did this boy come by such a letter from the Watchman?" said Scroope, licking his twisted lips as he slowly advanced on William.

William struggled for an answer. "I found it, sir. Along the road from Jamestown."

"Liar." Suddenly, the captain took his riding glove and slapped William across the face. "You come here with a coded message from one of our most sought after American spies and ask for Mr. Armistead and you expect me to believe you just found it?"

"I overheard the boy claim he was at the battle in Green Spring," spat Shaw. "It appears the Watchman gave it to him before he died."

On the edge of panic, William searched his mind for something that would satisfy Scroope. Two of the redcoats moved closer to him.

Captain Scroope flicked at the piece of shrapnel stuck in William's shoulder that poked through the tear in his shirt. Suddenly, he twisted the metal deeper into the flesh. "You've been wounded. Brave boy."

"Ah!" William nearly fainted from the pain. "I was just a drummer, sir!"

"I see." The captain's mouth turned down in mock sorrow. He released the shrapnel and patted William's head. "Poor boy. Poor little soldier."

William grabbed his shoulder and sank to his knees.

"And there you have it, Captain Scroope," said James Armistead. "I suggest you take the letter to Lord Cornwallis in all haste. Something like this cannot be delayed."

"That will be your mission, Mr. Armistead," said Scroope as he handed the letter to Armistead. "Several of my men will escort you across the James River to General Cornwallis's camp in the morning. I will remain here. The Colonies are filthy with American spies. Hunting couriers carrying secret messages is now our first priority, eh, Mr. Shaw?"

"Indeed it is, Captain Scroope," sneered Shaw. "I live for it."

"In the meantime, we will take over the Raleigh Tavern and lock it down. No one comes or goes. Mr. Armistead, you will join me for supper. Sergeant!"

"Yes, sir!" said one of the redcoats.

"Post a guard on the boy here in the barn."

"I don't see any further use for the boy, Captain," James Armistead said as he looked over at William. "I say let him go his way. He's just a drummer, after all."

"Nonsense, Mr. Armistead. He is obviously a traitor and now my prisoner of war. I will therefore set an example," snapped Captain Scroope. He took a step toward William, lightly touched his cheek, and then spoke softly in his ear. "I never forget a face." Abruptly, he turned on his heel and headed to the door. "We'll hang him on the Palace Green at dawn."

5

THE HANGING TREE

★ ★ ★ ★ ★ ★ ★ ★ ★ ★ ★ ★ ★ ★ ★ ★

William lay in the hay in the corner of the barn, shivering in terror as he waited for dawn. His hands were tied behind him, and his legs bound with a chain. A redcoat sat dozing at the table. Once in a while, he would rouse himself to make sure William was still secure, and then he would fall back to sleep, snoring, his hands on the Brown Bess musket that rested across his lap.

William strained against his leather bonds. The jackknife was still hidden deep in his breeches pocket. Try as he might, he could not twist his body far enough to reach it. He rolled to his side and felt the sharp metal piece of his drum in the other pocket against his leg. Its tip poked through a small hole in his breeches. He managed to pinch a piece of it between his thumb and index finger. Carefully, he pulled it from the hole. There! With his fingers, he slid the larger end of the shard into his palms, grasping as hard as he could. Using the tiniest of movements, he managed to move the sharp point of the metal against the ropes that bound his wrists. If he could saw through the ropes just enough before dawn, he could make his escape.

The quiet scrape of the barn door drew his attention from his task. He instantly froze. Again, there was the tiniest of scrapes. William shifted his body to face the door. He held his breath as the door slowly opened. Joshua's face appeared. The slave caught William's eye and put a finger to his lips. Carefully, the big blacksmith eased the door farther open and crept into the barn. He loomed behind the sleeping soldier and reached out with his powerful hands, grabbed the man's head, and gave it a violent twist. Joshua released the unsuspecting soldier, and the redcoat fell to the ground, dead.

"Stay quiet, Master Tuck. We're going to get you out of here." Joshua limped over to William and untied his leather bonds. Then he unwound the chain from around his legs and helped him to his feet. William staggered for an instant; then his legs gave way and he leaned against the man who'd saved him.

"Easy now." Joshua half carried William out of the barn and then leaned him against the corral fence. "Can you ride?"

"Yes," said William as he rubbed his wrists.

Joshua went back inside the barn and emerged with a saddle and bridle in his strong right hand, leading the big brown horse with the other. The gray mare gave a whinny of protest.

"With my leg, I can't ride horses so well. I can fix 'em though." Joshua tossed the saddle onto the horse's back, and William reached underneath and cinched the strap tight.

The big horse's dark-rimmed eyes studied him as he fastened the bridle, ears twitching in anticipation. William stuck his boot in the stirrup. His leg pained him as he struggled to climb onto the saddle. Joshua grabbed him by the belt with his huge right hand, lifted him into the air, and dropped him on the horse's back.

"He's young, but he's eager and learns fast." Joshua adjusted the stirrups. "I call him Honor."

William gave the stirrups a test for length. Honor skipped sideways, unsure of his rider. "Easy, boy."

Joshua handed William the reins. "Those soldiers are going to hang you if they catch you, so you ride out of here as fast as you can. Take this." He handed William the pamphlet that James Armistead had written his secret numbers on earlier that night.

"What do I do with it?" William put the paper in his pocket.

"Mr. Armistead says that letter has to go all the way to General Washington himself." Joshua's eyes glistened in the moonlight. "He needs you to take it to the courier as fast as you can. Lord Townsend."

"Where?" Honor began to jig sideways in excitement. William brought him around in a tight circle.

"Head to the other end of town. You'll see a sign for the Post Road over by William and Mary College."

"Yes, I noticed it last night," said William, struggling to keep Honor steady.

"Turn north toward Richmond, to Spencer's Ordinary. That's a tavern about six miles up the Post Road. Just the other side of the tavern is Lord Townsend's farm. Go there. It has a metal pineapple sculpture four feet tall on top of the main house. You'll see. Mr. Armistead says you tell him what all you did and about the Watchman and everything and the battle." Joshua stuck his massive hand out to William.

"Thank you, Joshua." William gripped the calloused hand and shook it. "You be sure and hide now. Those soldiers will be after you too."

"I will. I know just the place." Joshua smiled. "Now, you find Lord Townsend and give him Mr. Armistead's message."

"I will." William gripped the reins and leaned forward in the saddle, leading the horse across the wooden bridge. The message to George Washington burned in his pocket.

"Honor, go boy!" He urged the horse into a canter. William gave a quick look back toward the barn. Joshua had already disappeared. Fireflies twinkled along the creek. He stayed in the shadows as much as he could back toward town, until he came to Duke of Gloucester Street. A number of redcoat horses were tied to the railings several blocks away, by the Raleigh Tavern. He crept along the lonely streets of Williamsburg, looking for the Post Road. All was quiet. He kicked Honor into a gallop and tore down the street. He glanced to his right and saw the Governor's Palace. The hanging tree stood alone, as if waiting for the coming light.

★ ★ ★

William guided Honor over fallen trees that blocked the main road. The horse was breathing hard after the six-mile run. Early morning light revealed the destruction around Spencer's Ordinary. Fences had been torn down, barns had been torched, and some cattle lay dead in the green fields. He rode past the tavern until he spotted a farmhouse at the end of a long, pebbled drive. Part of the main house had been blackened by fire. On the roof was the metal sculpture of a pineapple, just like Joshua had said. He guided Honor through the woods that bordered Lord Townsend's farm. Two other burned structures sat on either side of the white wooden house. Wisps of smoke still drifted from the ruins. William dismounted, tied Honor to a tree, and then made his way through the bushes near the wooden fence that sat along the length of the drive. He needed to get a better look to see if whoever burned the house was still around. He lay quietly in the grass at the edge of the woods about fifty feet from the house.

"Don't move," said a young woman's voice from behind him. "I have a gun pointed at your head, and if you even twitch a muscle, I will see that your brains are scattered all over the yard."

William immediately froze and waited for the woman's next command.

"All right, now. Get up slowly and raise your hands."

William, ever so cautiously, got to his knees and stood. Slowly, he turned to his female captor. As she came from behind a pine tree, he met her eyes and was immediately stunned. Holding a deadly scattergun, a musketoon, was a pretty young woman. She had green eyes framed by reddish-blond curls and was dressed in a ruffled, white dress, somewhat darkened from ash. She was a little taller than William and perhaps a few years older. A smear of charcoal ran down her cheek.

"Who are you, and what are you doing on my land?" She kept the musketoon leveled at his chest.

"Please, Miss…uh." William struggled to speak.

"I won't ask you again," she stated simply, her green eyes challenging him. "I suggest you come out with it if you want to keep your head."

"My name is William Tuck. I have a message for Lord Townsend, miss," William stated shakily.

Just then, a tall black man in a soiled white cotton shirt emerged from the woods. In his hand was a long knife. He sheathed it, walked over, and stood by the girl.

"Everything all right, Miss Rebecca?" said the man.

"Yes, Daniel. It seems young Master Tuck here has a message for my father."

"More likely he was looking to steal from the house," said Daniel as he stroked his graying beard. Gently, he took the musketoon from Rebecca and pointed it at William.

"That is also my feeling. My instinct says he's nothing more than a common thief." Rebecca's green eyes bored into William's. "Just what is this message you would have for my father?"

"I can't say," explained William. "I am entrusted to give it only to Lord Townsend."

"I see. Entrusted by whom?" asked Rebecca, her eyes flashing with doubt.

"James Armistead, miss."

Rebecca Townsend blinked. She gave William a long look, as if she was working out in her mind just what to do with this war-torn mess of a young man. "See to it Master Tuck's horse is taken around to the back, out of sight."

"Yes, ma'am," replied Daniel.

"Looking at that blood on his shoulder, he is in obvious need of our help. Tell Macy and Loretta to prepare a bath for him. See that his clothes are washed. The poor boy is filthy. In fact, we could all stand to clean up a little."

"All right, ma'am." Daniel turned to retrieve Honor.

"Master Tuck," said Rebecca as she turned and headed toward the house. "Come with me."

★ ★ ★

William sat in his filthy underbreeches in the warm bath in the kitchen, soaking away the pain from the last two days. Rebecca scrubbed her own face and hands as William told her of his brother's death, the Battle of Green Spring, and his narrow escape from the hanging tree. Once clean, Rebecca turned to the task of repairing William's shoulder. She began to pull out the slivers of shrapnel from his chest and shoulder with a pair of tweezers.

"So this message is from James Armistead?" She nodded toward the table where the pamphlet lay along with the Watchman's watch, the jackknife, and the shard of William's drum.

"He said to trust no one but your father and that he should get it to George Washington."

"Scroope arrested my father, shackled him like an animal. His patrols have been tearing apart the countryside looking for couriers. Scroope charged Father with being a spy and sent him off to a prison boat in Yorktown." A tear formed in her eye and she quickly brushed it away with the back of her hand. "Then Banastre Tarleton's dragoons stormed the area and stole everything. Except for a few of our horses we had hidden in the woods, they took our livestock. Then they torched our barn and the smokehouse and tried to burn the main house. They would have succeeded if Daniel and some of the others hadn't been able to put it out after the dragoons left."

"What about your mother?" asked William.

"We lost her five years ago. She died from fever," she said, her eyes glistening with the memory. She gripped the one remaining large piece of shrapnel with the tweezers. "This may hurt."

"Go ahead," he said as he set his teeth against the pain. She yanked out the shrapnel and dropped it into a china bowl with a clink. "Ah!" he cried. Blood dripped from the tear. She swabbed the wound with a cloth and then reached for a needle and thread.

"Why does your house have a pineapple sculpture on the roof?" William winced as Rebecca began to sew the wound shut.

"It's a signal. We provide safe haven for patriots." She tied off her stitch and tucked away the needle, wiping the blood from his skin. Rebecca moved to the table and began to leaf through the pamphlet. "What did Armistead write on this?"

"I don't know. He said it was urgent and would change the war. You can't see it because it's invisible."

Rebecca's stared at William, her eyes shining in calculation. She reached for a cotton robe and tossed it to him. "Put this on. I want to show you something." She tucked Armistead's message down the neck of her dress and motioned for him to follow.

William caught the robe, wrapped it around his sore, damp body, and followed her out the kitchen door into the next room. The once-grand living room had been reduced to rubble. Elegant windows that looked out toward the front road had been broken, the wall on either side scorched from flame. Much of the furniture had been smashed and piled into the far corner near the fireplace. A beautiful rug had been shredded, and china plates lay scattered in pieces. A staircase led to the floor above. She stopped and gestured around the room at the mess.

"The redcoats pretty much destroyed everything we had, but they missed the most important thing. Come." Rebecca led William over to the wall opposite the fireplace where a massive mahogany bookshelf stood. Many of the books had been strewn about the room. A piece of decorative wooden trim ran up the wall beside the bookshelf. She picked up a silver dinner knife from the floor and pried open a foot-long piece of the trim. Inside was a small metal lever. She tossed the knife on the floor, twisted the lever, and leaned against the wall next to the bookcase. A wide panel of the wall began to move. "Help me."

William put his good shoulder against the wall and pushed. Gradually, the wall opened. She motioned for him to follow her through the doorway. Rebecca then picked up a candle from a small table and lit it with a match. The light revealed a secret stairway. Once they descended the dozen steps, Rebecca held up the candle, illuminating a room full of weapons. She proceeded to light other candles in the room. On one wall was a rack of guns. There were muskets and pistols of every kind. William picked up the most striking gun and ran his hand over the rifled, octagonal barrel. A patch box was built into the rich maple wooden stock. A number of greased cloth patches were stuffed inside, ready for reloading the musket ball. He closed the tiny door of the patch box and brought the butt to his shoulder and felt the rifle's balance. He squeezed one eye as he looked down the barrel through the rear sight.

"The one you're holding was made for my father in Williamsburg," said Rebecca as she took two American officer's pistols with silver mountings and hefted them. Suddenly, she turned as if toward some imaginary enemy and aimed, one in each hand. Satisfied, she returned them to the rack.

"I prefer my musketoon. I can load fast and hit anything up close with it. Fill it with a smaller ball shot, and whatever is in front of me will meet its fate. There is a certain redcoat captain I would like to have at the other end of its barrel!"

"I could hit a bird on the wing with this," said William, admiring the magnificent weapon. He put the gun back and ran his hand over a leather shot bag that hung on the peg next to it. Inside were extra lead balls and flints. A powder horn with a hollowed-out charger tip for measuring gunpowder dangled from a leather strap. Gold letters adorned the flap on the bag. *To my good friend, H.T. May this correct your errant ball! Your friend always, T. Jefferson.*

"It's from Thomas Jefferson. They used to hunt together. My father was a bad shot. Come over here. I've something to show you."

She led him to a large trunk. She knelt down beside it and lifted the heavy lid. William sat next to her, and she handed him a lit candle. Together they began to sort through the contents of the trunk. There were maps of all thirteen colonies. They opened the maps and spread them on the floor. Numbers had been written beside each town. Rebecca pulled out a small box filled with letters and a map.

"This one is the post route," she explained as she opened the map. "It goes through the colonies from South Carolina, all the way to New York, and up into Boston. It's a courier map called a thirty-five."

"What does 'thirty-five' stand for?" asked William.

"What's written inside this particular map is revealed in

code. A courier might include a message or a description of some kind for other riders to aid them. It means the third letter of every word containing five letters or more would spell the message. It's an old one all the couriers used when they ran information. I wrote messages to my father that way for fun."

William picked up the map and studied the writing beside Charles Town. "This just talks about how bad the weather is and how it's a slow year for crops."

"Typical. If you use the code, you'll most likely find it contains information on troops and gun powder," she explained. "You have to be clever though. What you think is the message might not be it at all. There could be a hidden code within."

"How would you know?" asked William, shaking his head in wonder.

"Like I said, you have to be clever. All these old letters were messages that had to get to George Washington, Lafayette, or Rochambeau. Since the British soon cracked the old thirty-five, my father used to copy them in invisible ink before he would send them north. Much like James Armistead did with this one." She pulled the pamphlet from her dress. "Look here."

Rebecca reached down into the trunk and pulled out several other pamphlets that looked just like the one Armistead had used. On further examination, each was a simple Virginia almanac. There was a record of weather, towns along the post route, taverns, Bible quotes, and numbers denoting the distances between towns.

"The last page is blank," mused William.

"That is where Father would write his message." Rebecca ran her fingers along the almanac. Her eyes began to glisten.

"I'm sorry about your father, Rebecca." William gently touched her shoulder.

"What are we to do?" she asked. William took a deep breath and faced Rebecca.

"Can you help me make sure this message gets to George Washington?"

For a moment she said nothing. Then the strength returned to her face, and she nodded her head. "Yes. It's what Father would want."

"My brother, Asher, would always say, 'for the good of our country.'"

"Precisely." She glanced again into the trunk and pulled out a pair of scissors. She turned her back to William as she handed him the scissors. She gathered her hair in her hand and pulled it away from her neck. "Cut my hair."

"What?" William looked at the scissors, then at Rebecca's golden curls. "But I can't. Your hair is—"

"I can't join the Continental Army looking like a proper girl," she said. "Cut it."

William took her hair in his hand and cut as best he could in a straight line along the base of her neck. Rebecca turned back to him, grabbed the hair and the scissors, and went to the bottom of the stairs.

"Daniel!" she called.

"Yes, ma'am!" boomed Daniel's voice from above.

"Ask your son if he can spare a clean pair of breeches and a shirt. Then head over to the beehive and collect some honeycombs. We need wax!"

"Yes, Miss Rebecca!"

"What's the wax for?" asked William.

"I'll have Daniel waterproof the message with it before we go. I used to help my father do it before each of his courier rides in case it rained. There's no telling what might happen on the road north, and we can't afford to lose a number on that paper." Rebecca dragged a heavy metal box from the corner of the room and opened the lid. "Do you know how to prepare ammunition?"

"A premade cartridge?" asked William.

"That's right," Rebecca said, tearing a strip of cloth from the hem of her dress. She quickly tied her hair back like a boy. Only a few inches stuck out from the end of the cloth.

"I need paper, a dowel to measure, musket balls, and gunpowder," he offered.

"It's all in here in the box. Use the shot and dowel that match the two American pistols and my father's gun. We'll be taking them with us. If you can shoot like you say, it'll come in handy. I'll be taking the musketoon, so set aside bird shot." She went over to the gun rack and pulled down the weapons. "You should carry a pistol. Which one do you want?"

"I'll take the Kentucky model," he said, glancing over to the rack. "How many cartridges do we need?"

"As many as you can make in an hour. When you're finished, come upstairs."

"Where are you going?" William asked as he stuck his hand into the box and brought out some musket balls.

"To get Lady Blue!"

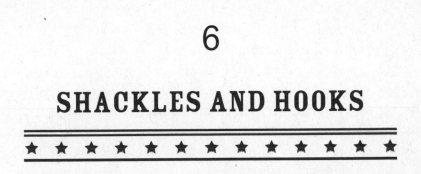

6

SHACKLES AND HOOKS

★ ★ ★ ★ ★ ★ ★ ★ ★ ★ ★ ★ ★ ★

William set down the shot bags and powder horns next to two canteens on the back porch. Daniel had finished waterproofing James Armistead's message and had carefully sewn it to the inside of William's breeches, next to his thigh. Honor shifted warily as Daniel's lanky son, Jeremiah, tied a bedroll to the saddle and slipped a tinderbox into the saddlebag.

"Jeremiah, you better run and bring Lady Blue's saddle from the cellar. Don't waste time, now. She'll be riding in on that crazy horse any minute."

"I won't," said Jeremiah as he ran to the side of the main house.

"Yes, sir. One look in her eyes you think the devil is coming to call." Daniel chuckled to himself.

"She sounds like a wild horse," William said as he tied the leather shot bag to Honor's saddle.

"Now, I'm talking about Miss Rebecca." Daniel nodded

toward the pasture. "Lady Blue is another story. See for yourself."

They turned in time to see Rebecca galloping bareback across the pasture on a pure white horse. Gone was the delicate form of young Miss Townsend. As she rode closer to the house, William saw what looked like a young man. Rebecca had transformed herself. She wore breeches, a hunting shirt with a vest, and a hat. Her boots flailed at the flanks of the spirited Lady Blue. Together they raced as one toward the house. Rebecca pulled the snorting horse to a fast stop, causing Honor to jerk nervously to the side. Lady Blue had a wild look in her eyes, so William grabbed Honor's reins and pulled him farther away as Rebecca swung her right leg over her horse's neck and slid to the ground.

"Daniel, I want everyone gathered. I wish to speak to all of you," said Rebecca.

"Yes, ma'am." Daniel went to the side of the house and rang a metal triangle with a steel rod. A half-dozen field-workers left the crops and headed toward the house. Several more who were repairing the barn set their tools down and hurried over. Jeremiah ran from the side of the house with Lady Blue's saddle and proceeded to strap it on the white horse. When all were present, they gathered in front of Rebecca. There were eight men and boys, three women, and one small girl.

"I love you all like family," said Rebecca. "I may only be sixteen years of age, but I am the lady of the house. I am going away on a mission with Master Tuck. Daniel, you will be in charge while I am gone."

"Yes, Miss Rebecca," said Daniel.

"I have here my father's will," said Rebecca as she held up an official-looking paper. "I do not expect to find him living again, for they have taken him aboard a prison boat. If my father should perish, and God forbid something should happen and I do not return, there is a law which says that because you saved our house, you would be entitled to your freedom."

"You mean we would be free to go, Miss Rebecca?" an older man asked tearfully.

"But where?" wondered a young woman.

"That you may decide in time, Loretta." She wrapped her arms around the woman and fought back tears. "For now, this is what I ask of you. While I am gone, take care of our farm. Defend it against the redcoats as best you can. Live in it as if it is your farm."

"Praise you, Miss Rebecca. We'll take care of everything." Loretta took Rebecca's hands in hers. "My, you do ever so look like a boy!"

Rebecca gave a short laugh, then walked over to the younger men at the end of the line.

"I say this to you. The British have promised that any slave who runs away and fights on their side will be declared free at the end of the war. I believe these promises to be more of their lies. But if you choose to join the redcoats, you will not be welcomed back, for I would not house any man who raises arms against my country. Do you understand?" Rebecca asked, her voice wavering a little.

The men nodded or shifted their feet, some meeting her stare.

"All loaded up, Miss Rebecca," said Daniel as he finished cinching the saddlebags to Lady Blue's saddle.

Rebecca said her good-byes to each man, pressing their hands. One by one, they headed back to the field and the barn. As she stopped to hug the women, William walked over to Honor and stroked the white blaze on his head. Then he grabbed the reins and eased himself onto the saddle. Honor whinnied as his new master guided him over to Lady Blue. He let the two horses sniff each other. Suddenly, Lady Blue nipped Honor's shoulder, causing him to buck. William struggled with the big horse for a few seconds but managed to settle him down.

"I wouldn't let your horse get too close for a few miles until she gets used to him," said Rebecca as she let Daniel give her a leg up onto the saddle. She handed Daniel the will. "Thank you, Daniel. Lock this in the secret room. See to everyone, please."

"Don't you worry, Miss Rebecca." Daniel tucked the paper into his pocket. "You be careful and hurry back."

"Master Tuck!" Rebecca pulled Lady Blue away from the house. As she did, she checked her musketoon and her two pistols that rested in their holsters on either side of the saddle. "Are you ready?"

"Ready!" called William as he urged Honor into a trot. He felt Armistead's message pressed against his leg.

"Pray try to keep up. She's a jumper!"

Rebecca gave Lady Blue a firm kick with her boots, and the horse shot forward, a white streak against the green grass.

"Honor! Go, boy!" William gave Honor a squeeze with his knees. The powerful horse hesitated at first and then bolted into a gallop. The black mane flew in the wind as he raced after the white horse. At the end of the field stood a fence that lined the road in front of the property. Lady Blue charged toward the fence and cleared it with ease. William set his teeth to this first challenge.

"Well, she said she was a jumper!" cried William as they neared the end of the pasture and closed in on the fence. "Up!" Honor stumbled and then gathered himself. Up and over they went, Honor's hooves slightly scraping the top board of the fence. They landed stiffly on the other side. Rebecca and Lady Blue shot down the road ahead of them. "Good boy. Now, let's see what you've got."

William gave Honor his head, and the young horse flattened out in a dead run. Gradually, they began to catch up with Lady Blue and pull alongside. As the two horses galloped side by side, Rebecca gave William a surprised nod of approval.

"Where are we headed?" yelled William as they raced along the road.

"Richmond!" cried Rebecca. Then she tugged her hat down tight, gave her horse a strong tap with her boots, and Lady Blue sped ahead.

"What do you think, Honor? Shall we let her go?" William

shouted. Honor took his own cue and launched himself after the blue-eyed horse.

The British were nowhere to be seen. They rode for miles past farms and forests in the July heat. They passed fields where many slaves were tending to the crops of tobacco and the waves of golden wheat. Hog farms dotted the vivid green landscape. The stench was ripe. Looking for shade and a place to rest, they brought the horses to a creek in the woods some fifty yards off the road. Satisfied they were well hidden in the trees, they dismounted and let the horses drink their fill. Not well-conditioned, Honor was breathing hard and sweating from pounding up the Post Road.

★ ★ ★

"You can smell those hogs before you can even see them," said William as he scooped some water in his hat and poured it on his head.

"I believe we've covered nearly twenty miles." Rebecca sat with her boots off, dipping her feet in the creek. The gentle tinkle of water sounded like music as it gurgled over the rocks. She took the map from her vest and opened it, spreading it beside her. "It looks like we'll make another fifteen miles, and then we'll have to make camp for the night. It's too hot to push it harder."

"How far is Richmond?" William asked as he splashed the cool water on his face and arms.

"Another day at this pace and we'll be there." She

studied a note written next to the capital city. "Using the thirty-five code, it looks like there is a courier right near the capitol building. If we can get to him, we might have some help."

"Let me see." William slid over next to Rebecca and studied the map.

"Right here. This line is the Post Road. This is where we are now. Go up an inch to Richmond. The sentence written here…this word, 'pretend,' you have *E*." She ran her finger over to the next word containing more than four letters. "Here is another, 'require.'"

"You would use the *Q*?" William looked at her questioningly.

"That's right. The next word has a *U*. That gives you *EQU*." Rebecca shot her eyebrows up as if to urge William to a conclusion. "Well?"

William sat for a moment, but for the life of him he could not come up with the answer. He shook his head. "I don't know."

"Now, think," she said, narrowing her eyes. "You're sitting right next to one."

William looked around at the rocks and trees, the leaves, and even the bugs that swarmed around them. He settled in on Honor as he continued to drink from the creek. Finally it hit him. "It's short for equine! A horse!"

"Yes! What a courier rides!" She gave him a punch on his good arm.

SNAP! They froze. *SNAP!* The sound echoed through the trees. They sat, searching the woods for intruders. *SNAP!* The sound came again and again. Rebecca went white as a sheet. She quickly put her boots on.

"I know that sound." She gathered the map and stood.

"What is it?" asked William.

"Once you've heard it, you will never forget it. It is the sound of pure evil."

"Redcoats?" William reached for Honor's reins. Immediately, the big horse began to stomp in anticipation.

"The whip." Rebecca grabbed Lady Blue's reins and gestured for William to follow her through the trees.

★ ★ ★

Rebecca lay hidden at the edge of the woods next to William, staring through a small telescope. Just over a hundred yards away, a brawny white man cracked his whip across the naked back of a black man tied to a tree. Several white men with guns stood guard as the head overseer then untied the slave from the tree and forced him to lie on the ground. Another white man threw a long rope with a steel hook on the end over a low-hanging branch. Dozens of other slaves stood witnessing the torture. Some were shackled at the feet with iron chains.

"They're going to hook the poor man. Look!" She handed him back the telescope.

"Hook him?" William looked in disbelief at the scene before him. The overseer held out the barbed hook to the crowd of black people and shook it at them.

"In the belly. Then they'll haul him up with the rope," explained Rebecca.

William could not believe the level of cruelty unfolding before his eyes. It had to be stopped. He tossed the telescope to Rebecca and ran a short distance through the woods to where they had tied the horses, and he pulled out the Virginia rifle. He grabbed the Kentucky pistol and shoved it into his breeches, throwing the shot bag over his shoulder.

"William, no!" said Rebecca urgently as she reached his side. "It's not our business. We've got to get to Richmond."

"We can't just let him die. Take Lady Blue fifty yards up the forest. When you see me fire, let loose with your pistols." William began to load the rifle as fast as he could.

"I'll never hit anything from there!"

"We don't need to. It will make them think there are more of us. They might take us for British coming to steal their slaves!" William moved the rifle's firelock into half-cock position and reached for a cartridge.

"All right, but hurry!" Rebecca mounted Lady Blue. "I'll meet you on the road." She gave her horse a stiff kick with her boot and shot off through the trees.

William crouched just inside the tree line. He bit off the paper end of the cartridge and shook some powder into the rifle's pan and shut it. He poured the powder down the barrel of the rifle and rammed home the patch and ball. Precious seconds ticked by. He replaced the ramrod and slammed the butt against his shoulder, cocking the firelock. He took a deep breath. He had one shot before all hell would break loose, so he had to make it count. He didn't want to kill the overseer, just frighten him. He lay down and took a deep breath, balancing the rifle. He sited in on the steel hook that hung just above the overseer's head. One of the white men raised the doomed slave to his knees and held him steady. Just as the overseer reached up to grab the hook and drive it into the belly of the black man, William fired.

The crack of the Virginia rifle scattered the crowd. The shot went low and the overseer spun to the ground, hit in the shoulder. The four white men jerked around to see where the shot came from. One of them pointed to the area where William lay hidden. The men ran toward him, ducking and weaving in the tall grass for cover, moving fast to close the distance. As William loaded his pistol, he saw a man rise from the wheat field and lift his gun. The crack of the gun followed the puff of smoke, and the musket ball smacked into the tree trunk just above William's head.

Suddenly, a pistol shot rang out fifty yards to William's left. Rebecca, riding through the woods, raced along the forest edge. Another blast from her second pistol set the men scrambling for cover. Just as the men set to fire toward Rebecca, William drew his Kentucky pistol and let loose. The men began to back slowly toward their horses near the plantation outbuildings. A loud bang from Rebecca's musketoon did the trick and sent everyone running. One of the unshackled black men from the crowd turned around and sprinted to the slave who had been whipped, freeing him of his bonds. Together, they raced past the fallen overseer toward the woods.

William ran to where Honor was tied and sheathed his rifle. He quickly mounted the horse, shoving his pistol into the holster on the saddle. The trees were thick. He tilted his hat in front of his face to protect his eyes from the branches as he kicked Honor into a run. Gradually, the trail widened by the creek and he picked up speed. They crashed through the water and tore along the path that led to the road. Up ahead, he could see Lady Blue leap over a fallen log. William gave Honor another squeeze with his knees, and they bolted after Lady Blue and eventually pulled alongside her and Rebecca.

"If they find out we're not the British, they'll be after us!" William yelled as they pounded down the road.

"They already know. They saw me for sure. Look behind you!"

William turned his head to see five men on horses bolt from a side road several hundred yards behind them. William knew that if their horses were fresh, they would certainly catch up with them. They had to try to lose them through the forest. Rebecca must have been thinking the same thing, for once they rounded a bend, she pointed to a pig trail that merged from the thick woods to the main road.

"Follow me!" she shouted as she urged Lady Blue in front.

"All right! Go!"

"Hold on tight! I see a lot of jumps ahead!" Rebecca turned her horse sharply to the left and raced through the trees, snapping her riding crop against Lady Blue's flank.

William gave Honor his head and he raced after the blue-eyed horse. Immediately, they encountered a series of fallen trees. Honor began to hesitate. Up ahead, Lady Blue leaped over a moss-covered tree trunk. Rebecca expertly handled the jump, glancing back at William. William took a deep breath and tried to relax his position as they closed in on the first jump. Honor cleared the tree with plenty to spare, but William was knocked back into the saddle with a jolt, pain shooting up his shoulder. He recovered quickly and readied himself for whatever would come next.

Their pursuers' shouts came from behind as they raced along the pig trail. For a second, it appeared they had eluded them, but a pistol shot drove them faster and deeper into the woods. William could make out the charging white shape through the thick forest ahead as Rebecca tore through the trees like some mythical young goddess. William had to force himself to let go and give in to the thundering hooves beneath him. After a few miles, he began to anticipate Honor's movements, feel the muscles of the horse's flanks. The more he relaxed, the faster he went. He closed the gap on Lady Blue. Fear gave way to the thrill of each jump as Honor began to trust him more and more. Together they ducked under the branches and leaped over rocks and streams until there was no sound of the overseers behind them.

They splashed into a deep creek, the horses surging beneath them in the mossy darkness, straining to get to the opposite side. The sun disappeared under the canopy of thick branches and a light rain began to fall. The woods dripped like some ancient, watery world.

"Keep your powder dry!" cried William as he grabbed the

hunting bag and held it over his head. The water rose to mid-thigh, and he raised his leg in order to keep the message dry.

"I know!" She had already reached for her shot bag.

"Where are we?" He inhaled the sulfur stink of a swamp as they moved deeper into darkness.

"Near the Chickahominy River. These swamps get worse every mile." She brought Lady Blue to the bank of the stream, kicked her up the muddy slope to the pig trail, and waited for William as he urged Honor up the bank next to her. They sat still, listening. The only sound was the rain that sifted through the leaves of the trees.

"I think we lost them," said William.

"We should keep moving just in case. It looks like we're in for some bad weather," said Rebecca. "This trail leads to the James River. If I'm not mistaken, there is an old ferryman a few miles ahead. We can cross the Chickahominy there and head to Richmond on the old plantation road. I didn't know you were going to shoot that overseer. Or was that a mistake?"

"I was aiming for the hook."

"I thought you backcountry boys were supposed to be good shots," she challenged.

"We are. I'll wager your father was a bad shot because the rear sight is off a little. It shot low and to the right."

★ ★ ★

William stood under a tree a few feet away from the rickety wooden ferry, holding the reins of the horses. The

Chickahominy River was rising as the merciless rain beat down. The heavy drops jumped like silver coins in the water. The front of his hat poured a steady stream and he tilted it to let the water run toward his back. He wiped his eyes and caught sight of Rebecca as she continued to negotiate a crossing fee with the stubborn ferryman. Because of the summer storm, the man was demanding an outrageous price to take them the hundred feet across the tossing river. Finally giving in to the relentless Miss Townsend, he nodded and accepted her coin. They shook hands and she jogged toward the ferry. The ferryman brought his mule over to a long line and began to fasten a towing harness to it. He then tugged the harness snug and walked the mule a few feet until the rope went taut. The line, attached to a pulley on the far side of the river, snapped from the surface. He signaled to them, and they led Honor and Lady Blue aboard the ferry.

"I am now known as Robert Townsend," said Rebecca with a husky laugh, playing her part as a teenaged boy. She hurried to tie Lady Blue to the railing. "He's not the ferryman I remember. He asked a lot of questions about us."

"What kind of questions?" William asked.

"He wanted to know where we were going and why two farm boys were traveling alone. He seemed to be particularly interested in the fact we're so heavily armed. It makes me wonder if he could be a spy for the British. The way he's looking at us makes me suspicious."

The ferryman stood watching them, his long black coat snapping in the wind.

"James Armistead says you can't trust anyone," replied William. "Should we take a different route?"

"There's the Frontier Road, but that's many miles west."

"There's no time," said William. "Better to take a chance on Richmond, then."

William gave the ferryman a wave, indicating they were ready to go. The man nodded and led the mule away from the river. The pulley squeaked and the ferry edged away from the bank with a jolt. He and Rebecca braced themselves as they began to move across the river. With the rain crashing all around them, they huddled closer to each other. Steam from the heated bodies of Honor and Lady Blue rose off their tough hides.

"William, we must make a pact." She nearly had to shout over the rain.

"What kind of pact?" asked William.

"That no matter what, we must trust each other. Agreed?"

William looked into her eyes and knew this was a person he could indeed trust. "Agreed."

A few minutes later, the ferry touched the bank. They untied the horses and walked them to the muddy road that would take them along the James River and northwest to Richmond. Rather than wait it out in the swamp-like shelter of the woods, they decided to forge ahead. The faster they could make it to Richmond, the sooner they could find a courier to help them in their mission.

They pressed on against the lashing storm, past several farmhouses that had been burned to the ground. The countryside had been stripped clean of livestock by the British procurement troops. No one passed them as they made their lonely trek. The only evidence of life were the sounds of frogs and the occasional rustle of a wild pig. Two hours later, they came upon another abandoned plantation. The main house had burned down, but several other structures remained intact. Soaked to the bone, they decided to head over to a wooden outbuilding that stood by itself in the middle of a blackened field.

Cautiously, William slid open the door and peered inside the dank wooden structure. He was immediately hit with a horrible stench of human sweat and filth. The room had been abandoned. Rotting blankets lay scattered in the dirt. Rows of wooden bunks three deep lined the walls. He motioned to Rebecca to follow, and they brought the horses inside.

"What is this place?" asked William, nearly gagging.

"It's where they kept their slaves, William," Rebecca said. "They had them stacked like cordwood."

A door half-off its hinges opened to another room. They went inside to investigate.

"It's the overseer's quarters," said Rebecca.

William stared in disbelief. Metal collars with spikes hung on the walls. Iron masks and shackles lay scattered nearby. Several whips, some with barbs, had been draped over a wooden desk. In the center of the macabre display on the wall was a large hook like the one they had seen just hours earlier. A faded sheet of paper and a quill pen still rested on top of the desk next to a black Bible. William picked up the paper and studied it.

"There must be fifty people listed here." He ran his fingers down the list. He handed Rebecca the paper. "They all have names from the Bible. Look."

Together they studied the list.

"What do you think happened to them?" asked William.

"My guess is the British took them." Rebecca set the list back down on the desk. "Or they ran away."

"Why would your slaves wait for you if they could just run away?" William asked after a long moment. It was difficult to understand the horror in the room.

"Some may very well run. But our family has always treated them well. There are those folks that put the fear of God into them, threaten them, force them to stay, kill them," Rebecca explained. "We feed them, house them, and take care of their needs. They have less reason to flee. Father had about forty at one time, fewer since the embargo. We had to give up some of our help to Thomas Jefferson."

"But Tom Jefferson is against slavery, isn't he?" William asked as he looked upon the arsenal of torture.

"It is said that he is, but he has many. George Washington owns three hundred," said Rebecca.

"Where I live, folks are not rich enough to own them."

"Who does the work on your farm?" Rebecca asked.

"Me," said William. "Asher did too."

"And you can produce enough to sell?"

"No." William shook his head. "To eat."

"Sorry. Of course." Rebecca walked over to the only window in the room and stared out at the blackened field.

The rain continued to beat down. The steel-gray sky swallowed the day's light. A crack of lightning lit up the iron masks. Thunder rolled in the distance.

William knelt next to an old iron stove, making a fist-size nest of torn paper on the floor. Using the back of his jackknife blade, he began to strike the flint from his tinderbox until he got a big enough spark to land on the paper. After blowing on the spark until it burst into flame, he picked up the burning nest by the edges and placed it into the stove. He tossed on more paper and then reached for a piece of wood from the rack and began to strip off thin slices for kindling. Soon they had a roaring fire.

With the fire burning, they brought in their wet saddles and gear, and spread everything out on the floor. Silently they checked their powder and shot. They wiped down their guns with old blankets that lay strewn about on the bunks. William adjusted the sight on the Virginia rifle. He slid the sight forward one click and then began to load the rifle.

Rebecca sat studying her father's map. "According to this, we need to find twenty-one Bristol Lane in Richmond. There's a courier named Arvy Montgomery there."

"What do we do when we find him?" asked William.

"I don't know, William. I hope he'll tell us." She folded the map carefully. "In any case, we'll need help. First light, we should head there. What are you doing?"

"Only one way to check the site." He rested the gun on the window ledge and aimed at a small branch that jutted out from a tree a hundred yards away. "With all the thunder, no one will hear."

William pulled back the cock and aimed at a branch. Flashes from the lightning made it seem crooked. Haunted. The lightning flashed again. He squeezed the trigger and the big rifle bucked in his grip. The branch flew from the tree, his shot dead center.

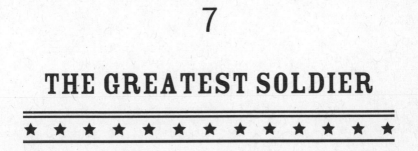

7

THE GREATEST SOLDIER

Richmond lay in ruins. The famous traitor Benedict Arnold had reduced much of the new capital to ash just six months before. All the hope of moving the Virginia government to Richmond from Williamsburg and away from the blows of war had been dashed. Though no redcoats were to be seen, William and Rebecca nonetheless rode cautiously along Courthouse Road, the steam rising from the street as the afternoon sun baked away the rainstorm. Shops had been destroyed, doors smashed, and windows broken. Majestic houses had been reduced to rubble. The few folks who stubbornly remained after the British siege walked head down, bending in defeat. Strangely, the government buildings had not been touched. They stood strong as if the center of Richmond, the heart, could not be broken. Slowly, they continued their search for Bristol Lane. Several streets past the courthouse, they found it.

They turned down the lane and counted the abandoned

shops along the way until they reached number twenty-one. It was still intact.

Mr. Arvy Montgomery
Fine Silver Ware
And
Watch Repaire

William tied off Honor to the railing outside the shop as Rebecca pocketed one of her pistols and slid from Lady Blue. Catching her eye, William grabbed his pistol and shoved it into his breeches. They stepped onto the boardwalk and peeked through the window of Mr. Montgomery's shop. It was dark inside. William tried the door. It was locked.

"Maybe we should look around for someone," suggested Rebecca. "They might know where to find him."

The faint *click-clack* of a horse carriage drew their attention away from the shop. They pressed themselves against the side of the building as the sound drew nearer. A wagon, loaded down with salvage items, edged into view. A lone driver hauling old furniture and picture frames passed down Courthouse Road.

"I have an idea," said William as he took out the jagged piece of his drum. He carefully twisted and bent the narrower end into a hooklike shape until it resembled a key. Slipping it into the keyhole, he twisted it until he heard a distinct click. He tried the handle and the door swung open.

"Where did you learn that trick?" asked Rebecca.

"You figure out how to make tools from nothing on a farm

like ours," William said as he pocketed the shard. "If anyone comes, we'll just say it was open."

They slipped inside the dark little shop. Several long wooden matches lay near a set of silver candlesticks. Quickly, they lit the candles, expecting to find the room destroyed. Instead, everything was in its proper place. There were silver cups and spoons lined side by side on the shelves. Fine silver chains and jewelry were displayed in glass cases. A brick oven sat against the far wall where all the work of melting and pouring, forming and hammering was done. William walked across to the oven and felt it. It was cold to the touch.

"It looks like Mr. Montgomery is still open for business," Rebecca mused as she moved behind the counter. She rummaged through some papers, bills of sale, and a ledger.

"What are we looking for?" said William as he examined the tools near the brick oven.

"Anything that might tell us that he really is a courier—or even if he is alive. Perhaps there is a button or a lever somewhere like the one Father had."

William kicked at the rug that lay in the center of the shop. All the wooden planks of the floor were the same. There were no signs of a trapdoor. As he replaced the rug, something caught his eye. He picked up a candle and walked over to a glass case that stood against the opposite wall. There, resting on a pillow in the display case behind a glass panel door was a beautiful watch, much like the one the Watchman had given William. He tried to slide the panel, but it wouldn't move. A small lock anchored the panel on the right of the case.

"Look," he whispered.

"What is it?" said Rebecca as she popped up from behind the counter.

"A watch like the one I have." He pulled his watch out from around his neck and compared it to the Watchman's piece. "They're nearly identical."

"There's our first clue." Rebecca walked over and examined the watch.

They ran their hands along the case and studied the wall around it.

"I think I see something," William said.

A slight gap appeared between the case and the wood and plaster wall behind it. Carefully, he slid the metal shard into the gap. He moved the jagged piece of his drum up and down. The piece suddenly stuck. *Click!* Slowly that end of the cabinet began to swing toward him. In the wall were six cubbyholes. William and Rebecca sorted through the cubbyholes, hardly daring to breathe. There were shoes, books, and an assortment of papers and maps. William picked up one of the shoes and inspected it. The heel was slightly separated from the shoe. With a gentle tug, the heel came off in his hand, revealing a secret hiding place for messages.

"Look at this," William said, holding up the shoe.

Rebecca pulled out several small bottles from one of the cubbyholes and showed them to William. "Invisible ink, I'll wager."

They put the items away and studied the shop. While not the scale of Lord Townsend's secret room, the hidden compartments still had much of what a spy might need. At least now they had enough information about the courier. Perhaps the secret message would be safe in the hands of the silversmith of Richmond.

"Prithee, gentlemen! I doubt Mr. Montgomery would approve of what you're doing." A woman's voice shook the silence of the room like a thunderclap.

William whirled around. Facing them in the doorway was a pleasant-looking older woman holding a musket. Dressed in white bib and bonnet, she looked like a plump little grandmother. Still, her eyes had the steely look of someone few would trifle with.

"I'll not stand for any thieving. I'd just as soon put a hole in you." She nodded her head toward the case. "Now, please close that up if you will."

"We're just wishing to speak with Mr. Montgomery, mum," said William as he shut the case.

"So why would you be messing with his things there?" She held the musket steady, her bony finger curled around the trigger. "And I don't see why, with the watches and silver, you would be interested in the papers and the shoes? Can you tell me that?"

"We're not here to take anything, mum," William explained. "We wish to give him something."

"William." Rebecca shot him a glance of warning.

"And what would that be, young man?"

"This." William held up his watch. Instantly, the woman's face lit up.

"Oh, my dear. Where did you get that?" Slowly, she lowered her musket. She walked over to William and touched the watch with a dainty finger.

"From a man last week. He gave it to me just before he died. I thought Mr. Montgomery would want it."

"Where did he give it to you?" Her eyes searched his.

William hesitated, not knowing just how much information to reveal to her. He glanced at Rebecca. She gave a quick nod of her head.

"Near Jamestown, mum." William cleared his throat as he explained. "He called himself the Watchman."

"Dear me," said the woman. "The Watchman, was it?" Suddenly, her face beamed. "Oh, my precious boys…very important, very important indeed. Mr. Montgomery will want to see you! Yes. He has been waiting for word from him."

"Where is he?" asked Rebecca.

"Why, just down the street at Hanover Tavern. I'll take you right to him." She reached into her bib pocket and brought out a key. Ushering them out the door, she locked it carefully behind her. "Please, hurry now."

"What about our horses?" asked William as he started to untie Honor's reins.

"No need. No. They'll be fine here." The woman urged him away. "Come, come. It's just a short walk away."

The old woman, musket still in hand, led them down the road toward the courthouse. They crossed the grounds of the new capital and turned up the street on the opposite side. A block later, they came to another road where several two-story buildings stood, undamaged. As exhausted as William was, he was excited to meet the courier, deliver the message, and fulfill his mission. Rebecca glanced at him with a look of concern as they turned down an alley. At the end of the alley, they turned again. William's breath rushed from his body. Directly in front of them was a corpse, dangling from a rope tied to the streetlamp just outside the Hanover Tavern. The word *spy* had been painted in red across the body. Several horses with British equipment were tied to a railing farther up the street. Suddenly, the old woman turned and faced them with her musket. She pointed to the hanging body.

"Look up there, boys!" The woman's eyes were glazed with excitement. "There's your Mr. Montgomery!" She threw a look over her shoulder. "Spies! Alarm. Alarm!" she yelled.

A British soldier appeared from the tavern door, a beer still in his hand. He had the same black-and-red plumed helmet worn by Scroope's men.

"Lads! You'll want to see this one." He laughed as the soldier motioned through the doorway. Two other redcoats appeared, drinks in hands. "Mrs. Tuey has brought us two dangerous spies. Thank you, mum!" The others laughed and toasted her, lifting their glasses. "Go away, you daft old woman."

"You'll owe me when I tell you this, Sergeant Donald!" Her face reddened. "You'll want to know who sent them to see Mr. Montgomery."

"And who would that be, mum?" One of the soldiers laughed. "Hear that, Montgomery? You have visitors!"

"Sorry, he's busy now." The other soldier slapped his thigh and swilled his drink. Montgomery's corpse twisted slightly in the breeze. A swollen, blue tongue protruded from his decomposing face. "He's gone a bit quiet, hasn't he, mates?"

"Rude, I'd say," Sergeant Donald answered. "C'mon, Arvy, mind your manners. You've got company."

"The Watchman sent 'em!" Mrs. Tuey could stand it no longer. She fairly sputtered with frustration.

With that piece of information, the three soldiers straightened up. The sergeant's face tightened with interest. He set his beer down.

"They had the secret panel open in the shop." She straightened with pride. "Say they have something for Mr. Montgomery from the Watchman. Captain Scroope promised me a bounty for bringing him a spy. Well, now I've caught two and I'll take double!"

As Mrs. Tuey glanced back at the redcoats, William lunged toward her, grabbed the barrel of her musket, and yanked it hard to the side. The old woman fell to the ground and the gun went off, the musket ball ricocheting harmlessly down the street. Rebecca drew her pistol and fired at the soldiers, sending them scrambling back into the tavern for their muskets.

"Run, William!" cried Rebecca.

They sprinted back toward the courthouse as fast as they could. Shouts of the British soldiers could be heard as they raced down the block. William shot a look back and saw Sergeant Donald and three of his men storming after them.

Sergeant Donald went down to one knee and took aim with his musket. William grabbed Rebecca's shirt and pulled her to the left as they tore across the grass of the courthouse lawn. They heard a blast and a chunk of bark exploded from a nearby tree. William grabbed for his pistol and cocked the firelock. He needed to slow the British charge. As they took the turn off Courthouse Road, he dove against a building, took aim, and fired. The three soldiers hit the ground for cover.

They turned up Bristol Lane and raced to their horses. Honor jigged away from William, skittish from the excitement. Rebecca leaped aboard Lady Blue and holstered her pistol. She reached over to help steady Honor by grabbing his bridle. William found the stirrup and hoisted himself up. He gathered the reins in his left hand and shoved his pistol into its holster. He kicked Honor into a gallop as Rebecca and Lady Blue dashed up the street. The three soldiers burst into view behind them and kneeled, in a firing position. By the time the redcoats fired, William and Rebecca were well out of range of the muskets.

"Keep the river on your left!" shouted Rebecca. "If we get separated, ride for the main road north!"

"All right!"

Together they tore down an alley and then raced along a road that ran parallel to the courthouse. Four mounted British dragoons galloped into view two blocks away. One of the soldiers saw them and signaled the others.

"Over here!" William led Honor toward a burned-out warehouse by the river. They stopped beside some old crates by the wall and reloaded their pistols. They could hear the soldiers shouting as they rode past, searching the streets for them. Once the hoofbeats died down, William and Rebecca emerged from hiding and slowly urged the horses through the river streets, making sure to keep the river in view. After a few minutes, they came to a shipyard that had been burned to the ground. Boats lay capsized or destroyed, the hulls beating dead against the riverbank. Carefully, they edged along the ruins, looking for signs of the dragoons. William caught a movement out of the corner of his eye. Two blocks ahead, an old man stood in a shop window, waving a small red, white, and blue flag about two feet in length. A patriot flag! He pointed the flag at them and then drew it to the left as if to guide them. Then he took out a Red Ensign British flag and pointed it in the other direction, indicating the redcoats' position.

"He's telling us to make a run for it," Rebecca said.

"Should we take the chance?"

Suddenly, a shot rang out. The window shattered above the old man's head and he quickly ducked inside his shop.

"To the left! Go!" Rebecca gave Lady Blue a smack on her flank with her riding crop.

"Come on, Honor! Come on, boy!" The big horse tore after Lady Blue, struggling at first to get his footing. As he passed the shop where the old man was, he glanced down the street to his right. The four redcoats were bearing down on them from two hundred yards away. "They've seen us!"

Together they raced for their lives, leaving the last of the blackened buildings behind them. As they galloped along the river, they came to a dirt lane that branched off the main road and led into the woods.

"Lose them in the woods!" Rebecca took Lady Blue hard to the right.

William threw a look over his shoulder. The redcoats were just one hundred yards behind. He knew what Rebecca was thinking. Lady Blue was in her element in the woods. If he could just keep up, they had a chance. Honor dug in and launched himself after Lady Blue. William ducked low, and the branches whipped and snapped as they tore through the trees. He leaned forward, urging Honor faster. "That's it, boy!"

A mile later, they shot out of the woods and found themselves back on the main road. William looked back. They'd put some distance between them, but the redcoats were coming on fast.

"They're still behind us!" William shouted. They drove the horses as hard as they could, but he knew the pace could not last forever. He figured if they could just stay ahead of the dragoons, endurance would win. It would depend on Honor. The young horse was immensely strong, but most of his short life had been spent as a workhorse, not racing at such speed. He fell in beside Lady Blue and matched her stride for stride as they galloped ahead of the redcoats.

William held on for all his might, the pounding hooves thundering beneath him. As they raced around a bend in the road, he spotted a wooden bridge.

"There's a bridge up ahead!" he shouted. "If we can beat them over the creek and up the hill on the other side, we can head into the woods again. It might be our only chance!"

The crack of a Brown Bess made them turn their heads. One of the soldiers was less than a hundred yards behind and closing, and the other three were gaining quickly.

"Come on, Honor!" William leaned forward and Honor shot past Lady Blue. He figured if he could get past the bridge, he might turn and risk a shot with his Virginia rifle and take down the lead redcoat. With a final burst of speed, they made it to the bridge and drove the horses hard across the wooden planks, desperate to reach the safety of the woods. They raced across to the other side and charged up the hill just as the dragoons made the creek.

Boom! A musket cracked and a puff of smoke appeared from the woods directly in front of them. William jerked Honor to a halt. Rebecca nearly crashed into him. He turned to see one of the redcoats writhing on the ground at the entrance to the bridge. The other soldiers stopped, their horses skittering on the wooden planks. Just then a huge man on a horse, a smoking musket in his hands, emerged from the woods. He was three hundred pounds of muscle dressed in a blue patriot uniform. Blood oozed from a gash in his right leg. A sword five feet long dangled from his waist. Calmly, he began to reload his gun, his hands swallowing up the ramrod as he shoved the musket ball home. He squinted in the sun, as if measuring the dragoons for battle.

"Are you boys loaded?" grumbled the giant soldier. "I see you've got a fine Virginia piece there."

"Yes, sir!" answered William.

"And your musketoon, lad?" He nodded at Rebecca.

"Yes, sir! It's loaded," Rebecca said.

"Good." He brought his musket into position and fired. The dragoons quickly turned and rode their horses to the farside of the bridge where they began to load their weapons. The wounded dragoon limped to the bridge railing for cover. The patriot giant reloaded, studying the situation. "This shouldn't take long. I'll charge them. You with the rifle, what's your name?"

"William, sir."

"Well, young William, when I say so, see if you can take out one of those redcoats. You'll only get one shot. Can you do that?"

"Yes, sir." William grabbed his rifle, slid off Honor, and took cover in the trees.

"What's your name, musketoon boy?"

"Robert," Rebecca said, keeping her voice low.

"Robert, be ready in case this goes bad and I go down. In any case, there'll be only one of them left, and the two of you can handle that, right?"

"Yes, I think...I mean, yes." Rebecca grabbed her musketoon and led Lady Blue off to the other side of the road. Then she slid behind a rock.

"Well then, here we go!"

The blue-clad soldier tugged at his hat and kicked his

horse into action. He slammed the butt of his musket against his shoulder and held it with one hand, the reins in the other. Fearlessly, he galloped toward the bridge and into the teeth of a fight.

William chose the soldier on the left, the one who looked the most ready for battle. Carefully, William cocked the firelock. The American rider dashed across the bridge and let loose with his musket, scattering the British dragoons. The wounded soldier still on the bridge stood weakly, attempting to fire his pistol. But the patriot swung his empty musket, smashing the man's head and sending him clear over the side and into the river. The giant soldier charged the other redcoats, firing his pistol just as one of the dragoons let loose with his Brown Bess. The redcoat collapsed in a heap. "Fire!" shouted the patriot.

William squeezed and fired. The big rifle bucked in his hands just as the targeted dragoon raised his musket. The soldier fell to the ground. Right when the remaining redcoat shifted his musket toward William, Rebecca let loose with her musketoon, causing the dragoon to dive for cover. William quickly reached for a cartridge and began to reload, his hands shaking as he bit off the top of the paper to pour the powder down the barrel. Finally, he rammed the ball home and raised the gun to fire, but there was no need. The patriot soldier had dismounted and had the fourth dragoon at the end of his five-foot sword, on his knees and begging for mercy. The American gestured for the man to rise. With the blade at his neck, the dragoon fired his weapon harmlessly into the air. It was a sign of surrender. Then all was quiet. The air smelled of spent gunpowder. The only sound was the buzzing of insects.

William and Rebecca watched as the American soldier helped the British dragoon collect the wounded soldier from the creek and put him on his horse. The patriot checked the two fallen redcoats, who looked to be dead. When the bodies were tied securely to their mounts, the two British dragoons were allowed to leave and ride back to Richmond. The patriot soldier limped to his horse and rode back across the bridge. Blood seeped from a fresh wound in his arm.

"Thank you, gentlemen," groaned the giant as he inspected his arm. "A fine job, you did. Fine job, indeed. I bade them take their time returning to Richmond. You two must be in quite a spot of trouble to have four of them after you like that."

"Did I kill the one?" asked William.

"A clean shot. I thank you for it. He went quick." The giant man nodded his head in appreciation. "Young Robert?"

"Yes, sir?" Rebecca looked at him.

"A musketoon loaded with bird shot is not my weapon of choice when firing through your own troops from behind." He scowled at Rebecca. "I may be picking at the one lead ball for days."

"Your arm! My shot?" Rebecca exclaimed.

"No, that was delivered by the first man's pistol. The ball went right through, so it won't be a problem." The patriot laughed. "It's this one little thing in the back of my neck!" He turned his neck, and there rested the tiny ball, a trickle of blood oozing from the wound. "However, you did manage to make a mess of the face of one of those dragoons. Young William?"

"Yes, sir?"

"We may need to put that magnificent rifle of yours into service again. I saw some wild turkeys just up the road. I say we three find a place to rest for the night and cook us up some supper! By the way, you must excuse my manners. Peter Francisco's the name."

William stood slack jawed. Rebecca's mouth dropped. They were speechless as they watched the huge patriot kick his horse and move up the road, for they now knew that they had just fought alongside the Virginia Hercules, the man considered to be America's greatest soldier.

★ ★ ★

William shoved a piece of turkey in his mouth. It had been a clean shot from a hundred yards.

"They say you fought at Cowpens," said William as he savored the taste of the roasted bird.

"Yes, and Saratoga, Guilford Courthouse, and everywhere else it would seem." A bashful smile flickered across Peter Francisco's face as he finished a massive chunk of turkey. "I go where I'm needed." Rebecca immediately handed him a leg. "Thank you, Robert." He gave Rebecca a sturdy pat on the back that nearly knocked her into the fire.

"My brother fought against Bloody Ban Tarleton at

Cowpens," offered William. "He was Virginia militia in the rifle company."

"The Virginia boys tore the Brits apart!" said Francisco, nodding his head. "Old Waggoner loved those fellows. He must have been a crack shot, your brother. Made my job with the light dragoons a lot easier. Where is he now?"

"He was executed last month." The words pained William as he spoke. "By a captain named Scroope."

"The same man who took my father," said Rebecca.

"Tarleton's lackey." Francisco grunted in recognition. "Wouldn't mind having him at the end of this sword someday." He reached behind him for the long sword and set the blade in the fire.

"Asher used to talk about you. He said you once picked a cannon up and carried it off on your own."

"It was bloody heavy," Francisco said as he licked his fingers. He hefted his sword and inspected the blade. Then he turned it over and placed it back in the flames. "Once you've heard the words of Patrick Henry and the like, you do things you never thought possible. Like you did today, William. I know how you feel about killing the man."

William nodded. He wondered if the soldier would have given it a thought if the soldier were alive and William were dead.

"I've shed a lot of blood for my country." He pointed to the second turkey leg. "Do you mind?"

"*Give me liberty or give me death*," quoted Rebecca as she passed Francisco the turkey leg.

"As an orphan boy, that speech meant a lot to me. I was there at Saint John's Church that day. Patrick Henry was an inspiration. He really packed them in." Suddenly he winced. His hand touched the stain on his coat and came away red with blood. He wiped it on his sleeve. "Now, what are you boys doing out here?" said Francisco as he ripped off a bite of turkey. "Are you looking to join up now? You both don't look old enough."

"I was a drummer at Green Spring." William reached into his pocket and pulled out the shrapnel of metal. "A cannonball hit my drum. This is all that's left of it."

"You're a lucky young lad." Francisco nodded in respect.

"We're headed north." Rebecca shot William a look, pausing in her explanation. "We have reason to get to New York."

"A long way, lads. Fredericksburg is where I'm going. There's a certain Mr. Weedon I'm charged to deal with." Then he began to take off his uniform coat. "You'll tag along. You may have to bury me by the side of the road if I don't stop this blood. A little skirmish I got into." Francisco rose from the fire and unwrapped the bandages from his torso. Blood trickled from a shot that had grazed his side. His arm ran with red from the day's fight. Then he stripped off his breeches. He ripped his underbreeches to expose a saber slash on his thigh.

"Dear Lord," whispered Rebecca when she saw the scars covering the man's body.

"What happened?" asked William, wondering how Francisco could have survived so many battles.

"Tarleton put the word out. Nine of his boys caught up

with me at a place called Ward's Tavern some ways east. They arrested me." Francisco reached into the fire and pulled out his sword. The end of the blade was red-hot. "They were holding me prisoner in a small room with just one guard, while the rest of them went to drink rum outside or in the main dining hall. The one guarding me wanted the silver buttons on my shoes. I took offense."

William's eyes shot up in amazement. "How did you get away?"

"I told him to take the buttons. The fool bent down and I grabbed his sword and dealt him a blow to the head. He fired his pistol and grazed me. See here?" Francisco pointed to the wound in his side. "I ran outside to my horse for my long sword and pistol. A few of them came at me from around the tavern. One charged me with his sword, and I managed to take his head off with this beauty and then lay open another one just as he shot me in the leg here with his Brown Bess." He handed the magnificent sword to William.

"It's heavy." William hefted it. He could barely hold it up. He handed it back.

"A gift from George Washington." He admired it, cutting the air with the blade. It made a deep whooshing sound. "Anyway, the one who gave me this little nick in my leg got a taste of the butt of his own musket. A few more soldiers came running out the tavern door. I shot one with my pistol. Some other bloke tried to jump me from behind, so I had to dispatch him. When I wasn't looking, two of the cowards mounted up and ran away with my horse, so I pulled this other dragoon off his ride as he was trying to get away, broke his neck, and escaped on his horse. He's a nice one but too small. I need a bigger mount." He counted on his fingers. Satisfied with the number, he nodded his head. "I think that's nine men."

"You fought against nine," wondered Rebecca. "And possibly killed three. Yet today at the bridge, you let those soldiers go."

"Make no mistake, Robert, I take no pleasure in killing." Francisco gnawed on his turkey. "Know that it is one thing to fight a battle, quite another when you have a man at the end of your sword asking for mercy. To kill him then would be murder. It's a point of honor."

William and Rebecca sat munching on their turkey in silence, marveling at his story.

"May I see that piece of your drum, young William? It'll make a good bite stick." Francisco held out his hand.

William gave the man the jagged piece of metal. Francisco offered the butt end of the sword to William and pointed to the bullet wound in his side.

"Press the blade as hard as you can against the hole for a count of five. Think of me as a piece of that turkey." He clamped the scrap of the drum between his teeth.

"One…two…three…" William counted as he pressed the blade against the giant man's flesh.

"Ah!" gasped Rebecca. The sound of skin sizzling was more than Rebecca could handle. She turned her head away and bit her lip.

"Good!" Francisco mumbled through clenched teeth. He took out the drum shard and indicated William's bleeding shoulder. "I see from your arm there you could use a little burn."

"No! I'll be all right." William felt the stitches Rebecca had sewn. While there was some blood still seeping from the painful wound, he felt no desire for a red-hot sword.

"Suit yourself." Francisco clamped his teeth on the shard, then twisted around and pointed to his back where the musket ball had exited. That hole was even bigger than the first one. William pressed the blade and began to count in his head. After five seconds, he removed the blade and Francisco turned to face them. He took the metal out of his mouth, peered at his thigh, and then gestured for William to cauterize the saber wound. "Two more and we'll have it." He stuck the jagged metal bite stick back in his mouth.

"One...two...three..." counted William as he seared the gash closed.

8

WEEDON'S TAVERN

They gathered themselves on Caroline Street at the edge of town, out of sight, and tucked along the Rappahannock River. Late afternoon sun bounced brightly off the water. It had taken two days of riding cautiously along the Post Road to get to Fredericksburg. No redcoats had appeared.

"It looks quiet enough," mumbled Francisco. "Weedon's Tavern is just a ways farther, lads. Williams Street."

William rested his palm on the butt of his pistol as they trotted down the road. His eyes shifted warily as he searched the streets and houses for signs of British soldiers. Rebecca, hand on her musketoon, brought up the rear with Lady Blue. Most of the buildings were still intact. It appeared that Fredericksburg had not suffered as much as other towns during the British invasion of Virginia. In a few minutes, they came to Weedon's Tavern. It was a fine-looking two-story redbrick building that rested on the street corner. Several horses were tied out front. None appeared to be military. Francisco held up his hand as they stopped in front. The tavern door began to creak slowly open, but then it suddenly shut with a thump.

"Here we go again," Francisco muttered to himself. "I thought we were over this. George! Mr. Weedon!" he then bellowed. They waited for several moments. No one opened the door. Suddenly, a shadow appeared behind the window next to the door. The window closed with a bang, followed by the click of a lock. After a few seconds, another window was slammed shut. "I bloody well know he's in there."

"I'll just give a knock on the door," said William as he slid off Honor and tied him to the railing by the other horses. Quickly, he hopped the stairs and gave the door a good rap with the knocker. He pressed his ear close, listening for sounds. A woman's angry voice could be heard followed by the low pleading tones of a man.

"Colonel Weedon!" roared Francisco derisively. "I'll have a word with you, like it or not!" He winced and put a hand to his side. "Sir! Open the door or I shall blast it down!"

"Perhaps we should move on, Mr. Francisco," said Rebecca. "It appears we are not welcome here."

"Nonsense. He just needs a little encouragement." He eyed Rebecca's musketoon. "Is it loaded?"

"Of course."

"Be a good boy," he said with a smile, indicating the gun. Rebecca knew it was useless to deny the man and handed him the weapon. "Thank you, Robert. William!"

"Yes, sir?" Unsure of what was about to happen, William took a few steps away from the door.

"That's a good lad." He waved him away a little farther. "Perhaps a bit more." Francisco nudged his horse a few feet closer to the tavern as William ducked behind a water trough. "Watch yourselves in there, George!" He took careful aim at the solid oak door. "Oh, and please give my regards to your lovely wife, Catherine!"

Great cursing and the scuffling of furniture could be heard from inside the tavern. *Boom!* The musketoon shot its load and blasted a pie-sized hole in the door.

Francisco sat on his horse with a satisfied grin. After a moment, an angry face appeared in the hole of the door. The man was sputtering with fury, his red face shaking.

"Curse you, Francisco! Damn you to bloody hell!"

"Hello, George! Nice to see you again." Francisco chuckled. "I see you've fixed the place up."

"No thanks to you, you crazy jollux!" replied the furious man. "And it's General Weedon! Or have you forgotten your station?"

"General you say?" Francisco let out a huge bellow of good-natured disdain. "I reserve that for real soldiers, you old hoddy peak!"

Suddenly the door opened and a woman brushed her way past Weedon and faced them defiantly in the doorway. Pinched faced and wide hipped, she stood like a block of granite. Her apron was stained with red wine and food. Auburn hair peeked out from a white bonnet. Curly, loose strands bounced along her trembling jaw. She pointed a finger at Francisco.

"Peter Francisco, you'll just have to take yourself out of here. We've no use for a bull of a man like you."

"So nice to see you, Catherine. Forgive my manners." Francisco doffed his hat gallantly. "I'll see the door is repaired."

"Never you mind about the door, Peter. You and these boys move on down the street. You'll not start up something in Weedon's Tavern. Took a month to get things right after what you did to those farmers." Mrs. Weedon crossed her arms and stood her ground.

"Got them to enlist, didn't I, George?"

"He's got a point, Catherine." Weedon calmed a bit and sighed. "Well, what do you want, now, Peter? I can see you've seen better days. Leave another tavern in ruins?"

"I've got word for you, George." Suddenly, Francisco slumped forward in the saddle. A groan escaped his lips. "It's from the top. Tom...Jefferson." He tried to grab his horse's neck but crumpled to the ground in a giant heap. William went to his side. Rebecca slid off Lady Blue.

"Dear me." Mrs. Weedon ran from the doorway to Francisco. Gently she picked up his head and held it in her lap. General Weedon joined her.

"He's been through it, all right. Can you hear me, Peter?" Weedon shook the big man's shoulders. "What about Tom Jefferson? Dear God, is he all right?"

"Yes, George," he said faintly. "He says..."

"Yes? What, Peter?"

"We need you."

"No, George," lamented Mrs. Weedon. "Not again. We've had enough fighting."

"Catherine…" Francisco motioned to Mrs. Weedon weakly. He closed his eyes as he struggled to speak.

"Oh. Dear Peter. Can you hear me?" She stroked his broad face tenderly.

"I…" He let out a pitiful groan.

"Yes, Peter?" Tears began to form in Mrs. Weedon's eyes.

William and Rebecca knelt beside the great hero as he struggled to speak.

"I love you!" Francisco let out a gleeful roar and kissed Catherine Weedon full on the cheek.

"Blast you!" Mrs. Weedon bolted up, red faced, as her husband couldn't help but laugh at the prank.

"Help me up, lads!" He continued to enjoy himself at the poor woman's expense. William grabbed Francisco's arm, and he and Rebecca helped the giant to his feet. "Take me to my old room!"

"George! Not our best room," protested Mrs. Weedon. "It's for our finer guests!" She hustled after her husband. "And not in the same bed…please, George, to think of all the great leaders of the world sleeping soundly…and now this hulk of a man!"

"It's the only bed that will fit him, Catherine." Weedon laughed and tried to soothe his wife. "He really had you this time, my sweet!"

"Don't you 'sweet' me, George." Her nose shot up in protest as they went inside. "He'll reduce it to firewood, mark my words!"

★ ★ ★

Mrs. Weedon opened the door for Peter Francisco and he limped into the middle of the elegant guest room, a huge smile on his face. William and Rebecca stood in the doorway, sharing a quiet laugh as they watched America's greatest soldier throw out his massive arms and do a clumsy pirouette.

"Lovely, Catherine!" Francisco bellowed. "Lovely!"

William had never seen such a room. A handsome four-poster, canopied bed rested majestically against the far wall. There were fine tapestries and paintings of faraway lands. It was easy to see why heads of state would be comfortable in the kingly lair. A necessary sat placed at the foot of the bed for those who had to relieve themselves in the night. The thick ornate chamber pot looked to be made of fine china. A beautiful gold and blue quilt covered the huge feather bed.

"Just look at this bed!" exclaimed Francisco joyfully. "I could sleep for a week!"

"Not on the quilt!" Mrs. Weedon rushed to protect the beautiful cover. Too late. The bed creaked in protest as Francisco flopped full length on the feather mattress.

"Curse you, Peter Francisco!" She rushed to the hallway. "Eunice! Jerusha! Bring plenty of soap and water on up here! And a bag for some filthy clothes!"

"All right, ma'am. Right away!"

"And start a fire under the tub! Strip the clothes off this rascal of a man. I'll not have this room plagued with bedbugs!"

"Yes, ma'am!"

"I am grateful, Catherine!" Francisco bellowed.

"You two boys come with me." Mrs. Weedon started down the hall. William caught Rebecca's eye and followed her. Just as they passed the stairs, General Weedon came up carrying a bottle and two glasses on a tray and went into the ornate room.

"God save us," muttered Mrs. Weedon. "Go easy, dear."

"Not to worry, love," said General Weedon. "Not to worry."

"Rum!" cried Francisco delightedly.

Mrs. Weedon led William and Rebecca down the hallway past several closed doors to the last room on the left. Taking the keys hooked to her waist, she sorted through them until she came up with the right one. Struggling with the lock, she finally managed to open the door. They entered and were met with an entirely different scene. Rather than the grandeur of Francisco's room, this one possessed all the charm of a broom closet. There were two small cots with rope webbing—but no mattresses—lined against the wall under a small window. Two wooden side tables held candles. Long matchsticks rested in a cup. A pitcher of water sat in a large bowl for bathing. There was only one necessary.

"Good enough, boys?" Mrs. Weedon, arms crossed defiantly, nodded to them. "From the sad looks of you, I should think you'll manage just fine."

"Yes, mum," William replied, not wanting to anger the woman any further.

"May we have a second necessary, at least?" Rebecca asked coolly.

"You'll have to make do," she snapped. "We'll allow you supper for one night. First thing in the morning, I want you gone from sight. Understood?"

"Yes, mum." William smiled as best he could. "First light."

Her eyes narrowed. "I must ask you, where did you meet up with the likes of Mr. Francisco?"

"Outside Richmond, mum," said William.

"Richmond?" She smiled stiffly. "My. A very dangerous place to be, I hear. Redcoats."

"Yes." Rebecca squared off and returned her smile. "Mr. Francisco was quite helpful."

"You're from Richmond, then?" asked Mrs. Weedon somewhat pleasantly.

"Near Williamsburg, ma'am," Rebecca answered as friendly as she could. "I'm Robert Townsend. This is my brother, William."

"We're traveling north."

Mrs. Weedon stared at them for a few seconds. "North where?"

William looked at Rebecca. They each waited for the other to respond. Something made them a little uneasy about the woman's sudden charm.

"Well. You just get comfortable. I shall have someone bring you each a clean nightshirt as well. I can smell the vermin on you. We'll boil your clothes along with Mr. Francisco's and have them ready for you in the morning."

"That's all right, Mrs. Weedon," protested Rebecca. "We'll manage with our clothes just fine as they are."

"Nonsense. My house, my rules." Mrs. Weedon refused to budge.

"Thank you just the same. There is no need." Rebecca, filthy clothes or not, stood her ground, knowing they had too much to hide.

"Very well. However, I want both of you to put your muddy boots outside the door now," she snapped.

Rebecca glanced at William, and they sat on the beds to take them off. Then they placed the boots into the hallway.

"Emanuel will give them a good polish before supper." She turned on her heel and trudged toward the stairs, mumbling as she went, "I'll not have mud all over the tavern!"

Rebecca closed the door with a thump. "Insufferable woman!" she whispered loudly. "William, would you mind if I wash up a bit?"

William hesitated, puzzled.

"I'd like a bit of privacy, if you don't mind?"

"Of course. Sorry." William nodded shyly. "I'll check on the horses and get the map. We'll need to make a plan for tomorrow." He headed out the door in his stocking feet.

William brought Honor and Lady Blue around the back toward the barn. He passed the cookhouse where a black woman was roasting a large pig on a spit. His mouth watered. He brought the horses into the barn; took the guns, saddles, and saddlebags off; and set them by the railing in the corner. Tossing down some hay, he began brushing the mud off first Honor and then Lady Blue. As he wiped down the guns, he glanced over at Rebecca's saddlebag. Curious, he reached into the bag for the map. It was getting dark out, so he went over by the blacksmith's fire and sat down. He opened it, drawing his finger up the Post Road past Richmond and into Fredericksburg. He stared at the notes that were neatly written on the map to the right of the Rappahannock River, just on the opposite side of Weedon's Tavern. A fine ink line pointed straight from the tavern to a smaller building one block west. A list containing four names of famous leaders of the country—G. Washington, B. Franklin, T. Jefferson, and N. Greene—was scribbled on either side of the line.

William stared at the names. Then it hit him. SAFE! The third letters of each last name spelled *safe*. The line pointing past the tavern and into the smaller structure might be a safe house for couriers!

William threw his shot bag over his shoulder, grabbed the Virginia rifle and the map, and walked briskly from the barn to William Street. He turned the corner on Caroline Street and quietly ducked between the tavern and the house next to it. A fenced yard across the road led to the back of a barn. Off to the side was a small building. As he stepped out to cross the street, a rider dressed in the clothes of a schoolmaster dismounted in front of the tavern and tied his horse to the railing. A satchel, most likely full of books, was hooked to the pommel. He stretched his back and rubbed the backside of his breeches, groaning slightly. He lifted his hat and touched the neat curls of his hair. Catching William's eye, he politely nodded, adjusting his wire glasses.

William tipped his hat to the man and watched him head

into the tavern. Satisfied he was now alone, he ran across the street and climbed the fence into the yard. Keeping low, he jogged past the barn. There were no signs of life, horses, or equipment. He peered through the windows on the back porch. Nothing stirred inside. He slid around the side to the front porch. He threw a quick look down the dirt lane that led to several other houses, making sure no one was watching. He tried to open the window next to the front door, but it was bolted shut. Straining to see through the glass, he could just make out shelves that had been turned over and smashed. A desk lay upside down and papers were strewn about the room.

The sound of boots scraped softly somewhere down the dirt lane. A spark of fear shot up the back of William's neck. He froze and listened as the boots drew closer. Ducking around the corner of the house, he quietly pulled back the cock of the rifle. A shadowy figure of a man appeared in the dimming light. The man stopped in the middle of the road and stared at the house. William held his breath, his finger on the trigger. The man swayed a few steps toward William and then drunkenly staggered back down the lane. Quickly, William retreated from the house and made his way back over the fence to Weedon's Tavern. He checked on the horses one last time and slipped into the back entrance. Carefully, he peered into the dining room. The bookish-looking traveler sat with his hat off, patiently listening to the ramblings of another man with long sideburns and a droopy mustache. It was the drunk. His hat tipped comically to the side; he waved his mug expansively, sloshing the grog on the floor. The schoolmaster seemed to tolerate him with polite amusement.

William took the stairs two at a time and hurried down the hall to his room. Two pairs of boots stood black and shiny against the door. He gave a swift knock.

"Rebecca, it's William."

"It's all right. You can come in," Rebecca called from inside.

He entered the candlelit room, setting his rifle and shot bag down. He reached for their boots and quietly closed the door behind him. Rebecca sat on one of the rope beds, freshly scrubbed and clean. She tugged at her hair and began tying it into a ponytail.

"I just found something." He spread the map out on the floor and pointed to the arrow. "You see these names? The letters using the code? It says 'safe.'"

Rebecca picked up a candle and knelt beside him, studying the map. "You're right, William. Could mean a courier or a secret hiding place."

"That's what I thought. The house is right across the street. I went over to look. It's been abandoned, and you can see things have been smashed inside."

"The redcoats may have gotten to it." She took out the Virginia almanac pamphlet from her breech's pocket and compared it to the map. "We need to ride out of here fast, William. My instinct is Mrs. Weedon is not to be trusted. I have a bad feeling about her."

"What if we were to leave Armistead's message with Peter

Francisco?" William felt the outline of the secret message with his palm. "Wouldn't he be best suited to deliver it to General Washington?"

"I doubt it. It's obvious the redcoats are after him. The man is a target." Rebecca concentrated on the almanac. "Perhaps we should make our way to Annapolis."

"That's nearly ninety miles," William mused as he added up the mileage noted on the map. "Once you get there, it looks like there is a lot of water to cross. According to this, you need to use Gunpowder Ferry and after that the Susquehanna Ferry."

"William, it's about three hundred miles to New York. Chances are we won't make it nearly that far without help. If we ride as fast as we can, it'll still take about ten days. And that's if we aren't caught or slowed down by British troops."

"We have to get help." William shook his head over the impossible task.

"But from where?" Rebecca searched his eyes.

"Philadelphia," said a faint voice.

William and Rebecca bolted up from the floor. They stood looking all around the room for the source of the voice. Suddenly, a panel of the wall against the adjacent bedroom began to slide open. Facing them from inside a false wall was Catherine Weedon.

William and Rebecca backed away as Mrs. Weedon slid the secret panel closed and stepped toward them.

"You should head to Philadelphia as fast as you can. And you were right not to trust me, Robert." Her smile played opposite her sharp stare. "As I was right about you. I had suspicions about you from the moment I saw you."

"Suspicions about what?" Rebecca said in her deeper voice.

"You see, dear, you are no more a boy than I am. Your wrists and hands—so fine and delicate. Your ankles and feet." Mrs. Weedon managed a pleasant smile. "With a little dirt off your face, I thought you to be quite the pretty young woman. I hid in the wall to make sure. My little secret. You would be surprised what I learn from my guests."

She pointed to the boots. "William. Go ahead, put them on."

William took his pair and sat down on the bed. He quickly pulled on his newly shined boots. Mrs. Weedon nodded to Rebecca. She sat down next to William and threw her right knee over her left one. As she began to pull on her boot, the woman stopped her.

"Dear girl, a woman crosses one knee over the other when she puts on her shoes. Like you just did. A man or boy will cross his ankle over his knee." She gave a sniff of satisfaction. "If you're going to play the boy, you'll have to do much better. Sharp eyes. I'm a very observant person."

"To a fault," sniped Rebecca. "Spying on a guest is not an admirable quality."

"What do you want?" William asked.

"I want to help you." She pulled up a chair and sat opposite them. "If what I discovered about you through these walls is true, you are carrying something of great value to New York. If you have a message from James Armistead, my guess is that means General Washington would very much like to see it. I should like to see it too."

William froze. He struggled to keep his hand from drifting to the secret message sewn into his breeches.

"I am familiar with hidden messages, William. Hand me your vest."

William caught Rebecca's eye. She nodded her head slightly in approval. He handed the woman his deerskin vest. Her nimble fingers flew over the creases and seams. She closed her eyes in concentration and finally shook her head.

"Very clever. Nothing in here or your boots. Whatever you're carrying must be on your person. No doubt your breeches?" She stared at William's pants.

Rebecca looked to William and shook her head.

"Young lady, you come from the Williamsburg Townsend family, you said?"

"That's right," offered Rebecca.

"I know of a Lord Henry Townsend. He has stayed in our tavern on occasion."

"That's..." She hesitated, surprised at the woman's information. "He's my father."

"That would make you Rebecca." Mrs. Weedon smiled pleasantly. "He spoke of you many times. You are here in his stead?"

"Yes." Rebecca slowly nodded her head. "The redcoats took him away."

Mrs. Weedon reached for Rebecca's hand. She nodded in empathy.

"You know, the British have been very clever. Their spies are everywhere. You will not find a courier anywhere near these parts. They are hunting them down like dogs."

"The one across the street?" William asked.

"Nigel Hopkins." She nodded. "He was hanged and his family imprisoned before the British troops marched south. My husband resigned his commission a few years ago, but we kept up a steady stream of information from our tavern. I learned a lot from these rooms. Mr. Hopkins made sure the news I gave to him traveled the Post Road until the British discovered what he did."

"You're a spy?" William asked incredulously.

"Was."

"So there is no one in Fredericksburg who can help?" asked Rebecca.

Mrs. Weedon rose from her chair and stood in the middle of the room. She looked long at William and Rebecca.

"My dears. My very brave children." Her eyes began to sparkle. "My husband and I have stayed out of the war for too long. Perhaps it is time to jump back in. Two young boys may just be the ticket to get that message to New York. The redcoats might be less suspicious of you. I'll help you get to Philadelphia. You'll need a contact there. I have one. He's a cobbler named Mr. Tweedle. William, please fetch General Weedon while I speak with Rebecca. Hopefully, the rum hasn't gotten the better of him yet."

"Yes, mum."

"And you will need a new shirt. The stains and powder

burns on the one you have say you have been in battle. Better to look like a farm boy. You will take on the guise of young boys heading north to apprentice with Mr. Tweedle. From there, he will supply you with the means to get you to New York. We must make up a story. You also need a coded decoy message. Here, in the lining of your vest. If the redcoats catch you, you must let them have it and not Armistead's."

"What will it say?" asked William.

"You will not know. It is better that way." A sly smile crossed Mrs. Weedon's lips. "Trust me."

William hurried down the hall to Francisco's room when—*Boom!* A huge explosion shook the tavern. William was thrown against the wall. He looked out the window and saw an orange ball of flame rising at the far end of town. The door from Peter Francisco's room flew open and General Weedon staggered out, cursing. "Redcoats have hit the munitions factory!"

Peter Francisco, bare chested, bellowing and waving his sword with one hand and the bottle of rum with the other, followed behind.

"Call out the Third, George!"

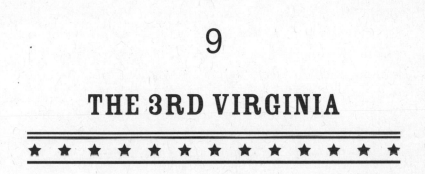

9

THE 3RD VIRGINIA

★ ★ ★ ★ ★ ★ ★ ★ ★ ★ ★ ★ ★ ★

The tavern bell rang all during the night. Over a hundred men of the 3rd Virginia Regiment gathered on horseback in the street, their blue coats with red facing shining proudly in the light of the torches. The newly energized General Weedon, now dressed in his uniform, commanded the troops from his horse, barking orders as the soldiers rode into town from their homes. Peter Francisco, his great sword at his side, was given a huge black stallion. He bellowed and cajoled as he rode among the twenty or so members of the ragtag militia. The famous Catawba Indian scout, Captain Peter Harris, along with three of his men, had ridden north to track the redcoats responsible for the destruction. Other riders had sped on ahead to towns and farms to alert more members of the 3rd Virginia.

William and Rebecca brought Honor and Lady Blue around to the front of the tavern and mounted up as General Weedon rode up and down the forming column of soldiers.

"Men! The word is Colonel Tarleton and his dragoons are on the move to lay waste to our beloved Virginia. You all know Bloody Ban's tactics in war. He will take no mercy on anyone who stands against the King." The light of the still-burning munitions factory shone in Weedon's eyes. "As God is my witness, I will not rest until we catch him!"

"Huzzah! We're with you, General!" cheered the patriot soldiers as they checked their equipment.

"Peter!" General Weedon motioned to Francisco with his saber.

"Yes, General!" Francisco kicked the black stallion over to Weedon's side.

"Have the men load. Reform the column. I want muskets in front and rifles to the rear."

"Yes, sir!" Francisco rode up and down the line, barking orders as Virginia dragoons loaded their weapons. "You heard the general. Half cock! Load! Muskets form in the front. Those with rifles to the rear!"

"Huzzah!" shouted the men, eager to head into battle. General Weedon caught Rebecca as she urged Lady Blue toward the front of the column.

"Young Robert!"

"Yes, sir!" said Rebecca.

"You and William must remain to the rear of the column and avoid all battle. It is agreed you will ride in the safety of the Third as far north as possible. I have given word to my wife that you will come to no harm while under my command."

"I am sixteen and of age to fight, sir." Rebecca took out her musketoon. "Tarleton's men stole our livestock and nearly burned us out. If I have him in my sites, I will put the man down." Rebecca stuck out her fine jaw defiantly.

"Can you load that musketoon in twenty seconds?" Weedon peered at her in challenge.

Rebecca nodded and proceeded to load her gun. Swiftly, professionally, she accomplished the task as well as any soldier. She presented the loaded musketoon to General Weedon in the Poise Firelock position.

"Well then. Go to the rear of the muskets," he ordered. "If we engage, ride in last."

"Yes, sir! Thank you, sir!" Rebecca shot William a big smile and kicked Lady Blue farther forward in the column.

"William!" barked Weedon.

"Yes, General."

"Now, do not make the fool of me and tell me you're sixteen."

"No, sir. Twelve." William lowered his head. The last thing he wanted was to be a burden to the troops. "But I could be of use with this." He pulled out his Virginia rifle.

General Weedon took the rifle and gazed at its beauty. "A farm boy with a piece like this. Formidable, I am sure."

"I'm good from at least two hundred yards," he pleaded.

"Son, I can see the courage in you. But law is law. You're too young. You remain in the rear with the rifles and keep well hidden," General Weedon said as he kicked his horse to the front. "That's an order!"

General Weedon and Peter Francisco led the column of

two hundred men on horses past the still-burning munitions factory. The yellow-and-blue flag of the 3rd Virginia snapped in the wind as they pounded up the Post Road in the morning light. More soldiers joined the swelling ranks as they swept along the countryside. Some had their uniforms; others looked to be in rags. They came from farms and hollows; at times, it seemed they appeared from nowhere.

Rebecca shot a look toward William as she galloped ahead of him in the column. She looked much more like a plain farm boy in a different shirt and vest, thanks to the keen eye of Catherine Weedon. The former spy was determined to keep Rebecca's identity secret. Even Catherine's husband did not know Rebecca was a girl.

They rode past scorched plantations and burned-out fields of corn and tobacco. Evidence of Banastre Tarleton's destruction was everywhere. It seemed nothing escaped his efforts to cut the lines to the north that supplied General Washington and the Continental Army.

They galloped across a green valley, past the smoking ruins of a church, when four bare-chested Catawba Indian scouts broke from the tree line ahead and raced straight toward the column. General Weedon gave the order to halt as the scouts closed in on the troops. One of the Indians turned and motioned toward the woods as he spoke to Weedon. He had two large blacksnake tattoos that wound up his back. The others had similarly placed but smaller tattoos, and their hair was decorated with deer tails. All were armed with old muskets as well as bows and arrows. Each wore a deerskin breechcloth, leggings, and moccasins. They carried long knives sheathed in leather belts. Weedon and the Indian kicked their horses to the mid-rank of the column.

"Men! We're close. Maybe five miles. Captain Harris here and his men say some of Tarleton's dragoons are heading to our supply houses. We don't have much time. Sergeant Macpherson!" General Weedon commanded.

"Yes, sir!" The blue-uniformed sergeant kicked his horse over to Weedon's side. A shock of red hair poured from his hat. The soldier's face looked to have been ravaged by smallpox.

"When we get to the supply depots, you take any of the militia carrying a rifle into the woods and cover our charge!" ordered Weedon. "We'll ride to the farside and you try to cut off any escape."

"Yes, sir!" Sergeant Macpherson snapped. He turned to the men in the rear of the column. "You heard him! Rifles, ride with me!"

They covered the remaining miles at a blistering pace. Sergeant Macpherson suddenly signaled the men to dismount. William grabbed his rifle and crept through the forest. There was no way he was going to hide from battle, he thought. He followed the rest of the soldiers as they went to the ground and inched forward on their bellies. With the Virginia rifle cradled in the crook of his arms and the ammunition pouch bouncing against his chest, he would at least be ready if needed. They had their orders and were to take their positions well away from the cavalry, which had ridden several hundred yards farther along the pig trail.

William knelt behind a large pine tree. He looked to either side of the trees. Rifle barrels began to emerge, poised and ready. Peering through the woods he could see a warehouse. About twenty British Light Dragoons had it surrounded and two Americans lay dead outside the building. Another man, wounded, was crawling toward the woods. A British soldier walked casually up to him and ran a bayonet through the poor man's back.

"Dear Lord," muttered a fifty-year-old veteran. He had a partially missing ear on his scarred face. "That one is mine." He pulled back the firelock on his rifle and sited on the redcoat. "Come on now, Weedon. Give the order," he whispered.

"Wait for it!" ordered Sergeant Macpherson as he ran low down the line of the Virginia militia riflemen.

"Fire!" Hidden rifles exploded with a volley of deadly lead. Immediately, four British soldiers went down, shot from more than two hundred yards away by the accurate back-country boys from Virginia. Several redcoats tossed burning torches through the main door of the building and then dove for cover. A huge blast of gunpowder came from inside the supply house, shooting flames through the open front door. All at once, a roar went up and General Weedon and his dragoons tore from the woods and raced toward the burning building. Rebecca, on Lady Blue, galloped at the rear of the column, musketoon in one hand and reins in the other.

The British let loose with their muskets and pistols and then scrambled for their horses. General Weedon and the cavalry fanned out and thundered down on the redcoats.

Tarleton's rearguard was no match for the 3rd Virginia, and they began to retreat. Two more British soldiers went down as the remaining Tarleton's Raiders sped away and headed for the trees. Dozens of patriots raced after them.

William and the riflemen ran back to their horses. Mounting quickly, they spurred toward the burning warehouse. The flames were spreading across the front door and along the wooden porch. There was no way to enter through the ball of flame, so they raced to the side of the building. Using swords and hatchets, they began to chop through the shutters and smash the windows. William and several other soldiers squeezed inside and into the growing smoke, collecting uniforms, shoes, and blankets. There was no way to stop the place from burning to the ground, but they got all they could. In the end, half of the supplies had perished.

★ ★ ★

It was late afternoon. The cavalry had returned to the makeshift camp with several British prisoners. The redcoats were being interrogated as to the whereabouts of Banastre Tarleton, but so far none of them would give up the location of their colonel.

William walked through the camp, carrying hardtack, salt pork, and canteens of water. He'd been instructed to give food to the prisoners. As he approached a soldier who'd been bayonetted in the leg, the man looked at him with a superior smile. Like many of his fellow dragoons, the soldier had a certain polished look despite his green jacket being somewhat worn from battle.

"Thank you, friend." The redcoat nodded his head in appreciation and then fixed his gaze on his bandaged leg. "Water, if you don't mind?"

William was struck by the man's polite nature and handed him a canteen. Even wounded and a prisoner, he seemed to know he would not suffer in the hands of his American captors. It was common knowledge that General Washington treated prisoners fairly, unlike Scroope, who had sent Asher to his grave.

"I wonder, sir," said William defiantly, "what you would do with me if I were in your camp and your prisoner." He watched him take a swig.

"It depends," said the soldier as he handed back the canteen.

"On what?"

"Who my commanding officer might be."

"Colonel Banastre Tarleton is your commanding officer, isn't he?"

"Well, then, sorry for you. It is likely that you would be swinging from this tree that hangs overhead." The soldier struggled to tighten the bandage around his wound. Dark blood seeped through the cloth.

"Or tied to the tree and shot like my brother was." William felt the anger building inside of him.

The soldier looked into William's eyes. "Was he militia?"

"He was a hero along with the rest. At Cowpens."

"Then he was a traitor to the Crown and deserved to be shot. It is war. We are the elite. Your so-called Continental

Army was lucky at Cowpens." The soldier chewed thoughtfully on his pork. "Ours is an army of trained and skilled men. The men of my family have served with honor and distinction for generations. Your lot is a bunch of thrown together ragtag, what, Yankee Doodles? Is that the expression? Led by idiots. You Americans are all the same to me. From your leaders to you, young man—one traitorous snake." He grimaced as he touched his wound. "We'll cut you in pieces, sever the head, and then lop off the tail. We missed him before."

"Who?" William asked.

"My secret. We'll bloody well take him this time. Cut off the head…" The dragoon choked on his words as the massive hand of Peter Francisco wrapped around his throat.

"An excellent question, my good man. Who?" Peter Francisco lifted the man by the throat and held him up against a tree. The dragoon squirmed like a fish at the end of a bear's claw.

"Point of honor!" gasped the dragoon. "I am a prisoner!"

"Honor, no. But a choice!" He drew his five-foot sword and held it against the man's neck. "I'll cut your head off quick or saw it off slow. Now, sir, answer the young man's question. What was it, William?"

"The head of the snake. I asked him who."

The terrified dragoon struggled helplessly in the grip of Francisco. He gurgled something painfully.

"I'm sorry. What was that?" Francisco drew his sword slightly until a line of blood trickled down the soldier's neck.

"Thomas Jefferson!" he managed to get out.

Satisfied, Francisco let the man loose and watched him crumple pitifully to the ground.

William left Francisco to deal with the prisoner and went to make a bed for himself. He spread out his blanket on some pine needles and made room for Rebecca as she set her saddle and musketoon down. The night air still smelled of burning wood and meat. "Tarleton is going after Tom Jefferson. Weedon is riding out after him in the morning."

The dragoons were roasting chunks of pork on sticks and swigging either rum or water from canteens. William took out his jackknife. He sliced off a piece of pork. It was not very good but would serve for the night. He offered Rebecca a piece, and she popped it into her mouth, still excited from the day.

"I heard. I only wish I could go with them, William. I would ride with these good men to the end of the earth," she whispered excitedly. "Look at this!" She pointed to her side. Her vest had been slashed by one of Tarleton's men. "You should have seen it!"

"Are you wounded?" William searched her side. No blood was showing.

"No. I fired off my piece just as he swung."

"Did you hit him?"

"I missed and so did he." She swigged from a small canteen, making a face before handing it to him. "Take a drink of this."

William took the canteen and lifted the cork top. He took a sniff and winced as the powerful smell wafted through the air. He shook his head.

"Awful, isn't it?" She gave a quiet laugh and poured it on the ground, out of view from the rest of the 3rd Virginia. "It'll rot you teeth, this stuff." Rebecca gave a wave to several dragoons who were sitting off to the side drinking.

"Well done, young Robert!" one of the soldiers said as he and the others toasted her. Rebecca pretended to drink from her canteen.

"We'll have to split off from them." William checked the map. "Head north through Maryland. It's about two hundred miles to Philadelphia."

"Should take us maybe five or six days," Rebecca said as she lay on her blanket beside William.

"Once we get that far, it should be safer. We can ride alone and make good time." William folded up the map.

"Good. That's good." Rebecca turned on her side toward him. Her hat slipped off. She opened her tired emerald eyes and smiled at William.

"Better hide your hair." He adjusted her hat back on her head. "No one has hair like that."

"I wish I had a brother like you, William." She yawned deeply, blinked, and closed her eyes. "I wish…"

William looked at his friend. As strong and hard as she seemed sometimes, he knew what she must be feeling inside. He felt so very grateful for Rebecca's help and companionship, for without her, where would he be? He turned over and waited for sleep, pressing his hand against Armistead's hidden message.

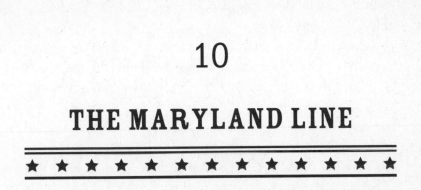

10

THE MARYLAND LINE

★ ★ ★ ★ ★ ★ ★ ★ ★ ★ ★ ★ ★ ★ ★

Splitting off from General Weedon's forces, William and Rebecca rode fast through Maryland. After three days, they were halfway to Philadelphia and they had not seen one redcoat. Wagonloads of tobacco or flour were being hauled along the Post Road. They passed slaves working the fields of the wealthier citizens who traveled between plantations in elaborate stagecoaches. There were many Maryland plantations, owned by both loyalists and patriots, but in a land where the British-aligned Tories once ruled the roost, the American Whigs were now in control. Maryland had escaped the redcoat destruction of the southern colonies.

They crossed the Potomac River on a flatboat and forded shallow creeks on horseback. They skirted Annapolis, covering most of their journey in the mornings and late afternoons. At times, Rebecca urged Lady Blue into a flat-out run, something Honor relished as a challenge. William would give Honor his head, and they would tear after the blue-eyed horse.

The midday July sun was strong and the heat was too much to push for long. They trotted into the shelter of the woods by a stream and decided to rest for part of the afternoon. William limped over to the stream. Large, painful blisters had formed from the ill-fitting boots. He stuck his sore feet in the creek and sat back with his rifle. Nothing stirred but the building rattle of cicadas. Rebecca sat next to him. She filled her hat with water and poured it over her head. She opened up the map and they were studying the route ahead when they heard the clip-clop of a horse above the buzzing of the insects. Grabbing their guns, they crept to the edge of the woods. They watched from the shelter of the trees as several wagons accompanied by a dozen Maryland Light Dragoons rumbled past them and then disappeared up the road.

"Looks like they're hauling supplies," said William as they ran back to the creek.

"They don't seem to be in too much of a hurry," offered Rebecca as she pored over the map.

"Are we near a town?" William asked.

"We must be close to Baltimore by now. Perhaps five or six miles. Look here." She pointed to some words scribbled just on the other side of Baltimore and the harbor.

"What is it?" William asked.

"There is a safe house a few miles north on the other side of town, Angler's Mill, according to this."

"How far to the Susquehanna River?"

"Forty miles or so." Rebecca folded the map and stuck it in her saddlebag.

"I say we keep going and follow the dragoons into town," said William as he hurried to put on his boots. "It'll save us time tomorrow."

They rode behind the troops and supply wagons, past the houses and shops along Baltimore Street. At the harbor, citizens and slaves scurried about on the docks sorting supplies for the Continental Army. They came to Charles Street and skirted past a line of ships, sails furled. Sacks of flour and tobacco, and crates of uniforms, shoes, and clothing of all kinds were being loaded aboard. A ripe smell filled the air as sweating men pushed wheelbarrows full of fish toward the taverns along the street. Baltimore was an important supply line for the armies of Washington and Lafayette, and one that was well guarded against the redcoats and the wealthy loyalists that lived among them.

Stopping in front of Kominski's Tavern, they were tempted to enter, but something about it persuaded William to move on. Perhaps it was his memory of the watchful Mr. Shaw in Williamsburg that made him think better about going inside and exposing themselves to the scrutiny of strangers. Instead, they picked up some food from the local merchants to supply themselves for the remainder of the journey to Philadelphia.

They took a left turn up York Road and headed out of town, cantering north on the Post Road. Several miles outside of Baltimore, they came to a fork in the road. Stopping to check their map, they decided to take a lane that headed into the woods. After a while, they came upon an old brick flour mill in a clearing.

Angler's Mill.

A giant wooden mill wheel still circled, squeaking softly in the current of the river. Off to the side sat a crooked wooden barn. There were no other buildings along the wooded shoreline of the thick forest across the water. The mill was quite isolated. The corral was intact with a mound of hay scattered on the ground. They led the horses to the riverbank to drink and then put them into the corral and let them eat the hay. Leaving their saddles on the horses, they grabbed the weapons and shot bags.

William walked up to the front of the mill as Rebecca checked the sides. He put his ear to the front door, listening for any signs of life.

"Doesn't look like anyone is around," said Rebecca as she returned and settled in beside him.

They opened the door and stepped onto a floor with white flour dust an inch deep. Sacks of flour, slashed across the middle, still sat along one wall. A huge circular flat stone with two stone grinders on top of it stood in the right side of the mill. Windows that faced the river let in the late sun, revealing several broken chairs and a desk. Tools and a broom lay scattered on the dusty floor.

"The place looks abandoned." Rebecca ran her finger along the white dust on the walls.

"There aren't even any footprints. Just ours." William noted the marks they made on the floor. "Look." William went to the opposite side of the room where a filthy old rug had been pulled off to one side and a trapdoor had been opened. A ladder led to a room below.

They climbed down the ladder to a dark room that was about fifteen feet square. A broken window with a wooden shutter hanging crookedly to the side faced the river. William stuck his head out and saw a narrow, planked walkway that ran the length of the mill just above the level of the river.

When William pulled his head back in, he saw that the wooden wall opposite the window had been smashed and only a few panels were left hanging. Behind the panels were shelves with some books and clothing. Bottles of ink, containers, and shoes had been tossed on the floor. A metal disk with a hole in it lay in the debris.

"Not a safe house anymore, is it?" said William. "Maybe we should move on."

"Look at this," said Rebecca as she picked up the copper disk. Letters lined the two-inch-wide rim like a watch.

"What is it?"

"Some kind of code wheel I think. See this hole? Something goes in here, I'll wager."

William looked around the room and spotted something shiny on the floor. "Over here." He went to the far wall and picked up a small, circular gold plate. It also had letters around the edge. He handed it to Rebecca. Together they sat on the floor, studying the code wheel.

"It's a really old one." She slid the smaller disk into the

hole and lined up the letters. "Right now, I have the letters lined up. A is A, B is B. See?"

"Turn the middle plate a little."

"Now W is A, I is M…"

"So my name is…AMPPMEQ!" William laughed.

"Yes, I shall now call you Amppmeq." Rebecca gave him a friendly punch on his good arm.

"So they could write their messages in this code and…"

"As long as the receiving side knew the starting letter, they could change it anytime."

"Brilliant."

Just then one of the horses gave a loud whinny.

"Lady Blue. I wonder what she wants." Rebecca rose and went to the ladder.

Lady Blue gave another whinny. A faint scraping sound suddenly came from the floor above them. William grabbed Rebecca as she reached the ladder, putting a finger to his lips. Another creak and some flour dust began to seep through the floor and sift down into the room.

"Shhh…" He quietly pulled back the cock on his rifle and felt for his pistol. "Are you loaded?" he whispered.

"Yes." Rebecca raised her musketoon. She indicated the handles of the two pistols she had stuck in her breeches.

They backed away from the ladder to the far corner of the room and aimed at the trapdoor. The floor creaked again. More flour sifted from the ceiling as the footsteps crept slowly to the trapdoor above. Finally they stopped. The barrel of a Brown Bess musket appeared in the opening followed by a black boot stepping down on the first rung of the ladder. William held his breath as he sighted down the barrel of his rifle.

Suddenly there was a quick movement in the window to the right. William turned to face a man in a hat, wire glasses. It was the schoolmaster he had seen at Weedon's Tavern. The man raised a pistol.

"Look out!" William pushed Rebecca to the side and dove to the floor. The man let loose with his pistol. The shot smashed into the spot where William's head had been. William fired his rifle at the schoolmaster. The lead ball blew apart the wooden shutter, sending splinters into the man's face. Cursing, the intruder grabbed his face and ducked below the window.

In a split second, the other man jumped down from the ladder. It was the same sloppy drunkard from Weedon's. Just as he swung his Brown Bess into place, Rebecca fired off her musketoon, catching the man in the shoulder with the scattergun. His musket fired wide as he hit the floor and lay still. William leveled his pistol at the drunk, determined to keep the man down.

"William! Behind you!" Rebecca cried.

William ducked underneath the window just as the schoolmaster reappeared and reached through the window with a second gun. William fired straight up at the man's arm and missed. In desperation, he grabbed the man's wrist, trying to wrestle his gun away. He held on with all his weight as the schoolmaster reached in with his other arm and tried to beat William with his free hand. Then he threw his arm around William's neck and started to choke him.

Suddenly, the drunk jumped up from the floor with a pistol. He let loose on Rebecca. Rebecca fired back, but her shot went wide. She dropped her empty gun and immediately grabbed her second pistol and held it on the man. The drunk pulled a knife and stood as if waiting for her next move.

"Let him go!" Rebecca demanded as she swung her pistol from one man to the other.

William felt himself growing faint from the choke hold around his neck. He could not move in the grasp of the man's arm. He brought his hands down and went limp, and the arm around his neck loosened. That was all he needed. In that instant, he reached into his pocket for the jackknife with his right hand and pulled out the blade with his left. Pivoting slightly, he plunged the blade deep into the schoolmaster's left arm.

"Ah!" the man screamed in pain as Rebecca ducked to the floor.

The schoolmaster's pistol fired into the wall above Rebecca's head. Dropping the gun, he grabbed for William's knife. William wrenched the blade away and turned and stood to stab him again, but the schoolmaster fell backward and splashed into the river.

Rebecca faced the other man with her pistol, but the wounded drunk scrambled up the ladder. William, jackknife still in hand, stood with Rebecca side by side in the middle of the room. The clatter of boots above them led to the front door.

"Reload!" William shouted, trying to catch his breath.

The two of them reloaded their weapons. After a minute William, pistol drawn, poked his head out the window and searched the river for signs of the schoolmaster. The only movement was the old mill wheel turning slowly in the current. The faint sound of hoofbeats clattered in the distance. William collected the discarded weapons of the drunk and the schoolmaster and tossed them into the river.

"I think they rode away." William glanced at Rebecca's arm and saw a patch of red on her shirt. "You're bleeding."

"Yes. Just a little. I'm all right." Rebecca ran her finger along her arm. She grabbed her musketoon and her shot bag. "Dear God, who were they? Scroope's men, do you think? Spies?"

"They have to be. I remember them from Weedon's."

They cocked their weapons and climbed back up the ladder. Blood and boot marks led to the door. Cautiously, they went outside, guns in hand, and studied their surroundings. The bloody trail led up the road, no doubt to where the men had tied up their horses. They checked on Lady Blue and Honor. The horses were nibbling on the hay. William took the pouch of food and they hurried back inside.

"I think it's better if we stay the night here rather than risk riding in the dark. They might still be in the woods." William shut the trapdoor. Then he grabbed some sacks of flour and dragged them across the floor and stacked them over the top of it.

"I don't expect they are in any shape to come at us again." Rebecca tugged at a massive wooden desk that lay on its side. "My guess is they're heading back to Baltimore to get fixed up. Help me with this?"

William took hold of a corner of the desk and together they managed to haul it across the room. Angled on its side facing the doors and windows, the heavy oak table would serve as a good shield. They sat down on the floor behind it.

"That musketoon of yours nearly took the man's arm off. And I hit bone with Asher's knife." He reached for his rifle, checked the frizzen and the pan, and set it to the side. He noticed Rebecca tremble a little as she inspected her wound through the hole in her shirt. "You're shaking."

"It's all right. Just a crease. We match." She smirked bravely at him and touched his shoulder. "Peter Francisco would just have you seal it shut for me with a hot knife, but don't get any ideas." William took out his knife and cut a strip of cloth from the hem of his shirt. Then he tied it tightly around her arm.

"Will you be able to ride in the morning?" William smiled a little.

"Definitely. This little thing won't stop me." She brought out a chunk of pork and tore it in half, handing a piece to William.

"I can take the first watch," said William as he chewed the meat. Then he picked up his rifle and rested it in the crook of his arm.

"Heavens no, William. Thank you." She pulled the

musketoon close. "We'll stay up together. Keep each other awake."

★ ★ ★

Honor and Lady Blue, chests heaving from the journey, pranced and snorted beneath William and Rebecca. The ride had been fierce and they had covered the remaining miles quickly, fearful their attackers might be following. They walked their horses toward Rodger's Tavern and tied them to the railing out front, next to a number of other horses, both military and civilian. They carefully took in the area around them. Not far down the road, the beautiful mile-wide Susquehanna River drifted to the east, toward the vast expanse of the Chesapeake Bay. Supplies for the Continental Army were stacked near the dock. Rodger's Crossing had been busy that afternoon.

William nodded to Rebecca as he shoved his pistol into his breeches and covered it with his vest. Following suit, she did the same and they walked up the steps to the door. As William reached for the handle, the door swung open, and they were ushered into soldiers' shouts of celebration. Crowded with patriots, the tavern hummed with life. Three civilians were huddled in the far corner of the room. William took note, silently memorizing their faces.

"To the Four Hundred!" went the cry. Eight blue-uniformed patriot soldiers of the 5th Maryland regiment toasted each other with tankards of ale. The owner, sleeves rolled to his elbows, began filling the empty mugs with more of the foamy brew.

"The Maryland Line!" the owner bellowed. "Everybody drink!" The speeches and war stories flowed as freely as the grog. A skinny old man with a fiddle started in with the popular tune, "The White Cockade."

"William," said Rebecca breathlessly as she grabbed his sleeve and led him to a table in the corner, away from the action. "These are men of the Maryland Four Hundred. They're among the toughest in all the Continental Army."

"The Battle of Long Island." William nodded, remembering the stories told by his brother. "They stood against thousands of redcoats so General Washington could retreat and save his men. Nearly all of the Four Hundred were killed."

"People say the war might well have been over quickly without them. We should get in their good graces," Rebecca said. "If there's any trouble, no one would dare stand up to these men."

They toasted again in unison, this time quoting the long wooden sign above the bar. "Good God! What brave fellows I must this day lose!" It was a quote by George Washington, and now it was a battle cry.

William and Rebecca sat at the table, counting what money they had. They would have to pay the ferryman for passage across the wide river. Two people and two horses would be expensive. William pulled out his paper Continental dollars and Rebecca produced some silver coins. The owner walked over with two mugs in his fists and introduced himself.

"Colonel John Rodgers is the name, boys. In here, everybody drinks. Compliments of the Fifth Maryland," said Rodgers as he slammed the mugs of cider on the table. "Bottom's up!"

Rebecca gave William a wink and grabbed her cider. Trying to fit in with the soldiers, she stood up and gave the men a cheer. "To the Four Hundred!"

"The Four Hundred!" the men raised their mugs. "Down the hatch! Drink her down! All at once, lad!"

William took a sip. It was sour to the taste but most likely safer to drink than any water served in the tavern. Rebecca put the mug to her lips, gasping as she managed to drain the last of it.

"Huzzah!!!" cheered the men. "Well done, young man."

"Are you looking to cross the river?" asked Colonel Rodgers as he noted the coins on the table. "No paper dollars, lad. They're—"

"Worthless, I know. We want to cross as soon as we can," said William.

"That'll be tomorrow most likely. Angus McCaron, the ferryman, is due back with his flatboat soon, but you won't have enough sun left to cross today. You best lay in for the night. You can bunk with the troops."

"With these men?" asked Rebecca, studying the raucous group. She licked the frothy cider from her lips.

"They're a good bunch when they're sober." Rodgers eyed the soldiers. There would be no shortage of drinking this night. "Looks like we're in for a long one. You work it out with

McCaron in the morning. I won't be up. You can pay him then. We all have to pay the ferryman!" He chuckled heartily. "Where are you two boys from? I haven't seen you around here."

"Virginia." William glanced at Rebecca.

"We're going to apprentice in Philadelphia," added Rebecca.

"A lot going on down in Virginia. The word is Tarleton is on the move again."

"It's true," said Rebecca. "He's burning the countryside. General Weedon and the Third Virginia had a fight with his rearguard the other day."

"They think Tarleton has gone after Jefferson. We got mixed up in it." William took a sip of cider and took a look around the tavern. He studied the civilians on the other side of the tavern.

"Weedon's back in?" Colonel Rodger's eyes lit up. He turned to face the men. "Hear that, boys? These two young men say Weedon's back in the game! Going after Bloody Ban!"

"Huzzah!" cried the soldiers. "To the Third Virginia!" They grabbed their mugs and swept toward William and Rebecca. The fiddler picked up his tune. One of the soldiers brought out a flute from his vest and joined in.

"I rode with Weedon!" shouted Rebecca above the din. She climbed up on the table, stood and raised her mug.

This caused laughter among the men, for Rebecca did not present a very formidable sight. Baggy clothes and hat, she looked like any poor young wilderness boy.

"Sit down, boy! Join up when you start shaving!" the men called.

"My name is Robert, and I fought Bloody Ban's men. I did!" she insisted defiantly. She pointed to the bloodied bandage on her arm. "Where do you think I got this? Good William was there!"

The room hushed. The music stopped. All looks went to William.

"He did. Robert rode with the light dragoons!" cried William. "Huzzah!"

"Huzzah!" shouted the soldiers. The fiddle and flute picked up again. Two of the men lifted Rebecca off the table. One sat her on his shoulders and marched her around the great room. "Well done, young master Robert!"

"To the Third Virginia!" shouted Rebecca delightedly. "To the battle of Guilford Courthouse!"

William stood and moved away from the growing celebration as they twirled a laughing Rebecca around the room. Out of the corner of his eye, he could see the ferryman through the window as he drifted ghostlike toward the riverbank. William slipped through the tavern door and walked down to the river as McCaron guided the ferry to the wooden dock. The ferryman wore a hooded dark coat that draped his tall frame like a shroud. Black hair, long and unkempt, blew behind him in the breeze. His bony hands handled the boat expertly as he closed in on the dock, gnarled fingers playing the long oar like an instrument. He picked up a coiled rope and tossed it on the dock, motioning to William to move away. As McCaron bent down to secure the flatboat, he looked up and gave

William the slightest smile. His eyes were almost without color, the palest blue. The gaze sent a slight shiver down William's back.

11

THE CITY OF
BROTHERLY LOVE

★ ★ ★ ★ ★ ★ ★ ★ ★ ★ ★ ★ ★

The morning sun shone bright in the distance, reflecting
off the Chesapeake Bay. They were already halfway across
the river, the flatboat beating hard against the choppy current. The drinking had lasted most of the night. By celebration's end, the soldiers, William, and Rebecca had collapsed
in the beds and cots of the tavern, exhausted from the night's
revelry. Rebecca had professed over and over that she had
had the royal time of her young life. The Four Hundred had
practically adopted her.

The darkly cloaked ferryman pulled on his oar. His strokes
were long and precise. His burly young helper matched him
from the opposite side of the boat as if they were in some
ancient ballet. Rebecca was busy studying the map.

"My young brother, I must say that is a fine-looking
watch you have there." Angus McCaron smiled serenely as
he stroked.

William looked up from his task of securing the horses

to the railing. The Susquehanna's waves were picking up in the wind, and Honor and Lady Blue began to shift around dangerously in the shallow-bottomed ferry. He glanced down at the Watchmaker's gold watch that bounced on his chest.

"Would you mind if I took a look at it?" McCaron asked politely. "My father, rest his soul, was a jeweler. It makes me think of him."

William stood and faced the tall gaunt man. It seemed a harmless enough request, so he lifted the watch for the ferry-man to see. He kept the chain around his neck and held on to the railing. McCaron laid down his oar and moved closer to William, resting a bony hand on his shoulder. His face lit up as he inspected the beautiful piece. He turned it over with his fingers and then settled it against William's chest.

"I don't think I've ever seen such a watch. Yes, a very fine one as ever made. May I ask where you got it?"

"It's been in my family," answered William. Deciding to remove temptation, he pulled the chain over his head and tucked the watch safely into his saddlebag, buckling the flap shut.

"I see. Is that where you're heading? To your family?" McCaron picked up his long wooden oar and began to stroke. The other oarsman pulled from the opposite side of the long, flat ferry. Together, they stroked in a practiced rhythm as they drew nearer to the shore.

"No. My family is in Virginia. We're sent to apprentice in Philadelphia." William started to explain his story the way Mrs. Weedon told him when Rebecca looked up from her map.

"Apprentice? With a silversmith?" asked the ferryman.

"A cobbler if you must know. Our farm was destroyed. Our family hopes Philadelphia will provide opportunity," offered Rebecca as politely as she could.

"A shoemaker. I see." McCaron smiled in empathy, but his ghostly blue eyes seemed to look right through them. "Fallen on hard times, have you? Many are forced to apprentice. The war will do that. How long is your contract, may I ask?"

"Five years," said Rebecca as she glanced at William.

"Not too long. No," McCaron mused. "Of course, you could take that watch to a silversmith in Philadelphia. No doubt you could fetch a good price for it, even in these times."

"Yes, you're right I suppose." William smiled stiffly and turned back to the horses.

"That is our intention, sir," Rebecca said, attempting to dismiss the conversation.

"Well, my young brothers, I wish you Godspeed. You will fulfill your obligations to your master and return home wearing your freeman suits in no time." The ferryman turned away from them and dug his oar deep into the Susquehanna, matching his burly partner in perfect rhythm once again.

Rebecca motioned William over to look at the map. She pretended to study it with great interest but kept one eye on the ferryman.

"I don't like that man; he asks too many questions."

"I know what you mean." William glanced at the map. "How far do we have once we reach the other side?"

"I'd say two days' ride. There are several creeks and ferries. Newcastle is about twenty miles ahead, but we should make Naamans Creek by tonight. My guess is we'll get to Philadelphia by late tomorrow afternoon."

"Sixty-nine miles to be exact." Angus McCaron twisted his head around and smiled. "Stay on the Post Road all the way." He turned back to his rowing as the ferry drew ever closer to the bank.

★ ★ ★

William gazed in awe at the city before them as they trotted through Philadelphia along Cedar Street. He had never seen such a big city. All around them, people hawked their wares, and horses pulled the fine carriages of the wealthy. Vendors pushed carts loaded with food. The aroma of cooked meals mingled with smells of horse manure and the Delaware River. Brick buildings and houses lined the streets. Some houses had goats or chickens penned in their yards. They passed many people along the way; some were rich and powdered, others raggedy and poor. Patriot soldiers limped by, a few missing arms or legs.

For a moment, they stopped to look at the small map Mrs. Weedon had given them to navigate Philadelphia's grid of roadways. They decided to turn left onto Second Street, keeping the river on their right side. As they made their way on the cobblestone road past City Tavern, they could hear men yelling from inside. It was the bellow of men and their politics. Several blocks away, an enormous church rose tall against the sinking sun on its left. Sunlight bounced off the steeple.

"That has to be Christ Church," said Rebecca. "We're getting closer."

"Look for High Street. The cobbler shop is supposed to be around the corner near a printer." William urged Honor to the right, studying the stores and buildings along the way. He noticed a copy of the Declaration of Independence affixed to the glass window of a shop. "Dunlap's Printers. Here it is."

They made the turn down High Street toward the river. An ornate one-horse carriage was parked on the right, its driver sitting contentedly and smoking his pipe. Next to the carriage was a small sign tucked between two taller buildings, hanging on a rickety old fence.

The Buckle and Shoe
Joseph R. Tweedle
Proprietor

A stone walkway led to a small, white, wooden shop. Two windows displayed belts, bags, boots, and shoes. William and Rebecca tied the horses to a rail and headed down the walk to the shop porch. They opened the door to the light tinkling of a bell. The shop was filled with the rich and pungent smell of freshly tanned leather. The sound of hammering came from a curtained room in the back of the tiny shop. Across the room to their left, an older, paunchy man with a leather apron knelt before a groaning rotund woman. Tufts of white hair stuck out comically from his balding head and bushy eyebrows twitched over wire glasses. He was struggling mightily to slip a yellow shoe on the woman's large foot.

"Careful, Mr. Tweedle!" screeched the woman. "My heel!"

The man turned to William and Rebecca and held up a finger. Sweat dripped from his face. "A moment! Wait outside, gentlemen." He gestured impatiently to the front door. He turned apologetically to the woman inside. William and Rebecca opened the door and sat on a bench on the front porch. They listened as Mr. Tweedle pleaded with his customer.

"Sorry to say, I think it has been stretched as far as humanly possible, Mrs. Fortenaut," said the old man. "You really need a new pair. You would be much more comfortable with a little more room. One's foot tends to change over time."

"Nonsense, Mr. Tweedle. These are my favorites and I have no time to wait. I need them tonight."

"Here, now," Mr. Tweedle urged in a gentle voice. "Try this one."

"Dear Lord!" cried Mrs. Fortenaut. "I will not be seen clip-clopping around in society like a Clydesdale!"

"Well, I'm afraid we've run out of options."

"I don't consider myself an option, Mr. Tweedle. Good day!" Mrs. Fortenaut marched through the door and tossed the offending shoe over her shoulder. Carrying her own precious shoes, she stormed barefoot down the walkway. The driver of the fancy carriage hopped off his seat and helped the woman aboard.

"Thomas! Fleur de Paris, fast as you can!"

She settled back into the seat and snapped open a parasol. In an instant, Mrs. Fortenaut was whisked away down High Street.

"Dear me," said Tweedle in the doorway as he shook his head and wiped his brow. "The woman always wears me out. Now, what can I do for you young men? I am closing for the day, so make it quick." He gestured for them to come inside.

They followed the man into his shop. Rebecca reached into her vest and pulled out Mrs. Weedon's letter and handed it to the cobbler.

"What is this you have?" He turned the letter over in his hands and examined the wax seal.

"It is a letter for you, sir," Rebecca said cautiously.

"I can see that."

"Are we alone?" asked William, glancing at the curtained room. "We need to speak in private."

"Young men, do not waste my time. I have had a very long day."

"It's from Mrs. Weedon of Fredericksburg," whispered Rebecca.

Mr. Tweedle froze for several seconds. Then he slowly went to the curtain and pulled it aside. A red-haired boy of about fourteen stood at a workbench busily attaching a buckle to a leather belt.

"Johnny, you may quit for the day. See me back here in the morning."

"Yes, Master Tweedle. Thank you, sir. Will it be eight, then?" asked Johnny as he dropped the belt and buckle.

"Yes, fine. Take a key and open up the shop. I will be in later."

"Yes, sir. Very good, sir." Johnny quickly left and shut the door behind him.

Tweedle went to the door and threw the bolt, locking it from the inside. He reached for a "Closed" sign and hooked it above the window. Drawing the curtains, he motioned William and Rebecca into the back room. Picking up a lantern, he lit the wick with a match and then used a knife to slit the wax seal on the letter. He studied the letter for a few seconds with a puzzled expression.

"This is a contract for apprenticeship?" Tweedle's bushy eyebrows twitched above his spectacles. "As you can see, I have no need for another apprentice. Johnny will be with me for three more years, until his family debt is paid."

"That is what it says," answered William, "but…"

"Not what it means," Rebecca said. "Mrs. Weedon said you are the only person in all Philadelphia she can trust with this information—this message, I should say."

"I see." Tweedle sat studying the letter. "Clever she is, Catherine. What better way to send a message? Two boys. Let us see just how clever."

The cobbler reached under his workbench. After a moment, a click was heard and a secret drawer popped out from below. He fished around and brought out a small corked bottle and a brush. Then he spread out the letter and began to lightly brush a liquid between the handwritten lines of the letter. Carefully, he blew on the liquid until it dried.

"Well, Mrs. Weedon. Back in the game, are we?" He motioned for William and Rebecca to come closer and held the light above the letter. "And here is her message to me. Look." Gradually, writing began to form between the lines as the invisible ink appeared. When the cobbler read the letter, he gasped. "My heavens. You carry correspondence from James Armistead. You're to take it to..."

"General Washington himself," William said. "A courier called the Watchman gave it to me before he died."

"The Watchman, you say? Dear me, poor man. Where is this correspondence?" The old man began to blink rapidly. Craftsman that he was, he could hardly control the shaking of his hands.

"Hidden, sir," replied Rebecca.

"Yes. Hidden well, I'm sure. Quite brilliant to send boys, I must say." The cobbler placed the letter on the table. He took off his spectacles and wiped the lenses with a cloth. When he was done, he placed them carefully back on his nose. Then he picked up a large threaded needle and turned to William. "Your name is?"

"William Tuck."

"And that makes you Robert, then." Mr. Tweedle studied them thoughtfully. "Brave boys. Brave boys. William, hand me your vest."

"My vest, sir?"

"I feel the need to make a minor repair," he said as he

pointed to a small tear in the seam around the left armhole. "Just there."

William took off his vest and handed it to the cobbler. The craftsman's experienced fingers flew over the leather vest as he probed the tear and began to sew.

"The trick is to get you past the British and up river to Washington's camp in New York. That is not an easy proposition. The closer you get to New York, the more dangerous it is. Redcoat patrols are everywhere. There are checkpoints along the lower Hudson River." The cobbler tied off the thread, examined the vest for any other irregularities, and then handed it back to William. "Here you are, William. That takes care of the vest. But your boots—I can see they are not yours. Painfully big, they must be."

"I was given them off a dead soldier." William flexed his toes, willing away the pain of his blistered feet.

"Forgive me. A cobbler can't help but notice. I could fix you up with another pair."

"No need, Mr. Tweedle. Thank you, these'll do for me. How fast can we make the trip?" asked William as he slipped the vest on, anxious to move forward with the mission.

"We need to get there as quickly as possible," said Rebecca.

"Quickly yes, but caution is essential. I have just the man for the job." Tweedle held Mrs. Weedon's letter over the lantern until it caught fire, letting the ashes fall into a dish. "We must find you a safe place for the night. And food?"

"Yes, sir." William's stomach rumbled at the thought.

"The City Tavern?" asked Rebecca.

"No. No, taverns are nests for spies, even in Philadelphia." He ushered them to the door and threw open the bolt. "Head to the State House. You can't miss it. Go two blocks down, then east on Walnut Street. Find the largest oak tree in the square and wait. I'll send word quickly."

A few minutes later, William and Rebecca found Walnut Street and rode slowly toward the State House. As they passed along the street, they saw two prisons on their left near a long earthen mound, the burial site of patriot soldiers. Several windows with steel bars hid the poor souls and criminals who shouted and begged, arms reaching toward them. On the opposite side of the street rose the spire of the State House. A crowd of a hundred people stood before a raised wooden platform. A dozen soldiers of the Pennsylvania militia were lined up in front of the stage. The doors of the State House opened, and the Continental Congress delegates walked out after another day's work of debating America's many issues. An angry roar rose from the crowd. The delegates climbed the three steps to the platform and patiently waved for the crowd to be silent.

"There's the oak tree," said William, pointing to the largest tree that stood off to the side of the platform.

They slid their pistols under their shirts and tied off the horses. Shouldering their way through the protesting citizens, they took their position under the massive tree.

"Our soldiers in the southern colonies who have been captured and taken aboard the evil prison ships must be compensated!" shouted one of the delegates. The intense-looking man in a long blue coat and white shirt turned to his colleagues and raised his arms in frustration. Others began to pound their canes on the wooden platform in agreement.

"Hear, hear!" shouted the crowd in agreement.

"By whom, Mr. Bee?" answered another, who stood to the left side of the platform. Dressed in a red suit and vest, he loosened the ruffled collar of his shirt. A stout man, he appeared somewhat frail. He raised his hat with a shaking hand and began to fan his face.

"Our newly formed government, sir! The one you so painstakingly helped create, Mr. Adams!" answered Bee. "Dear God, man, they've lost everything and have been treated in so vile a manner. They and their families deserve our help! Or has the delegate from Massachusetts forgotten our southern sacrifice?"

"William, that's Sam Adams," Rebecca said, sucking in her breath. "Would you have ever thought you would see something like this?"

"Never." Roanoke was a long way from the center of the revolution.

"How dare you, sir!" Samuel Adams slammed down his cane on the platform. One of the other delegates, a man much younger with delicate features and pursed lips, reached out a hand to steady him. "We've all sacrificed! The worst of the prison ships that hold these unfortunates are in New York. We have no money! How, Thomas, are we to compensate every one?"

"Prisoner exchange, I'll wager." Rebecca nodded to the

proceedings. "My father had been pushing for that for a long time. More men are dying on the ships than in battle."

As Samuel Adams began to make his point, the younger delegate put a hand on the older man's shoulder and whispered something into his ear. He then rose, straightened his brown jacket, and faced the room. Though he was perhaps just thirty years old, he nonetheless was a man of considerable authority.

"What the esteemed Mr. Adams will tell you is this." Everyone in the square grew quiet as the young delegate spoke. "First off, we will step up prisoner exchange. We need to get our most important officers and citizens and whatever belongings they have removed from this terrible confinement."

William and Rebecca stood, riveted. To be this close to the heart of the new government was something William had never imagined. Just then, a plump woman in a white bib, pushing a wheeled cart, stopped beside them. In the basket of the cart were cooked chickens wrapped in newspaper.

"Roasted chickens on Fridays!" she yelled to the bystanders. She then leaned in toward William and whispered, "The proof is in the stuffing." She handed him a chicken and then wheeled the cart among the spectators.

"Tweedle?" William looked at Rebecca. She nodded in agreement. Then they carefully unwrapped the paper from around chicken and looked for a message. There was nothing of note, so they began to eat as they watched the debate unfold.

"It's as if we are in the State House with them." Rebecca, transfixed by the proceedings, chewed her chicken slowly.

"Not good enough, Mr. Madison!" cried Bee. "We all know Washington's stance on exchange! He's against it. To him, one of our men isn't on the same level as a British officer. He'd rather let ours rot than give them back one of theirs."

"We will increase political pressure on the redcoats to agree to exchange by extracting all monies and properties from those loyalists we know are still faithful to the King. At the very least it will help compensate our own unfortunates!" announced James Madison.

"I say we hold debate on the subject tomorrow, Saturday!" Bee turned to his colleagues for approval.

"Hear, hear!" All the delegates voiced their agreement, and as quickly as that, America's leaders began to file off the platform and the crowd of people began to disperse.

William felt something hard in the breast cavity of the chicken. He reached inside and pulled out a small corked bottle. He wiped away the stuffing and popped off the cork. A handwritten note was hidden inside.

"Look at this." He held out the paper.

"Careful," she cautioned. "Someone may be watching."

William glanced around at the faces. He lowered the note and unrolled it.

"What does it say?" Rebecca asked as she finished her chicken and wiped her hands on the newspaper.

"It says, 'North on Eighth Street. Laundry. Mrs. Howell. Three white, one black.'"

"Eighth Street? Laundry?" she asked, puzzled. "Obviously a signal. What else?"

"*In all haste.*" William met her eyes.

"All right, then." She tugged at his arm. "Let's go."

12

HUNTED

It was nearly dark as William and Rebecca rode north on Eighth Street. The two of them slipped through the streets virtually unnoticed as they closely studied the houses and buildings along the way. After a while, they spotted a small wooden house on the left, at the edge of the city. An old woman, her white hair cascading from a blue bonnet, stood collecting laundry from a clothesline in the glow of a lantern that hung on a post. There were three white shirts and a black coat.

"Mrs. Howell?" asked William as they drew closer.

The woman turned to them and motioned them closer with a crook of her bony finger. William threw a glance over his shoulder to Rebecca. They dismounted and walked the horses over to the wooden fence.

"Take the horses between the houses here, to the back alley," said the woman quietly as she took down the remaining laundry. "You'll find a room off the stable that is lit with a candle. Stay there and don't leave. Ride out at dawn."

"Ride where?" asked William.

"Up the Post Road past Burlington to Crofwick's Bridge. We've sent word. The Hunter will be expecting you."

"How do we find him?" asked William.

"He'll find you. Move along now." She bent over, picked up her basket, and limped toward the house.

They led the horses down a path that ran the length of the house, to the back alley. Turning right, they came to a rickety wooden corral in front of an old stable that had a shed built on the left side. A light flickered through the cracks in the wall. They opened a gate and let the horses in. Water and hay had been left for them. Honor and Lady Blue immediately began to eat and drink. William and Rebecca grabbed their guns and opened the door to the shed. A single candle on a table revealed two cots. Resting on one of the cots was a pair of boots, a note peeking out from one of them.

William leaned his rifle against the wall and reached for the note and sat on the cot.

"It's from Mr. Tweedle," William said as he read the note. "He says to make an old cobbler happy and accept the boots as his gift."

"He's a good man." Rebecca inspected her arm. Then she collapsed in exhaustion on the other cot. "I'm so tired, I could sleep for a week." She rested the musketoon at her side.

"Until morning, anyway." William sat and admired the fresh boots. He began to remove the old ones from his blistered feet. He straightened out his bloodied stockings and pulled on his new boots. He stood and wiggled his toes.

The fit was nearly perfect. He silently thanked the kindly Mr. Tweedle.

★ ★ ★

Dawn came early. They sped past the outskirts of the city. For fifteen miles, they cantered along the Post Road. They passed the small farms that dotted the Pennsylvania landscape. Eventually, they entered a thick forest with small log huts, ghostly reminders of the terrible winter of 1778 at Valley Forge. William shuddered to think of the starving and diseased soldiers of the Continental Army who must have lived in them. For several hours, they continued north. A few riders and wagons appeared here and there along the way, but so far there were no British or American troops. Finally, they crested a hill. Below them was a wooden bridge that spanned a flowing stream. A sign stating "Crofwick's Bridge" stood beside the road that led across the bridge and disappeared into the woods on the other side.

"There doesn't seem to be anyone around," said Rebecca, studying the surroundings.

"Let's get out of this heat and wait by the stream." William wiped the sweat from his brow.

They pulled the horses into the shade below Crofwick's Bridge, dismounted, and let them drink in the moss-shrouded river as they waited for the Hunter. After a few minutes, they heard the sound of a horse-drawn carriage on the bridge. A black man in a dark suit and white wig snapped a whip and the horse picked up the pace. The carriage, carrying a well-dressed traveler, disappeared into the dark, wet woods. Just then, a wiry man leading a black horse walked slowly across the bridge from the other side of the creek. He was dressed in leather skins and his horse was loaded with animal furs. Bags of other items were tied to the saddle. The man stopped in the middle of the bridge, reached for a pipe in his pocket, and loaded it with tobacco. Peering over the side of the bridge, he nodded his head in greeting.

"Well, young men?" he said matter-of-factly as he lit his pipe. "Time's a wasting."

William and Rebecca looked at each other questioningly and then emerged from under the bridge leading Honor and Lady Blue.

"Are you the Hunter?" asked William.

"Names aren't important." The man smiled as he studied them. "I've been called lots of things. The Hunter will do just fine. I understand you have a great need to see the general."

"Yes, sir," answered William. "At all possible speed."

"Slower and cautious is better. Come closer and I'll fix you up with some of my load." The Hunter began to untie some of the skins. As Rebecca and William approached him, the man began to transfer some of his furs and skins to Honor and Lady Blue. "If we go as fast as we can, we could get there in two days. It's about seventy-five miles. Help me with these."

William and Rebecca assisted him with the load.

"Of course you run the risk of being shot." Seeing the uncertainty on William's face, he explained, "Redcoats patrol the Post Road between Cranberry-Brook and Flat-Bush. They've been shooting or hanging every courier they can catch. If you look like an express rider, they'll take you down. Better to do it my way. An extra day or two won't hurt— maybe even do some trading along the way. The point is to make sure Washington gets it, not the British. Trust me." He cinched the last of the load to the back of Honor's saddle. "That should do it. Now we go. So, William and Robert, is it?" He mounted his horse and began to trot across the bridge.

"Yes, sir," William said, glancing at Rebecca for reassurance.

"Let's go, then." She nodded her head and kicked Lady Blue over to Honor. Together they followed the Hunter into the dark woods.

Mr. Tweedle was right: the Hunter proved to be a most resourceful guide. They had moved easily along the Post Road for the better part of two days. They rode untroubled through Allen's-Town and spent the night in the woods near Cranberry-Brook. William hunted for food and, once again, shot a prize turkey for supper. As they traveled, the Hunter traded many of his furs for whatever silverware, cups, or lead he could find to one day be melted down to make ball shot, his most profitable trade bait. His black horse clanked with the bags of metal tied to the saddle. As they rode through Amboy, they came to a winding, narrow pass, and the Hunter held up his arm to stop.

"Wait here." He kicked his horse up a low rise and began to search the area with his telescope. He rode back to them, shaking his head. "Didn't see anything, but my instinct tells me there might be trouble ahead. We'll make a detour along the old Indian trail."

He veered into the thick woods off the Post Road and beckoned for them to follow him along a narrow path. They made good time through Pennsylvania and into New Jersey, past creeks and lakes, beaver dams and families of deer. If they kept up a fast trot through the woods, they would make it beyond the Narrows, and another day of careful travel would put them near the Continental Army and George Washington.

They guided the horses over a creek and came to the crest of a hill. A steep, rocky trail wound its way through the woods to a valley below.

"We'll have to go one at a time," said the Hunter. "Take it slow."

The Hunter rode first and they watched him pick his way expertly down the trail. Reaching the valley's edge, he turned and waved. Rebecca kicked Lady Blue forward, and she carefully guided the white horse down the slope. Once she hit the bottom, it was time for William to descend. He eased Honor ahead and leaned far back in the saddle as they took their first steps, thrusting his boots forward into the stirrups. Honor nervously made his way down the trail. As the trail got steeper, something spooked the big horse and it began to lose its footing on the loose rocks. Honor's hind hooves skidded out from under him. William's heart went into his mouth as he tried to lead the big horse away from the jutting rocks on the side of the trail. He yanked hard on the reins, fighting to keep them upright. Just then, a movement in the woods caught William's eye. He thought it must have been a deer. A shape slipped quietly among the trees and a quick flash of gold and red disappeared behind a rock. William managed to get Honor under control and forced him faster down the hill. Another shape darted through the dark woods on his right. A headdress of feathers appeared from behind a tree. William pulled Honor to a stop and reached for his pistol. In an instant, a dozen Indians with fierce black-painted faces emerged from hiding and surrounded him. The hairs on his neck stood up and he raised his pistol to fire.

"Hold your powder!" cried the Hunter from below.

William sat motionless as the Indians edged forward with muskets and bows and arrows ready. He carefully holstered his pistol.

"Come down slowly, William!" called the Hunter. "You're all right. It's trade they want."

William led Honor carefully down the steep slope as the Hunter began to loosen his bundles. Several Indians rode from the woods. The leader, dressed in deerskins and adorned with a brass necklace and bracelets, raised his hand in greeting to the Hunter. On his head was a leather helmet decorated with hawk feathers that stood straight up. The other twenty or so Indians were dressed in a similar fashion, but with plainer necklaces and feathers. They spread out to cover all sides. There would be no escape.

"These are Seneca Indians. The leader is Maska, Chief

Cornplanter's man." The Hunter, calm as can be, raised his hand in greeting.

"Chief Cornplanter? Of the Wyoming Massacre?" Rebecca placed both hands on the butts of her pistols. William followed suit and edged his hand toward his.

"I trade with all men. I know them well," said the Hunter.

"They tortured and killed patriots after they had surrendered! They're loyal to the British," Rebecca whispered urgently.

"Stay your hand. They want to trade for lead shot." The Hunter gave her a shake of his head and then turned to the Seneca leader. "Greetings, friends!"

Rebecca and William moved their hands away from their pistols.

"We have gifts for you, Hunter," said the leader as he motioned to several of his men. They trotted forward with horses laden with goods. "We heard you coming. We've been following you for many miles."

"I know." The Hunter untied a leather bag from his saddle. "I spotted you some ways back. You caught me at a good time, Maska. Look what I have for you." He held the bag out to the Indian.

Maska took the leather bag and reached inside. He pulled out a handful of lead musket balls. A smile appeared across his dark face. "For this we will give you our best bear skins."

"A few of those blankets will do nicely too."

Maska signaled to the other Indians and spoke in his

native language. Two of the Indians began to spread out black bearskins and blankets on the ground. Another of the hunters motioned to William and Rebecca. He edged his horse over to Lady Blue. Lady Blue jigged sideways and tried to nip the Indian's horse.

"She doesn't like anyone coming up on her." Rebecca jerked the reins and tried to move away, but the Indian continued to advance. Rebecca reached for her pistol. Several of the other Indians drew their muskets and trained them on Rebecca.

Another Seneca hunter came alongside Honor. He reached out for Honor's bridle. William almost fell off as Honor reared up and lashed out with his hooves. The bridle tore from the Indian's hands. William pulled back on the reins and backed Honor away from the man.

"Maska!" shouted the Hunter. "Friends! Easy now. Go easy."

The Seneca warriors began to converse among themselves while pointing out the pistols and muskets carried by William and Rebecca. The Hunter spoke to them in their native tongue at length, smiling, reassuring the Indians. Maska pulled the Hunter aside and the two of them engaged in a heated discussion. After a few minutes, the Hunter walked over to William and Rebecca.

"What do they want?" asked William nervously.

"Your horses and weapons." The Hunter turned and smiled at Maska.

"They could just murder us here and take them," said Rebecca in a low voice.

"There was a time they would do exactly that—take your weapons and your hair too."

"Then why don't they?" asked Rebecca warily.

"I told Maska that you are my new young partners." The Hunter stroked Lady Blue's head gently. "He's a good man. I made a deal with him."

"What kind of a deal?" William wondered.

"It doesn't matter. Something I'll work out with him later. In the meantime, stay calm. Let's get these skins and blankets together." The Hunter walked over to the bearskins and inspected them.

William slid off Honor and began to roll up the blankets. The Seneca hunters were dividing up the lead shot. Rebecca dismounted, keeping a careful eye on the Indians. She struggled to fold the bearskins with one hand, but her other hand never strayed far from her pistol. After they had tied everything to the saddles, they were ready to travel. Maska and the Hunter shook hands, and the Indians then mounted their horses and rode back up the steep slope. In seconds, they disappeared into the thick forest.

"That was close," said Rebecca as she mounted Lady Blue.

"Turned out pretty well. I think I made a bit of profit on this one." The Hunter chuckled. "Let's move on. Two more hours from here, there's a place we can put our feet up."

"Where?" asked William as he threw his leg over Honor, who was busy nuzzling Lady Blue. The white horse seemed to bask in the attention.

"Square in the lap of luxury, my young friends." The Hunter mounted and kicked his horse east. "The lap of luxury."

★ ★ ★

A massive redbrick farmhouse sat majestically in the green valley before them. The cookhouse and smokehouse stood off to the right. The stable and servants' quarters were farther away on the left. Dozens of sheep and goats were contained by a fenced pasture. Smoke rose from the cookhouse. Even at a quarter mile away, they could smell roasting mutton. They walked the horses along the gravel road toward the circular drive that led to the house.

"The Pendleton estate. Biggest in the valley." The Hunter smiled and smacked his lips. "Looks as though we're in time for supper."

"They're expecting us?" asked William.

"More or less. I always stop here on my trade route. They'll want everything we've got. Furs and Indian blankets from America are big in England and France. What we have, they'll ship out on the next boat. We're about ten miles from the Hudson River."

"What about the embargo?" asked Rebecca. She threw William a puzzled look as they followed the Hunter. "How would they get a ship past the British?"

"The Pendletons have their ways," he said simply. "Money talks. Money talks."

As they rode closer, the immense door of the main house

opened and a tall, elegantly dressed man in a burgundy coat and white breeches and shirt stepped out onto the porch. His white wig lit up as he faced the late afternoon sun.

He turned and called inside the house. "Mr. Able!" Instantly, a black man, also dressed formally in a black suit and white shirt and wig, stepped outside. "See to the guests, won't you?"

"Abraham, Isaac!" Mr. Able called out as he walked briskly toward the stables. He disappeared inside for a few seconds. Then, two young black males ran out to collect the horses. They were dressed in buff-colored vests, breeches, and white shirts, and looked to be about fourteen and sixteen years old.

"Well, Arthur, I see you've been expecting us!" the Hunter called out to the man. "Is that Olivia's roast I smell?"

"It is, my good man! You are just in time. We sup at nine." A charming smile stretched across Arthur Pendleton's face. "I see you have two hungry boys with you!"

"And some very nice bearskins and blankets, as you see."

"I do. I'll have my hands collect everything and we'll figure out a price." He gestured to the side of the estate. "In the meantime, you three can use the guest quarters by the pond to wash away the journey." He waved and stepped into the house.

"Kind of you, Arthur. But first, I need a word."

"Certainly." Pendleton paused in the doorway.

The Hunter turned to the two young servants as they led the horses to the stable. "Unload my horse but keep him saddled. I've a short errand to run."

"Yes, sir!" replied the older of the boys.

"Robert, William? Prepare for the best meal of your young lives," said the Hunter. "The servants will help with the horses and take you around to the guesthouse. I should be back by supper." The Hunter walked over to Pendleton. As the two men spoke, Pendleton glanced at William and Rebecca, his pleasant aristocratic demeanor giving way to a cold, stern look.

"See the way he's looking at us?" whispered William.

"Yes. I wonder what that's about," said Rebecca in agreement.

They followed the servants and horses into the long, wooden barn. Two-dozen stalls lined the walls and held beautiful and well-kept horses. The prize steeds stood chewing their feed, curious about the new arrivals. The two boys led Honor and Lady Blue into a double stall and began to unpack the supplies, furs, and Indian blankets. They then set down fresh hay and went outside to a pump to fill the water buckets.

"Odd, isn't it?" Rebecca whispered. "Look at all these horses. Well fed and pampered. I'm surprised the British haven't taken them."

"I was thinking that. And there must be a hundred goats and sheep outside," William noted. "Maybe the redcoats can't take them because the Continental Army is nearby."

"Perhaps. But then, wouldn't the livestock be given to our own soldiers?"

The servants returned with water buckets overflowing and

filled the trough in the stall. Honor and Lady Blue began to greedily drink together. The older boy smiled and clasped his hands behind his back.

"My name is Abraham. We'll take good care of the horses for you. Lord Pendleton says to show you the guest quarters. You can rest there until supper." He turned and indicted that they should follow.

"That would be excellent. Thank you, Abraham." Rebecca let out a sigh at the prospect of relaxing.

"This way, please." Abraham led them out of the barn and along a graveled path, toward a thatch of trees by the side of the main house. They walked through the woods, and after a hundred yards, a lovely pond came into view. Next to it sat a beautiful little brick cottage. To the side of the cottage, two servants were pouring steaming water into a large tub that sat outside on some bricks. Mr. Able directed a black woman as she carried tea and cups on a silver tray into the cottage.

William and Rebecca stepped into the guesthouse. The room was alive with bright-colored tapestries hanging from the walls and ornate vases filled with flowers. Windows along the side of the cottage provided a spectacular view of the pond. Swans glided across the water, glowing white against the green of the woods. A large four-poster bed with a red quilt sat against the wall opposite the windows. Two smaller beds for servants rested against the walls on either side. The woman set down the tea tray, turned down the beds, and left quickly through the side door. Everything seemed perfect. That they could have one night of luxury before they rode out to find Washington's camp in the morning filled them with bliss.

"You may wish to bathe before supper," said Mr. Able. "Shall I leave Abraham to assist?"

"No, thank you very much," said Rebecca quickly. "We'll be fine on our own."

"Very good. Dinner is in one hour." He snapped his fingers and headed out the door. The boys immediately followed him. Rebecca stared at the steaming bath like she had found a pot of gold.

"Go ahead," William said, knowing Rebecca would give anything to soak away the dust and sweat from their journey. "I want to look around. I'll wash up later."

"Thank you, William," she said happily. "Oh my, thank you." She turned her back and began to shuck her boots.

William smiled bashfully and went out to the pond. He walked along the beautiful setting, taking in the swans and the buzzing of insects. Stretching his arms, he sat on the ground and rested his head against a rock. He picked up a stone and tossed it into the water, watching the ripples spread, contemplating how far he and Rebecca had come. He had traveled nearly four hundred miles since that fateful battle at Green Spring. It was nearing the end of July. He pressed his hand against his thigh and felt for James Armistead's message. In one just day, he would complete his task. In that short time, the balance of the war could shift. He glanced at the setting sun, closed his sleepy eyes, and thought of his last moments with the Watchman.

Hoofbeats and the grinding wheels of wagons jerked him back to his senses. The sound grew closer until William could see the wagons pass beyond the trees. He got up and walked along the path through the woods until he came upon a dirt service lane that connected to the main gravel road. Three wagons pulled up to the back of the barn. The door slid open, and the drivers hopped down and disappeared into the barn. William ducked back into the tree line and moved closer to get a better look. He edged forward and knelt behind a fallen log. The drivers and several servants emerged, struggling as they carried large, heavy barrels and hoisted them onto the wagons, then went back in and returned with long, wooden boxes and stacked them next to the barrels. For twenty minutes, the men brought out supplies, blankets, and clothing, packing it around the barrels and boxes. Once everything was loaded, the drivers then settled into their seats and turned the wagons around and headed back toward the main road. As they passed by William, the last wagon hit a dip on the dirt road. One of the boxes tipped over and half a dozen muskets spilled out into the back of the wagon.

William rose from his hiding place and walked back toward the cottage. As he passed along the pond, he could see Rebecca's head above the lip of the bathtub. Her eyes were closed and she looked sound asleep. He went inside the cottage to wash off the filth. He poured some water from a pitcher into a bowl, took off his shirt, and toweled off his chest and back. Rebecca's stitches had held and his wound was much better. He took off his new boots and inspected his feet. The blisters were healing. He said another silent thanks to Mr. Tweedle. He pushed back his hair and started to retie it when Rebecca came into the room, already dressed.

"Here, your hair is in knots. Hardly presentable, Lord William. Allow me." She ran her fingers through his hair and tied it back. "I fell asleep in the bath, it felt so good. I dreamed we were in New York and there were so many shops and houses. I could hear horses and wagons."

"The wagons were real. These men drove to the barn and loaded them with guns and supplies."

"How many wagons?" Rebecca asked.

"Three. And there were large barrels. Gunpowder, I think."

"Strange. Most likely Lord Pendleton is selling supplies to the Continental Army. I wonder where he gets it. Were there any soldiers?"

"No."

Just then they heard a horse from the barn let loose with a loud whinny.

"Sounds like Lady Blue," said Rebecca as she tied her hair up her hair. "I think I'll go see if she's all right, maybe brush her awhile. She gets nervous if there are a lot of strangers around."

"I think we have to head over for supper right about now."

"You go on ahead, William. I'll catch up with you in a few minutes." Rebecca put her hat on and jogged toward the barn. "Tell them I won't be long."

William walked along the circular drive toward the main house. Abraham the servant lit torches on the porch from a long taper. William climbed the steps to the massive wooden door, lifted the large brass knocker, and let it swing down with a bang. After several seconds, Mr. Able opened the door and bowed his head slightly. He held a burning taper in his hand.

"Welcome, young man. A moment please," he said formally as he lit the last candle of a large chandelier in the entrance hall. Then he reached for a velvet rope fastened to a hook on the gilded wall and hauled the chandelier up. He tied it off and tested it to make sure it was secure. "Lord Pendleton and Lady Anne are waiting in the dining room. Come with me, please."

William stepped inside. Dozens of muskets decorated the walls of the foyer. He followed Mr. Able through a large living room. Antiques and gaming tables, tufted chairs and couches filled the oak room. They passed through a door into a huge dining room. Lord Pendleton, in a formal coat, white breeches, and a ruffled shirt, stood at the end of a long, mahogany table that had many chairs around it. A crystal chandelier dangling from the ceiling lit up Lady Pendleton like a porcelain doll. Dressed in a richly ruffled tangerine dress, she sat regally at the far end, closest to the service door. Her blond wig, perfectly curled and swept up high on her head, was held in place by tangerine silk. In her delicate, manicured hand was a half-full glass of red wine.

"Please, my dear boy, come join us," Pendleton said as he adjusted his freshly powdered wig with his fingers. He then indicated William should sit with his back to the wall of windows. "Have a seat. Pour our young man a glass of Madeira." He raised his eyebrows. "Oh, you do take wine, don't you? I'm sorry, what is your name?"

"William Tuck, sir." He glanced outside the bank of windows and saw that Abraham was still outside lighting torches. "I've never tasted Madeira, actually."

Mr. Able went to the antique side bar, filled a crystal goblet, and set it down near one of the six elaborate place settings. William sat, picked up the wine, and gave it a sniff. He took a sip and let it sit on his tongue. It was sharp and bitter to the taste. "Yes, that is very good. Thank you, Lord Pendleton," he said, wanting to be polite.

"And where is your young companion?"

"Robert went to check on his horse. Lady Blue gets a bit nervous sometimes. There were a lot of wagons being loaded at the barn, so that might be the reason. He'll be here in a few minutes."

"They'll be loading wagons through the night, I'm afraid." Lord Pendleton took a long sip of Madeira.

"I was wondering about where they were going. Are they heading to Washington's camp and the Continental Army?"

"No." Pendleton leveled his eyes at William.

"Arthur," Lady Pendleton said quickly, "perhaps William would care for some of this wonderful cheese. Mr. Able, please."

"The reason I ask is…I mean," William said, struggling with how much to reveal about what he had seen, "I saw gunpowder and cases of muskets."

Arthur Pendleton stared at William for a long time and then sat at the head of the table. "My boy, the Continental Army is a sinking ship run by completely incompetent men. It's just a matter of time before this whole mess goes away and we are back to normal." He indicated the cheese Mr. Able set down for William. "Please, enjoy. It truly is the best around."

"Then where are the arms going?" William was getting a sinking feeling in the pit of his stomach.

"To General Clinton in New York, of course."

"To the redcoats? You're loyalists?"

The Pendletons sat in silence before responding. Lady Pendleton then smiled; the corners of her mouth seemed to crack her porcelain face before she spoke. "We believe in what is best for our country. We owe a lot to the King. Why not pay his taxes? They have protected us for many years," she reasoned in a clipped voice.

Lord Pendleton popped a piece of cheese into his mouth and chuckled. "The taxes I don't like much, my dear. Can't say that I do, no. But it is better to feed an army of professionals than the Yankee Doodles under that idiot George Washington, a general who hasn't really won a single battle by the way." Lord Pendleton then took out his snuffbox and injected a pinch up his aristocratic nose.

"Speaking of feeding, I am ravenous for my favorite roast," said Lady Pendleton as she picked up a silver bell and gave it a jingle. "I simply cannot wait much longer. Perhaps we should serve. Olivia!"

Immediately, a black woman in a white wig, dressed in

a black dress and white bib, entered the dining room. Her gracious smile lit up the room.

"Yes, ma'am?" she asked eagerly. "Would you like me to serve the first course now?"

"A moment, Olivia." Lord Pendleton put up his hand. "Unless my ears deceive me, I believe our guests have arrived."

"Yes, sir." Olivia turned and disappeared into the kitchen.

William heard the sound of metal and hooves, a sound he knew well. Dragoons!

"William!" Rebecca's faint cry launched William out of his chair and to the window. He pressed his face against the glass, straining to see what was going on outside. She rode into the pool of lantern light on Lady Blue with Honor's reins held tight in her fist.

"In here!" William pounded on the glass, smashing a pane with his hand. They locked eyes as she struggled to hold Honor. Unable to control both horses, she let go of Honor and reached for her pistol.

"It's a trap!" cried Rebecca. "Get out!"

"Halt!" a deep voice commanded from outside the house. The sharp crack of a musket spurred Rebecca into action. She whirled in her saddle and let loose with her pistol. Immediately she was answered by more British fire.

"William, run!" Rebecca holstered her pistol and brought out her musketoon. With one hand guiding Lady Blue, she shouldered the musketoon and fired. Then she spurred Lady Blue straight out the circular drive, leaving Honor behind.

William turned to discover that all the doors were blocked

by servants. He had no weapon, no answer. Blood dripped from his hand onto the fine, embroidered rug. He felt like he was going to faint. The room filled with four armed redcoats. Following them came the Hunter. Another man then stepped slowly into the room. He stopped and took a long look at William, his dark eyes staring from under a simple tricorn hat. There were spots of what looked like dried blood on the right side of his face. His left arm rested in a black sling. After some time, he spoke.

"You're a long way from home, Master Tuck."

William stared at his bloodied hand. There was something about the man's voice. He staggered forward and caught himself on dining table. The man smiled and painfully removed his hat and gloves and handed them to Mr. Able.

"So. We meet again, young William." He adjusted the sling on his arm and turned to Lady Pendleton. "My, what is that delicious aroma, Lady Anne? Do I detect Olivia's famous roast?"

"Finally, we can eat." Lady Anne Pendleton rang the silver bell and Olivia entered from the kitchen. "Olivia, serve please. But first, find a wrap for the boy's hand. I'll not have him bleeding all over my fine tablecloth."

"From the looks of that wound, I would prepare a hot poker. It should be cauterized. Quite painful having just had that done to me, no thanks to you." The blood-spattered traveler reached into his vest pocket. "Oh, Hunter. I believe this is yours. Two hundred in silver upon delivery." He winked at William. "The going rate for catching a courier, my boy."

"You're the schoolmaster." William stared in wonder, for the man now looked nothing like the assailant he had stabbed at Angler's Mill.

"I am a man of many disguises, Master Tuck," the man said simply. "When one roams the colonies tracking down American spies and couriers, one cannot afford to be recognized."

"I promised the Seneca Indians another six muskets to let the boys keep their heads," said the Hunter as he hefted the bag of silver. "They wanted their horses and guns."

"See to it, Sergeant. Six of the Brown Bess."

"Very good, sir. Shall we ride after the other boy?" asked the redcoat.

"Don't bother. I believe we have the one we want."

William stared at the man, who smiled smugly in return.

"Go further back, William. Think." The man held William's gaze. "Imagine me with whiskers and you just hours away from a noose."

"In Williamsburg. You're Shaw…" William's knees began to buckle. He collapsed into a chair. One of the servants began to wrap a cloth around William's bleeding hand.

"Very good." He turned to Lord Pendleton. "I believe I'll have some of that Madeira, Arthur."

"Mr. Able? Fill the glasses." Pendleton nodded to his servant. Mr. Able went to Shaw and the Hunter and handed them full goblets of wine. "The finest this side of Spain. A toast." He lifted his glass. "To the King!"

"To the King!" replied Shaw.

William's head swirled with questions as his heart sank in despair.

"I found you such a personal challenge, Master Tuck," Shaw said as he moved closer to William. "A boy escapes in the night, leaving behind a dead soldier. That immense black man disappears. And Mr. James Armistead, well, I've always had my suspicions about him. Putting two and two together, I decided you might be more than the drummer boy you appeared to be."

"You were following me all this time," said William weakly.

"Hunting, to be more precise. Captain Scroope's men missed you in Richmond. I almost caught you at Weedon's Tavern. Save for that maniacal Peter Francisco, we would have taken you there, but I did not like the idea of my head being stricken from my shoulders by that sword of his. I should have just let you ride on to Philadelphia. It would have spared me this embarrassment at Angler's Mill." He raised his wounded arm painfully. "My best man nearly lost his arm from your friend's blasted musketoon. Not to worry. We'll find him one day. It is you that I am mainly interested in."

"How did you know I was going to Philadelphia?"

"Mrs. Weedon is a very clever woman. If you were carrying something of importance, like a message from the Watchman, she would send you there."

"But James Armistead has that message," William protested.

"Perhaps." He sat and took another sip of his wine. Then he held out his glass for more. Mr. Able quickly filled it. "Perhaps not. He's a clever one, that Mr. Armistead."

"My, such intrigue," Lord Pendleton said with a snort. "You'd think we're dining with the Culper Ring itself!"

"Ha! Arthur, it is my personal mission to bring an end to that Yankee spy network. I've half succeeded. Just how many have we caught here so far, by the way?"

"Seven, I believe," answered Lord Pendleton, nodding his head in approval."

"Seven and counting. I've taken down just about everyone of import. The Americans are good, but we're just that much better now. My people are in place everywhere. Nothing gets by me or the better of me."

"The ferryman at the Susquehanna River?" William interrupted, wondering if perhaps the ferryman had told Shaw about their plans in Philadelphia. His vision began to blur. "Is he your man?"

"McCaron?" He shook his head. "A good guess, but no. I've been working on him, but he is his own man. And a strange one at that."

"Who, then?"

"Bring me the boy's boots," Shaw snapped.

The sergeant signaled to his men. Two of the redcoats went to William. One of them held him by the neck as the other soldier roughly pulled off his boots.

"Cut the heel off," ordered Shaw.

The redcoat took out his saber and sliced the heel off with a quick slash. The soldier held up the shoe for Shaw's inspection.

"Nothing, sir."

"The other one."

The dragoon cut off the heel of the second one. A piece of paper stuck out from the boot. The soldier handed it to the spy.

"Ah! There we are." Shaw studied the note and chuckled. "Mr. Tweedle has quite a sense of humor. The man plays games with me. It's a bill for his services."

"Mr. Tweedle…" William said under his breath. "He's Mrs. Weedon's most trusted man, she said."

"*Was*, Master Tuck. Was." Shaw shook his head in mock sadness. He could not keep a wry smile from creasing his face. "Mrs. Weedon is somewhat behind the times. We've had Tweedle in our pocket for months. I paid him a visit. He assured me Hunter was taking you here the long way around. I rode posthaste to this very spot. Just about killed me with this arm, but I beat you by a day. I only needed to wait for your arrival. We're not fools, you know. Now, young man, hand over the message."

William sat frozen. He knew he was finished. He sat and waited for Shaw's next move.

"It's in the vest. Cut it out," Shaw said after glancing at Tweedle's note.

The soldier reached down and pulled William's vest from his body. He then began to rip the seams apart with a knife. His face lit up as he pulled out a small almanac. He handed it to the British agent.

"Now we shall see just how bloody important the Watchman's message is and just whose side Mr. Armistead is on." Shaw studied the almanac as he held it over the flame of a candle. "Nothing. Most likely a chemical message. Sergeant, in my saddlebag is a pouch with several small bottles. Bring it to me. In a few moments, we will learn much of Master Tuck's secret mission."

"Yes, sir." The sergeant started toward the door. "What shall we do about the boy? Hang him?"

"No. I have something much better in mind." Shaw's voice turned to ice as he massaged his wounded arm. "We'll send him to hell."

William felt strong hands grab his arms and stretch them across the table. He could no longer keep his eyes open.

"Dear Lord, not on my table!" William heard Lady Pendleton say.

Suddenly a searing pain shot up William's arm. He screamed in agony. The sizzle of the burning flesh of his hand from a red-hot poker was the last sound he heard before everything went black.

13

HELL

★ ★ ★ ★ ★ ★ ★ ★ ★ ★ ★ ★ ★ ★

William was on his stomach, fighting for consciousness, trying to will his way back to life. Terrible visions of his crying mother and father, arms outstretched and unreachable, haunted him. He opened his eyes. The taste in his mouth from the foul air made his guts heave yet again. His hand and wrist, burned and blistered from the red-hot poker, throbbed unbearably. Searing pain flooded up his arm to his shoulder. He tried to fight back the nausea but found himself at the mercy of the constant rocking of his world. He weakly raised his head and looked at his surroundings. All around him were half-naked men, stripped to just their torn breeches. What clothes others had hung from their emaciated bodies as though they were scarecrows. The pitiful moans of dying prisoners that rose from the lower depths of an inhuman nightmare told him all he needed to know. He had been taken aboard a prison ship. Morning light glowed faintly through the cross of iron bars. The stench inside the black hulk was gut-wrenching. Foul odors from disease and infection, decay and death lay thick as smoke. Tubs of human excrement rested near the ladder that lead to the hatch and the deck above. Crates and boxes lay stacked in rows ten feet away from the wooden hull. Many men clung to them, sleeping. Others pressed their faces toward small holes in the hull that were covered by iron bars just to breathe fresh air. The heat created by the many hundreds of bodies was unbearable. William's face rolled back and forth on the rough flooring. There was the sound of a metal chain slapping against a bulkhead, and then sunlight poured through a hatch above.

"Rebels, turn out your dead!" commanded a voice.

William turned his head to see two redcoats with sabers standing guard beside an open hatch at the top of the ladder that led to the main deck. The starving men stirred slowly to life from hammocks and bunks. One of the men shook a body lying on the deck. It didn't move.

"Poor Peter. Been dead for days," he said as he turned over the corpse. The man had been reduced to skin and bones. His limbs were black with infection.

"Bring up the dead!" A green-uniformed guard stormed down the ladder, saber in hand. He walked among the prisoners, striking the men with the flat of his blade. Prisoners scrambled to pick up the body and take it topside, eager to escape the guard's black boot and take in fresh air.

The guard walked over to William. "Congratulations, you made it through one night." Suddenly he lashed out with his boot and kicked William in his ribs. "Get up, boy!"

William curled into a ball and tried to cover his head. "Please, sir…" He gasped for air. He looked pleadingly into the eyes of the guard. The soldier had a cloth tied over his mouth.

"Sergeant Wood to you, you little scum." He reached down and wrapped a fist around William's shirtfront. "Welcome to the HMS *Jersey*. We like to call it Hell."

"Another one here, Sergeant!" called one of the prisoners as he held up a man's head by the hair. Hollow eyes stared lifelessly from the skull. The stronger men began to move the body toward the ladder to the main deck. Suddenly the man thought to be dead lifted his hand in protest.

"Not yet, you bastard," gasped the man weakly to Sergeant Wood. The men stopped and set him down on the deck.

"You'll not curse at me, vermin." He pointed to the poor man. "This is the uniform of a King's man. One more word and I'll take your head."

"I wish you would," said the dying man.

"Bring him up. Let him see the sun for the last time." The sergeant gestured to the prisoners to bring the man topside.

A redcoat shouted from the hatch above. "There is no boat for the bodies, Sergeant Wood! We can stack them and wait or throw them overboard!"

"Toss 'em into the drink!" ordered the sergeant. "Let the tide take 'em out."

"Water," cried a prisoner lying next to William. "Water…"

"Shut your yap!" barked Sergeant Wood. "No point in giving water to a dying man. Bring up the dead from below!"

A redcoat guard walked over and opened another hatch that went to a third deck below. Instantly, more hot, wretched air of vermin-infested men permeated the middle deck. Sergeant Wood tossed prisoners out of his path and climbed the ladder to the main deck.

William, gasping for breath, propped himself up on his elbows and managed to sit up. Gone were his boots, hat, and vest. His stockings were in shreds and his shirt was torn. He reached into his pockets. Asher's knife was gone, but he still had some Continental dollars and the metal shard of his drum. His hand went to his thigh. Miraculously, Armistead's message was still sewn safely into his breeches. Mrs. Weedon, with her dummy message, had outsmarted Mr. Shaw after all. Whatever she had written must have satisfied the spy. A memory of Rebecca galloping away on Lady Blue hit him, and he hoped deep in his heart that somehow she had been able to escape.

William felt his left hand gingerly. The flesh was bubbled, but the cut from the broken windowpane was sealed, melted from the hot poker. He tried to flex his fingers, but the pain was too great. He took out his metal shard and sliced off part of his breeches above his knee. With his good hand he tried to tie the cloth around his wound.

"Prisoners on deck!" came the order from above. Several guards appeared by the hatch, sabers drawn.

All at once, the suffering patriots began to take down and store the hammocks and then shuffle toward the ladder. William, caught in the middle, dragged himself farther toward the stern of the ship to get away from the ragged mass of men. Dozens of other prisoners came from the deck below, anxious to escape the dread and find sunlight. William pressed himself against a door of a bulkhead and waited as the last man dragged himself to the top of the ladder. Just then, there was a scrape of the door behind him and he fell backward.

"I see you made it through the night," said a voice. William looked up to see a man standing in the doorway. Dressed in remnants of a patriot sailor's uniform, his graying hair was tied back neatly and he was freshly, albeit raggedly, shaved. "Let me help you with that hand." He stooped beside William and began to wrap his hand. "Stay away from Sergeant Wood if you can. He's a refugee guard, and they're the worst. Don't dare look him in the eye. 'Yes, sir; no, sir' is all you say to him. Name's Ned Mull. What's yours?"

"William Tuck."

"I saw them drag you in last night."

"You're a sailor?" replied William as Mull tied off the bandage.

"Captain of the *Hawk*. She went down under British fire two months ago. The redcoats took us off before we sank. They let us salvage our belongings and then stuck us in our new home in the gunroom." He pointed over his shoulder. William took a look inside the room and saw some men sitting on a number of bunks and crates along the hull. The prisoners looked to be in better condition than most. All were shaved and somewhat presentable. "Officers only in there. Have you been inoculated for smallpox?" Mull closed the door to the gunroom.

"Smallpox? No."

"Where are you from?"

"Virginia."

"That makes sense. They are among the last to do it down there. We better cut you and get it done today or you won't last. That's how most of the men die on this boat. That and cholera. Come with me."

Captain Mull half carried William up the ladder to the deck above and into the brilliant sunlight. Immediately, he breathed in fresh air. As his eyes adjusted, William saw red-coats standing under a canvas awning, armed with muskets and sabers, watching the prisoners exercise as they lurched from bow to stern on the deck. He looked up at the single mast of the black ship. It had been snapped in half and there were no sails. Two massive anchor chains held the boat in a harbor about a quarter mile from shore. On the opposite side of the ship, he could see British vessels sailing down river past many buildings that lay far in the distance. The HMS *Jersey* was a ghost ship going nowhere.

"We're anchored in Wallabout Bay, New York," Mull explained.

They passed several men who were struggling with a tub of human waste. They slopped the contents as they emptied it over the side of the *Jersey* and into the water, drawing more curses from the guards. Four other prisoners were sewing corpses into flea-ridden blankets. Nine bodies had been brought from the lower depths and were being readied for the outgoing tide.

"No burial detail today," said Captain Mull. "But if you ever get the chance, go ashore with the internment party. You'll get to set your foot on land, smell the earth."

The prisoners picked up the bodies and threw them overboard. One by one, the sewn-up corpses splashed into the river. Mull helped William toward the bow of the ship, near the galley.

"First mess!" shouted a voice.

"That's us. Follow me, William. His Majesty is serving."

"His Majesty?"

"The cook. Used to be a prisoner like the rest of us," said Mull. "He's been promoted more or less. He eats about as much as he serves."

A fat cook was busy chopping up the carcass of some animal with a hatchet. In front of him was a giant kettle divided by metal into two sides, burbling with seawater. Men stood by the kettle, each holding a four-foot line with a different-colored tag on one end. The prisoners stuck the rancid-looking pieces of flesh onto hooks at the other end of the lines and tossed the meat into the bubbling kettle. After a minute or so, a bell was rung and each man pulled up his morsel.

"Thank you, Majesty!" the prisoners called sarcastically to the fat cook. They hungrily stuffed the food into their mouths.

"Don't eat from the copper side. It's for cooking meat, but it's poisonous. Contaminated by saltwater," Mull explained as he held out a bowl toward the other side of the pot. The cook dished out a clump of brown meal. He handed the bowl to William.

"What is it?" William sniffed at the food.

"Mainly peas and oatmeal. Other things. If you know, you'll not eat it, but it's better than wormy bread." He nodded his head toward a man who sat banging a rock-hard bread roll on the deck. "He's trying to knock the worms out." Then he gestured to the cook's assistant who was bashing another carcass with a mallet. "They smash sheep and cow parts and mash it into the oatmeal. Looks like today it's a sheep's head."

William gagged and held back his urge to wretch. He gave the oatmeal back to Mull.

"Listen to me. You will have to eat or you will die." Mull handed the bowl to the man who was busy with his wormy biscuit. The prisoner took it gratefully. "The way to survive is to volunteer every day for the working party. You'll slave all day long, scrubbing decks, emptying slop, and burying bodies. But you'll get better meat, some fresh water, and a half-pint of rum. Trade the rum for more meat."

William looked at the mass of diseased and starving men crowded on the main deck. It was hard to believe the living hell that was now his life. It seemed to be happening to someone else. A distant clang of a ship's bell interrupted his thoughts. The prisoners began to crowd toward the larboard side of the *Jersey*. Captain Mull led William along the gangway to get a better look.

"Dame Grant!" called the men. They began to beat the

sides of the *Jersey* as a small boat, manned by two boys, oared its way closer. In the stern sat a rotund woman. Her white bib that covered a black frock blew up over her face and revealed her enormous girth. A matching scarf held her brown curly hair in place.

"Here is where you pay. If you have the means, you tell Dame Grant what you need from shore and she'll bring it—soap, tobacco, a good piece of meat. She'll even post a letter."

"Hello, my merry men!" she cried as the two boys pulled in their oars and the boat settled alongside the *Jersey*. The prisoners crowded to the platform of the gangway. "I've got three today! John Rivers, Abraham Smith, and Charles Tyler!" She held out three letters to reaching hands. Instantly, the prisoners snapped them up. Each man clutched them briefly, dearly, as if receiving news from their own loved ones. The letters were then passed to two rightful recipients. The third letter was given back to Dame Grant.

"Tyler is dead, but good for the other two," said Mull to William as they watched the scene from above.

A few prisoners began to shout orders and hand Dame Grant coins. The boys collected the money, which the woman tucked away in a box. Some of the men got too close and she pushed them back. "You know the rules! Pay first. Hard money only."

William held on to the rail, struggling to stand, and watched as Captain Mull descended the accommodation ladder. Mull held out a few coins to one of the boys. He picked up tobacco and writing paper from the woman. All about him were diseased, skinny men who, unable to purchase anything, sighed and groaned longingly. The captain tossed a few pieces of fruit to the prisoners.

"Who's the miserable young boy there, Mull?" Dame Grant asked, indicating William.

"Say hello to William Tuck, Dame." He turned and threw William an orange. William caught it with his good hand. Immediately, one of the prisoners began to plead for it. William, glancing into the pockmarked face, gave the man the orange and stepped to the side.

"A shame. So young. Younger than my boys here." She shook her head sadly. "William Tuck!"

"Yes, mum?" he replied weakly.

"I'll pray for you!" she said kindly.

"Away now with you!" came the call from above. Sergeant Wood and the Royalist guards began to beat back the prisoners with clubs and herd them to the stern of the *Jersey*. "All on deck! Walk!"

Captain Mull climbed up the ladder and took William by the elbow. He helped him away from the crowd to the side of the galley. The guards standing by the forecastle near the ship's crew and officers' quarters beat their clubs and hilts of their swords against the rails. The prisoners began to walk the deck from stern to bow, then back, lurching and limping to the beat.

"Come with me," said Mull. "We need to fix you up."

As the prisoners marched toward them, Captain Mull and William worked their way through them to the hatch.

A redcoat guard gave them a curt nod, indicating they could climb down the ladder to the center deck. There, the sick or dying had been placed in bunks while the working party scrubbed the bottom deck below.

Mull led him into the gunroom. Two officers sat on their bunks, munching on hard bread and fruit. A third man lay in his bunk. He was emaciated and barely conscious. His face and torso were covered with the smallpox rash.

"Men, meet Mr. William Tuck." Mull closed the door. Light poured through the iron bars at the stern, casting shadows of crosses on the black hull inside. "First Officer Tiddle of the *Hawk* and Captain Deacon Murphy of the *Bold*."

"Master Tuck," said Tiddle. He stuck out his hand, managing a smile. William took the hand, noting that the right side of his face was healing from smallpox. The officer looked to be in good spirits, though his ribs stuck out from his bony body.

William turned to Captain Murphy and offered his hand. "William Tuck, sir."

"Cabin boy, I expect?" Captain Murphy shook his hand briefly and then got up and opened the lid of an ornate chest that sat next to his bunk. "Ship go down? What was she?"

"I was a drummer, sir," answered William. "At Green Spring."

"Green Spring? Never heard of it." Murphy reached deep inside his chest of belongings and took out a shirt. "Well, bad luck."

Captain Mull continued to rummage around in his own

trunk. His movements were slow and deliberate as his hands lingered over the items. He briefly organized the contents and then locked the chest and hung the key around his neck. He noticed William studying him.

"I thought I had a knife somewhere." Captain Mull walked over to the sick man and gently shook his shoulder. It was hard to tell the victim's age, he was so ravaged by smallpox. "Frederick, I have young Master Tuck here." The stricken man turned his head to look at William. Small blisters covered much of his skin.

"Are you going to stick the boy?" said Frederick. "You should stick him, yes."

"Master Frederick has smallpox. See?" Mull fished in his breeches' pockets, muttered to himself, and shook his head. "Have you got something sharp, William?"

"Just this." William pulled out his metal shard.

"That'll do fine. Hold out your arm, lad." Mull took the sharp end and touched William's arm.

"No!" He quickly pulled his arm away.

"Do it, young man, or what you see will be you." Frederick gestured weakly to his own disfigured and pocked face.

"Listen to me, William. If you don't do it, you'll end up like the thousands of men who have perished on this boat. My own boy died from the pox. I'll not let it happen to you," Captain Mull said firmly.

"I don't want it!" William tried to back away, but the other men took hold of him and held him down. "Please, no!"

They stretched out his arm. Captain Mull made a small

cut on his bicep. Then he scraped some putrid matter from the open rash on the neck of the other man and wiped it on William's arm.

"Done."

"What now?" asked William, fearful of what might come.

"You'll get the pox," the captain said matter-of-factly.

★ ★ ★

"Rebels, turn out your dead!" came the call from above. The hatch opened with a bang. Morning sunlight streamed down the ladder to the center deck.

William shifted away from the crack in the black hull. For two weeks, he had protected that life-giving slice of fresh air, face pressed close to the hole. The air was precious relief from the vomit stench of the middle deck. Strength was returning to his pox-ridden body. The fever was gone, and he was no longer shaking. The rashes on his face and chest were hardening and beginning to heal. It had been his worst nightmare, but it was over. Captain Mull had saved his life, and he had survived the mild case of smallpox given to him.

"Working party!" bellowed the captain, who was to be boatswain that day. Now in charge, he motioned to William to join him. "Can you do it, William?"

William nodded and flexed his hand. It was stiff, but he could finally spread his fingers. He slowly stood and headed to the ladder to join several men who were struggling with a tub of excrement. Gagging, he helped the men haul it up the ladder and pour it over the side. When he looked up from his filthy task, he gasped. A dozen huge British warships had docked in the harbor. Rowboats were carrying supplies to and from the accommodation ladders.

"I see some life is finally returning."

William turned to the smiling face of Captain Mull.

"Barely." He nodded to his friend. "When did those ships enter the harbor?"

"Two days ago," said Mull, shaking his head sadly. He nodded toward the vast Atlantic Ocean. Eight more seventy-four-gun man-of-wars loomed under full sail, the misty sun lighting up the British flags. "It looks like something very big is about to happen. We've got nothing that will stand up to this."

William headed back down the ladder to assist with the other tubs. His mind raced as he tried to figure a way off the boat. Whatever he carried sewn into his breeches might very well play some part in the war, even at this late stage. He dug deep and threw himself into his work. When all the tubs were emptied and cleaned, they were replaced at the bottom of the deck ladders. Then he helped the sick and dying prisoners up from the lowest deck to the center deck and laid them out on the bunks. When that task was finished, William and the other men went below to swab the lower deck. Through the hours, the men talked eagerly of rum and meat, of tobacco and tea. The August heat was brutal, but William dared not drink from the kegs of putrid water on deck. He would wait for fresh water from His Majesty, the cook.

William sat down with the others of the working party and devoured his meat for the day. It was pork and somewhat edible. The sun was setting over New York as they watched Dame Grant and her boys row away from the *Jersey*, past the hulks of the warships. He knocked a hard roll on the deck to shake loose the worms, which he then flicked away with his fingers. After a quick inspection, he broke off the better parts of the bread and ate, swallowing them with tea. The rum he received he traded for more meat. His body craved sustenance, and the rum was most valuable as currency.

"Can I do the burying? Go to shore?" William asked Mull as he looked out across the water. Somewhere in the distance was the landing so spoken of by the prisoners. It was a chance to set foot on dry land and perhaps find a way off the *Jersey*.

"Rebels below!" The call came from the Sergeant Wood.

"I'll see to it. Internment detail, first thing in the morning. Get some sleep." Captain Mull patted him on the shoulder and headed down the ladder to the gunroom and disappeared through the door.

William stretched out on his vermin-infested blanket. He refused to let his situation eat him up like so many of the others. He thought of jumping over the side of the ship and swimming to freedom. It was a quarter mile to shore. Surely he could make it. But he'd heard that those who had tried before had been shot or captured. He also knew Armistead's message would not survive the saltwater. His spirits brightened with the thought of internment detail and the opportunity to walk on land. Perhaps even a chance to run for it. He pressed his face to the hole in the black hull and breathed the clean air. Somehow he was getting used to the creaks and the moans of center deck. Soon, he drifted off to sleep.

★ ★ ★

William, Captain Mull, and six other prisoners of the internment party lowered the bodies of ten men over the side of the *Jersey*, onto a boat tied to the landing at the bottom of the gangway. Master Frederick Smith was among the dead, smallpox having taken its toll. Once all the bodies had been stowed, William and the others of the burial detail began to row toward shore under the watch of four Hessian guards. It was still early morning and already terribly hot. The bodies were getting stiff from rigor mortis.

"Raise oars!" shouted one of the guards.

William and the other prisoners raised their oars as they drifted toward the dock. William stepped out of the boat onto dry land for the first time in weeks. As rubbery as his legs were, it felt good to have solid ground under him again. The guards led them to a hut where they picked up shovels and wheelbarrows. William took the feet of a dead man as another prisoner helped to place the body in a wheelbarrow. He struggled as he carted the body along the trench near the riverbank, passing half-buried corpses in shallow, sandy graves along the way. Seagulls swooped overhead, calling and squawking for food. Several of the birds landed in the sand and stood watching as William dug his shovel into the sand. Once he had the hole deep enough, he tipped the wheelbarrow and the body fell to the ground. A flap of the blanket fell open. It was Master Smith, the pock-ridden sailor who in, some way, had perhaps saved William's life.

Having known the young officer made it more difficult for William. He covered the poor man until only a hand remained. It opened to the sky as if asking for hope. Tucking the hand into the sand, he then tamped the earth around him. Satisfied that Master Smith was fully covered, William bent down and picked up a chunk of grass and dirt, inhaling the earthiness. He put it into his pocket to take to the men aboard the *Jersey*, thinking if they too sniffed it, touched it, it would ease their souls. Despair swept over him as they finished burying the corpses and walked back to the dock. Closely guarded, there was no way to run.

The internment party stowed the shovels and wheelbarrows back in the hut and then assembled in the boat to row the quarter mile back to the *Jersey*. Fifty yards down the road from the dock, a young woman, dressed in a yellow dress and bonnet, stood off to the side, speaking with several of the British soldiers. She then took a few steps in the direction of the internment party and faced them, shielding her eyes from the sun.

The prisoners sat frozen, oars in hands, as if imprinting the vision of the girl in the yellow dress. William felt as if he were struck by lightning. His heart began to beat faster. A cry nearly left his throat. It couldn't be, he thought. Then the woman lifted her bonnet for a few seconds. The brilliant red-blond hair lit up in the sun. She placed the bonnet back on her head and gave the slightest wave. It was Rebecca.

William stared at the distant shore from the railing of the *Jersey's* main deck. Rebecca was alive! How he longed to see her. He had to force himself not to jump over the side and swim to shore. She had found him, come for him.

★ ★ ★

Bing rang the bell that signaled Dame Grant's approach. William rushed to the accommodation ladder and waited as the boat edged closer, hoping for word from his friend. The two Grant boys flew into action, gathering coins and offering up the goods to the prisoners who had already climbed down and were waiting on the landing. Their hands shot out as they begged for food.

"Master Tuck!" called Dame Grant. She held up a piece of paper. "A letter from that lovely sister of yours."

"Rebecca!" William blurted out. Saying her name sent a shock through his body. He flew down the ladder and reached for the letter.

"My, she's got the Brits eating out of her hands. Quite smitten are the men." She gave William a smile. "She's been asking about you for a week. Dear Lord, we all thought the pox got you. The redcoats are much taken with her—suppers at the Iron Inn, buying her trinkets. She begged them to have me deliver this to you. She's a pistol, that one."

"Away! Prisoners below!" The order to go below decks came from Sergeant Wood.

Dame Grant gave the signal, and the boys pushed the boat away from the *Jersey*. William clutched his letter and climbed the ladder. He raced below to his space on the blanket and pressed against the iron bars to read the letter in the last light of the day. His hands shook. The seal had already been broken. No doubt the letter had been inspected by the guards for any possible information or deception before allowing it on board. Hungrily, he poured over the precious words.

My Dear William,

We all miss you so. We Wait. In each day is a Tomorrow. If only I may Trade my Life for Yours. I long for play in Father's room, our chats in State House Square. Would that we might ride together in better Tomorrows someday. Mother is well and begs you Mull over these Words. Keep them close to your Heart. "It Behooves you to Spite ill and let love leap, Ending hate will fill you, and give calm Sleep."

Your loving Sister,
Rebecca

William stared at the letter, his mind whirling with the potential information in the message. It was just a question of deciphering the code. She repeated the word *tomorrow*.

That meant something was going to happen. She mentioned riding, so she still had Lady Blue. Her father's room is where he discovered all the weapons and she explained the thirty-five code to him. He read the letter again with that in mind. The thirty-five code did not make sense. He focused on "State House Square," trying to remember what they'd talked about. They were eating the chicken then and listening to the country's leaders arguing. About what? *Of course*, he thought, *exchange!* She used the word *trade*. The delegates argued about prisoner exchange on prison boats. She was telling him there would be an exchange tomorrow. William returned to the text of the letter. Rebecca's mother was dead, so that must mean there was something in that sentence out of the ordinary. Mull. Simple. His friend, Captain Mull, was to be exchanged. He stared at the quote attributed to his mother. The words within quotations held her second message. That would be where the thirty-five code applied.

"It Behooves you to Spite ill and let love leap, Ending hate will fill you, and give calm Sleep."

h…i…d…e

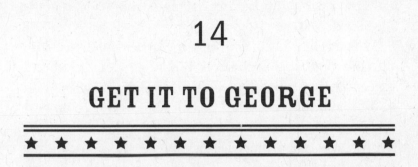

14

GET IT TO GEORGE

★ ★ ★ ★ ★ ★ ★ ★ ★ ★ ★ ★ ★ ★

William watched from the bow of the ship as a British rowboat oared its way toward them. The massive British warships lay anchored in the harbor, sails furled. The working party had begun the routine of bringing up the kegs of waste and moving the sick to the middle deck. The dead were being prepared for burial at sea by the internment party. Prisoners were sewing up the bodies in ragged blankets. They would not be going to shore this day. William knew he had only minutes if he were to succeed with his plan. It was still first mess, so all the American officers were near the copper cooking kettle, waiting for their meal. Slowly, so as not to arouse attention, he made his way toward the hatch. He shot a careful glance toward the officers' quarters. Two Hessian guards with muskets kept a careful watch on the morning ritual. Sergeant Wood stood speaking with Captain Mull and Captain Murphy. Murphy, most likely hearing the news about the exchange, gave Mull a reassuring clap on the shoulder. The Royalist guards, sabers in hand, began to move the prisoners away from the accommodation ladder as the rowboat drew closer.

William climbed quickly down the ladder and slipped into the gunroom. He shut the door behind him and breathed a sigh of relief. He was alone. Captain Mull's wooden chest sat in the middle of the room, ready for removal. He could hear the shouts of the guards, ordering the prisoners away from the hatch. William tried the lock on the chest, hoping the captain had left it open. It was locked. He reached for his metal shard and tried to bend the tip into a hook. It slipped and gashed his finger. He silently cursed and forced himself to slow down and remain calm. Ripping off a piece of his breeches, he wrapped the tip of the shard and bent the metal. Then he inserted it into the lock. He wiggled the shard in the lock until he heard it give. Voices grew louder as prisoners and guards climbed down from the main deck. William popped the lid and climbed into the chest, burying himself as best he could in Captain Mull's clothes. Just as footsteps reached the door of the gunroom, he placed the open lock on the ring that was attached to the side of the chest. Then he closed the lid, sliding his metal shard between the lid and the chest to create a small sliver of space for air, praying that Captain Mull would simply snap the lock shut. He pulled the clothes around him and held his breath, waiting in blackness.

The creak of the gunroom door preceded voices and footsteps. He felt himself being lifted briefly, but then the chest hit the floor with a jolt. He could hear Captain Mull curse while he fumbled with the heavy brass lock. There was the grating of metal and a slap of the latch. And then, the final snap of the lock. William let out a sigh of relief as he was hoisted into the air and carried by unseen hands. His head smashed painfully against the chest as he was carried roughly up the ladder to the deck above. Cries of farewell could be heard as the prisoners gave Mull a spirited send-off. Then, as the men lowered the chest down the accommodation ladder, William was tilted toward his feet until the chest hit the bottom of the rowboat hard. His head snapped back and cracked against the inside of the chest again. Finally, he heard the muffled, rhythmic calls of a British officer as the men rowed the boat toward shore. The minutes ticked by and the chest, exposed to the sun, began to heat up, making it difficult for William to breathe. William shook away fears of suffocation and thoughts of being tossed to the bottom of the sea. He had to believe that he would survive. He had faith in Rebecca, trusting that his resourceful friend would be somewhere at the other end to aid him.

"Oars up!" came the muffled call, and the boat struck the wooden landing. Once again the chest was lifted into the air by unseen hands. In a few minutes, the chest was lowered onto something and then slid sideways. More muffled voices gave way to a sudden jolt. The clip-clop of horse hooves and the rattle of wagon wheels over cobblestones shuddered through Captain Mull's wooden chest. William was sweating and his breathing was becoming labored. He was close to passing out and fought to stay conscious. The journey continued for at least fifteen minutes until, finally, the wagon came to a stop. Another voice could be heard crying out his name. A woman's!

"No, I'll not!" Captain Mull's voice raised in protest.

"Sir, please! Open the chest!" the woman answered loudly.

Rebecca! William listened as she argued and cajoled. Mull's muffled refusals were answered by Rebecca's ultimate threat.

"We have no time for this, Captain Mull! My friend William Tuck is in your trunk!" Rebecca threatened. "Do as I say or I shall blow it open!"

"William!" Mull's voice boomed. "Dear God, girl!"

William heard someone climb aboard the wagon. There was a clatter of a key in the brass lock. He could hear Captain Mull cursing and rattling the key. The lock would not open. William began to pound on the inside of the chest. He yelled Rebecca's name as loud as he could.

"Stand back!" shouted Rebecca.

William struggled to put Mull's clothes between himself and the lock. *Bang!* There was a blinding light and the smell of gunpowder as the lid was thrown open. William, gasping for air, sat up from his bed of clothes. Shielding his eyes from the sun, he saw Rebecca standing on the wagon, dressed in a yellow dress, her smoking musketoon in her hands.

"Good Lord!" exclaimed Captain Mull. He turned to the civilian driver. "Wait here."

Mull climbed to the back of the wagon, and he and Rebecca lifted William from the chest. At the last second, William reached back and picked up the piece of his drum.

"William," gushed Rebecca, smiling from ear to ear as

they helped him to the ground. William wobbled on shaky legs. Then she embraced him and held her to him, kissing his cheek over and over. "Dear William! Look at you! You've had the pox! Poor boy. And your hand!" She kissed the burn scar on his wrist and fingers.

"I'll be all right," he said. Black spots appeared before his eyes. "Water?"

"Yes, and much more than that. Come this way. We've no time to lose."

Captain Mull picked him up and carried him off the Hudson River Road to a grove of trees. In the center of the grove were massive boulders. A high-pitched whinny of a horse came from the other side of the boulders.

"That's Lady Blue," said William.

"Yes. And not just her." Rebecca had a smile on her face. "Your friend is here."

They rounded the rocks and came to a clearing. Lady Blue and Honor stood munching on some grass.

"Honor!" cried William happily. Upon seeing William, the horse tossed his head up and down in recognition.

Mull set William gently down against the rocks near Honor. William stood and took the big horse's head in his hands, stroking its muzzle.

"He wouldn't leave Lady Blue," said Rebecca, handing him a canteen of water. "Followed us the whole way."

"How did you know I was on the *Jersey*?" William gulped from the canteen. Squinting into the sun, he could see Manhattan across the Hudson River.

"When the redcoats took you from the Pendleton Estate, I hid in the woods. After they cleared out, I paid Lord Pendleton a visit. I had him at the end of my musketoon. He quickly told me about the prison boat. It took a few days to find it. I began to investigate when I met up with Dame Grant and learned there was a boy named William Tuck on board." Rebecca gestured to her rock fort. "I've been using this place for many days, looking for a way to get you out."

"Your message was perfect," said William.

"That was a brave thing you did, William," said Captain Mull. "You took quite a chance. They would have hanged you if they had caught you. How did you know of my release? I only found out early this morning."

"It's something I've been working on for some time," said Rebecca. "Word got out that General Washington was ordering more prisoner exchanges. I heard there was a certain Captain Mull in line for it and that there would be a wagon needed for transporting his belongings. It was my hope William would find a way out in the baggage." Rebecca reached into one of her saddlebags, pulled out a satchel full of food, and handed it to William. William drained the canteen of water. Then he took a hind of pork from the satchel, tore off a piece with his teeth, and chewed hungrily.

"Who told you this?" Captain Mull wondered. "How did you manage to get word aboard the ship?"

"Dame Grant had a hand in it. Cleaned myself up thanks to her and a bar of soap. I spoke with the British soldiers every day and sometimes let them buy me supper.

Suffice to say, men have their weaknesses. They'll tell more stories to a girl than a simple boy." She gave William a wink. "We can thank Catherine Weedon for that particular tactic. William, she was quite knowledgeable in ways of gathering information. She put this frilly yellow dress in my saddlebags and bade me use it. Now I shall get rid of it."

Rebecca grabbed her old clothes from her saddlebag and went behind the rocks.

William and Captain Mull sat and ate in silence. The Hudson River below was awash with activity. The huge British warships, sails now billowing, cruised before the great cluster of buildings that lined the island of Manhattan on the opposite shore. Supply boats full of British seamen rowed up and down the waterway.

"It looks like General Clinton got his wish," Captain Mull said. "There must be twenty new ships at least. We'll never stand up to the British navy without help. If Washington tries to engage, he'll lose everything."

"Will you return to battle?"

"I can't. The Brits have officially paroled me. The terms of my release state that I may never again raise arms against them. It is a point of honor," Mull said sadly.

"I need to get a message to General Washington's camp." William gulped the last of his meat and stood watching the action in the harbor. "Can you help us?"

"A message?" asked Mull.

"I'm a courier," said William simply.

"A courier! A boy your age?" Mull looked somewhat confused.

"It's a long story. Perhaps I should have told you, but I didn't know who I could trust," explained William. "I still held out hope that I would get off the ship."

"Washington is camped in Dobbs Ferry. It's—"

"Ten miles up the Hudson River, yes, I know." Rebecca appeared from behind the boulders dressed in her farm-boy attire.

"Good heavens." Captain Mull, at first startled at the sight of her, quickly added, "Yes, ten miles. He's there with General Rochambeau's army along with the light dragoons. You'll have to cross the river."

"William, can you ride?" asked Rebecca as she readied Lady Blue. Honor nodded his head up and down in excitement. "You have no boots."

"I'm a country boy. I don't need much." William grabbed Honor's reins and Mull helped him into the saddle. To William, a saddle was a luxury. He'd ride bareback if he had to.

"I had best be on my way, then. I have a driver who's been waiting quite patiently for me," Mull said as he looked down upon the massing ships. He held out his hand. "Good luck, son."

"Thank you, sir." William shook Mull's hand.

"Young lady." The captain nodded to Rebecca and then turned and walked around the boulders back to the driver.

William reached for his Virginia rifle and saw that Rebecca had loaded it along with the pistol.

"This road is crawling with redcoats," said Rebecca. "We have one final checkpoint to get through. Ready, William?"

"Straight up the river. We stop for nothing." He looked into Rebecca's eyes and nodded.

"Follow me," said Rebecca as she urged Lady Blue around the boulder and through the trees.

William guided Honor in behind Lady Blue. He set his heart and his mind for this one last leg. Weak as he was, William knew he had to succeed in his mission or die trying. A one-hour canter would take them into Washington's camp. He felt for Armistead's message. It fairly burned his thigh. Then he shortened his grip on the reins, held tight with his right hand, and leaned forward in the saddle. For good measure, he gripped a handful of Honor's mane with his burned left hand. With the Hudson River on their right and the woods on the left, they shot hell-for-leather up the road toward Dobbs Ferry.

"See any way around?" William asked as he and Rebecca hid with the horses in the woods off the river road.

"No. It looks like they've blocked off the bridge with that wagon."

For several minutes, they had scouted the creek that fed into the Hudson River. A dozen redcoats stood guarding the narrow bridge less than two hundred yards away, stoking a cook fire twenty feet off the road in the shade. One of the soldiers held a man at gunpoint while two others went through the contents of a small wagon. They smashed boxes with the butts of their Brown Bess muskets and stabbed at the contents with their bayonets.

"We could try to talk our way through," Rebecca offered.

"From the looks of how they are treating that man with his wagon, I don't think it would work. Look, they're taking his horse."

One of the redcoats unhitched the horse from the wagon and walked it over to where the soldiers had the other horses tied up. Then they roped the American's hands behind his back and sat him by the fire on a log. Several of the redcoats then set down their guns near the fire, passing plates and cups to each other, preparing for their afternoon meal.

"We should wait until they move away from the bridge to eat. Maybe they'll let their guard down," said William.

"Can you make that jump over the wagon if they don't move it?" asked Rebecca.

"Yes."

They watched for a few minutes, until every soldier had gathered to eat in the shade of the trees around the campfire. Only one soldier remained on guard, and he was stationed on the farside of the bridge. The small wagon blocked the entrance. William and Rebecca walked their horses from the cover of the trees.

"Let's not alarm them. We're just two boys on the river road. We should ride in slowly and in the open, get as close to them as we can," suggested Rebecca. "We'll have the advantage of surprise."

"Yes. And five loaded guns." William moved his hand to his rifle and lifted it slightly from its scabbard. He wanted to make sure it was free and would not get stuck. "If they go for their muskets, we can scatter them and then ride like the devil."

They closed the distance calmly. One of the redcoats looked up from his meal. He gestured to the others. They turned to look at them, but no one made a move or put down their food.

"Wave." Rebecca smiled nervously at William and gave the soldiers a casual wave of her hand.

William raised his hand and waved briefly, forcing himself to stay calm. They continued to close to fifty yards when two of the redcoats put their plates on the ground and stood to face them.

"Get ready," said Rebecca under her breath. She slowly moved her hand to the butt of her musketoon.

William reached back and felt for the stock of his rifle. "The guard on the other side of the bridge just saw us. He's got his musket ready," warned William. He could feel his blood pounding in his ears.

Suddenly, the two standing redcoats went for their muskets.

"Now!" Rebecca pulled her musketoon and kicked Lady Blue into a gallop. She fired into the center of the redcoats and then shoved the gun back into the scabbard and reached for one of her pistols. William let loose with his rifle, driving the soldiers behind the trees and logs. He sheathed the rifle and yanked his pistol from its holster on the saddle. He leveled it at one of the redcoats just as the man raised his musket. The shot went wild but caused the other man to miss as well. William holstered the gun, grabbed a handful of Honor's mane, and raced him toward the wagon a split second behind Lady Blue.

"Go, Honor!"

Rebecca fired her pistol just as she jumped Lady Blue over the wagon. Her horse skittered on the wooden bridge, and Rebecca struggled to keep them from falling as she tried to holster the empty gun. The lone guard at the end of the bridge knelt and raised his Brown Bess. With a surge of power, Honor cleared the wagon, moving in front of Lady Blue just as the guard fired. The lead ball grazed Honor across his left shoulder and drops of blood spattered William in the face. He kicked Honor straight toward the still-kneeling redcoat. Rebecca galloped behind him and fired off a shot with her second pistol. The soldier leaped to his right and rolled down the bank and into the creek. Honor and Lady Blue streaked side by side across the bridge and up the river road at a dead run.

"Are you hit?" called Rebecca, seeing the blood on William's face.

"No!" cried William. He glanced at the blood on Honor's shoulder. The gunshot didn't seem to faze the big horse. "He got Honor, but it's not bad!"

He shot a look back to the bridge. The redcoats had mounted and were riding fast behind them. "They're after us!"

"Dobbs Ferry must be a few miles more! Give it everything you have!" shouted Rebecca.

Several more musket blasts rang out. Honor flattened out his head and charged ahead of Lady Blue. They flew along the river road across the bluffs by the Hudson River, through the woods, and over the streams. Lady Blue, not a horse to give up a lead, pulled even and matched the bigger horse stride for stride. For several minutes, the British kept up. But Honor and Lady Blue had traveled far and wide with their young riders and raced together as one. William balanced perfectly in rhythm atop the sweating, heaving four-legged fury, while Rebecca kept pace on the wild, blue-eyed mare. The British soldiers lagged farther and farther behind.

William looked back over his shoulder and saw the redcoats pull up. "They're stopping!"

"William, look!" shouted Rebecca. She stood straight up in her stirrups and pointed ahead of her.

William turned in the saddle to see what she was pointing at. Immediately, his heart began to swell with joy and relief for directly in front of them, a half mile away, a formation of Rochambeau's French army stood in perfect order, bayonets glistening in the sun.

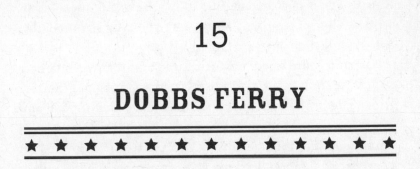

15

DOBBS FERRY

★ ★ ★ ★ ★ ★ ★ ★ ★ ★ ★ ★ ★ ★ ★

Two hours later, William and Rebecca rode slowly toward General Washington's command post. Honor's wound, a slight one, had been stitched closed by one of the French dragoons. Along the way, they had passed white tents that housed the thousands of troops gathered across the river at Dobbs Ferry. French Captain Anton Moreau, atop a battle-scarred black stallion, trotted ahead of them. Precious time spent pleading with the captain to see General Washington had finally produced an audience. Rebecca's details of William's escape from the HMS *Jersey* coupled with William's intricate description of the prison boat and the journey from Virginia had convinced the captain to take them to the heavily protected command tent.

They rode up a hill past a sea of ragged soldiers of the Continental Army. Many of the patriot soldiers did not have shoes or boots, but still they drilled to the shouted orders of commanding officers. The French infantry, in splendid green-plumed hats, the artillerists in gray coats and red velvet trim stood in marked contrast to Washington's men. Field artillery, horses, hospital tents, and cook fires dotted the countryside near the wide Hudson River.

Captain Moreau led them to a large tent that was guarded by soldiers of both armies. Six of each stood at attention on either side of the opening flap. Moreau signaled to William and Rebecca to dismount and told them to wait at a long hitching post to the side of the tent. A gray horse, covered in sweat, stood tied and drinking water from a trough. Shouting from inside the tent could be heard. William and Rebecca secured the horses to the rail and stepped toward the open flap of the tent. Peering inside, they first laid eyes on the imposing figure of General George Washington pacing angrily in front of two officers seated at a desk. One of them was looking over a piece of paper. A rough-looking man dressed in civilian clothes stood sweating and exhausted with his hat in his hands. A pleasant-looking, avuncular man in his fifties, dressed in a decorated French uniform, sat quietly in a plain wooden chair. William and Rebecca stood transfixed as they watched the most powerful man of the American Revolution stroll about the tent.

"Obviously, it's a ruse!" said General Washington. "My dear Rochambeau, it is exactly what Clinton wants! If we leave New York for the southern colonies, the British will control the entire north. We must fight him here and soon! And there is also the fact that my man in New York has it that Cornwallis and his army will move here to support Clinton."

"George, you've been adamant about that plan for years. It will not work," General Rochambeau reasoned calmly. "Twenty of Britain's largest fighting ships have sailed into the harbor. We have word General Clinton now has another fifteen hundred men at his disposal. Without Admiral de Grasse and his fleet, there is no way to match them."

"If we can get de Grasse up here with more troops and combine them with ours, it is quite possible we will succeed."

"Clearly, the dispatch says he is sailing for the Chesapeake at this very moment, my dear general," explained Rochambeau.

"And how do we know this man here, this courier, is not a spy planted by General Clinton?" Washington gestured to the exhausted man standing hat in hand. "Good man, you say you received this message last night at Newport Harbor?"

"Yes, sir," said the courier.

"And you say Admiral de Grasse had a ship deliver it in one week from the West Indies? Impossible! There was not time enough, either for the ride or the sail. I say it is false!" Washington fumed.

"A fast ship and a fast horse, sir," the man insisted.

"It does appear to be nearly impossible. And yet, the dispatch looks authentic." An older American intelligence officer said as he sat at the desk examining the message. Several small bottles of liquid were off to the side.

"My dear Captain Perrin, I ask you, can a man of your experience in espionage fake a dispatch like that?" Washington was not convinced. A long pause filled the tent. The logic of what General Washington was saying spread doubt among the officers.

"Yes."

"My point exactly."

"Excuse me, Your Excellencies." Captain Moreau stepped farther into the tent. "Another dispatch has arrived."

"From where? Who?" demanded Washington.

"A boy, General." Moreau swallowed hard. "From Virginia. William Tuck."

"A boy from Virginia?" Washington asked. "Since when do we use boys as express riders?"

"Never," answered Captain Perrin.

The French captain motioned William and Rebecca to enter the tent. William took a few steps to the center of the room. "He claims to have escaped imprisonment aboard the HMS *Jersey*. He has described the ship in its entirety. I believe his story is true."

"Dear God." Washington stood mouth agape, feet planted, and hands on his hips, staring at the battered and pockmarked young man before him. "Tell me, Master Tuck. You escaped the *Jersey*?"

"Yes, sir." William stared at his own dirty bare feet and then raised his eyes to meet the general's. Washington, dressed regally in his buff-colored breeches and blue coat with shiny brass buttons, seemed tall as a statue.

"How on earth did you manage that?" Washington looked mystified. He peered down his long, straight nose from his six-foot-two-inch height. "I don't believe anyone has ever escaped that hellhole."

"In a trunk, sir." William shook his head, incredulous at his own journey. "Just this morning."

"It was a prisoner exchange." Rebecca stepped closer to William and held his arm. "He went off in Captain Mull's belongings. I managed to smuggle a coded message, a thirty-five, on board in time with the information. William deciphered its meaning and hid in the trunk."

"It's an old code, General," offered Captain Perrin at the desk.

"The thirty-five, I know. I invented it." Washington dismissed the captain with a wave of his hand. He eyed Rebecca with a mixture of curiosity and respect. "That was very clever. And who are you, young man?"

"I…" Rebecca paused, thinking hard. After a moment, she nodded to herself. She doffed her hat and dropped her pretense of being a farm boy. "My name is Rebecca Townsend, the daughter of Lord Henry Townsend. My father is, or was, one of your men. British soldiers captured him and sent him aboard a prison ship near Yorktown. It was William who brought the message to our house. We tried to find a courier to bring it to you, but…"

"The British have hunted them all down," said William.

"Dear girl!" exclaimed General Washington.

"I did not know she was a girl, General!" stated Captain Moreau.

"Never mind that. Henry Townsend is one of the finest of

our intelligence bureau." His eyes crinkled with sympathy. "We had heard he was taken."

"Please, General. I need to…can you…" William nodded to a chair. "May I sit?"

"Well, get the boy a chair!" Washington commanded. "And bring the poor lad some water."

The French officer sitting at the table bolted up and brought over a chair and a cup of water. William sat, drank greedily, and then handed him back the empty cup.

"The message, sir. I have it here." He gestured to his breeches. "Sewn inside."

"It appears that he has had this dispatch for some time," offered Captain Moreau.

"How long?" asked Washington.

"I…I think over a month, sir." William struggled to remember just how long it had been since Green Spring.

"Who gave it to you?" General Rochambeau rose from his chair and stood next to Washington.

"James Armistead, sir. In Williamsburg." William took out his metal shard and ripped at the stitches in his breeches that held the precious message.

"Armistead!" exclaimed Rochambeau. "But he has been silent for some time. Most likely gone underground."

"Why would our most prized double agent entrust you with this?" asked Washington, suddenly suspicious. "This sounds preposterous."

"Because I brought it to him first." He pulled out the almanac and offered it to Washington. "It's covered in beeswax."

"You brought it to him?" The general took the pamphlet and examined it closely. He then handed it to the soldier at the desk, who began to remove the waxed protective paper from the almanac. "And where did you get it?"

William realized his story must have made little sense to the soldiers in the command tent. His thinking was slow and he struggled for an explanation. Then it hit him. The gold watch!

"Please, I need to get something from my saddlebag."

William limped out of the tent to where Honor was hitched to the rail. Unbuckling his saddlebag, he prayed the gold watch was still where he had put it some weeks before. He reached in, fingers searching until he felt the cold metal. It was there! Clutching the watch to his chest, he half staggered back inside.

"There was a battle at Green Spring. I was a drummer. I came upon a dying man. He handed me a letter and said to get it to James Armistead. That the war depended on it."

"Who was this man?" asked Washington.

"He called himself the Watchman, sir." William held out the gold watch. "He gave me this."

"The Watchman!" gasped Rochambeau as he examined the watch. He flipped open the gold cover. "Yes, I see it is his by the mark. It is sad to lose such a man. I've been awaiting word from him for a month. This message must be Admiral de Grasse's plan!"

"Mr. Armistead said that what was in the letter would change the war."

General Washington held the watch, weighing it in his hand as if pondering what to do with the filthy boy in front of him. After a moment, he motioned for William to sit and then walked over and stood before him.

"Please, William. Tell us everything. Start at the beginning," said the general.

As William told his story, everyone in the tent paid rapt attention to each detail. Captain Perrin cut the wax from around the almanac carefully and began to examine the contents. William went over every minute of his adventure. The French soldier scribbled furiously at the desk, writing down every word. After a few minutes, William stopped. There was not a sound from anyone. Washington stood, arms folded, gazing at his army through the flap of the tent.

Captain Perrin raised his head and cleared his throat softly.

"Well?" Washington turned to face the officer.

"It is authentic," said Captain Perrin. "James Armistead's mark is clear. In ink. You say he wrote his message, though, in lemon juice?"

"Yes, sir. It's on the inside of the last page. I saw him write it."

"That is odd." The captain lit a candle on the desk. Then he carefully held the paper above the flame so as not to burn it. "It's forming now. In one moment we shall see…yes, here it is." He took out a codebook and leafed through the pages. Every now and then he would write something down. The generals and soldiers in the room leaned forward in their chairs in anticipation of the news from America's greatest spy.

The soldier looked up and nodded his head.

"Yes?" Washington wiped the sweat from his brow with a handkerchief.

"Admiral de Grasse will sail to New York with half his fleet for the attack on Clinton!"

Washington looked sharply at the exhausted courier who stood trembling and sweating in the far corner of the tent.

"No!" General Rochambeau fell back in his chair, shocked at the news. "When?"

"The end of August." The captain set the pamphlet down and scratched his head.

Washington walked over and stood face-to-face with the courier. "Well, my friend, I will have you hanged for this. Your fast ship and fast ride with news of a different story looks to be designed to have my army leave New York and Admiral de Grasse unprotected once he arrives with half his fleet. I imagine Cornwallis and his troops will work their way here as well. That way the British destroy de Grasse and control the entire north. Very clever."

"George, wait." Rochambeau rose from his chair and poured himself a glass of water.

"Take this man into custody!" Washington ordered the men outside the tent. Two soldiers of the Continental Army rushed in and held the courier.

"Hear me, George!" Rochambeau exclaimed. Washington turned and faced the French general. "It appears the British have intercepted Armistead's message. Perhaps that is why their ships have just now arrived?"

"Yes, obviously!" he snapped. Suddenly his face softened in understanding. "I see. That would mean Armistead meant for them to take it." He motioned to the guards holding the courier. "Belay that." He turned to William. "Master Tuck?"

"Yes, sir?" William stood at attention.

"You say Armistead gave the British the Watchman's message? Did he say what that message said before he wrote his own on the almanac? Take your time, son. Think."

William closed his eyes in an effort to recall what the double agent had revealed in the barn. "I remember he was surprised, General."

"About what?" asked Rochambeau.

"It was the same as the message I brought you. That Admiral de Grasse was going to sail to New York with the French fleet and that Cornwallis and his redcoats were coming north to join Clinton. There was to be a battle here. But Mr. Armistead was positive Cornwallis and his men were going south."

"I trust James with all my heart," Washington said. "And yet, why would we and the British receive the same message?"

"Perhaps he altered the Watchman's," Rochambeau mused.

"Yes. That would make sense," Washington concurred.

"A country being born..." whispered William. Suddenly his mind jolted to life. "Sirs, I remember!"

"What, William?" General Washington turned to William and gripped his shoulders.

"The Watchman's letter was triple coded!"

"Triple coded?" asked Captain Perrin at the desk.

"Yes!" exclaimed William. "The real message was on the opposite side. That's when he said something about a country being born!"

"Perhaps Armistead has also included another message," Washington suggested quickly. "Examine the back!"

Perrin studied Armistead's message. He turned it over and waved the backside of the paper over the flame. After a few moments he shook his head. "Nothing here." Then he picked up one of the bottles on his desk and stared at it. "Master Tuck?"

"Yes, sir?"

"Did you perhaps see a bottle like this in Mr. Armistead's possession?"

"Yes, there were! Just like the ones you have!"

Perrin uncorked one of the bottles. Then he picked up a brush and began to paint the liquid over the back page of the almanac. "Invisible ink. I've got something."

"What is it, man?" Washington moved behind the decoding officer and peered at the paper.

"It's Culper Code." Captain Perrin opened a codebook and began to decipher the message.

"I would expect that of Armistead. Yes." Rochambeau went to Washington's side. His lips moved as he mumbled the code. "193 3000 635 586 38 72 739 49 711 3."

William looked over at Rebecca in anticipation as Perrin patiently scribbled on a paper and studied his codebook. After a moment, he looked up and leaned back in his chair.

"Admiral de Grasse is sailing to Yorktown to attack the British fleet." Perrin removed his glasses and wiped his forehead with a handkerchief.

"*Je savais qu'il!*" exclaimed General Rochambeau. "*Fantastique!*" The French general uncharacteristically drew Washington into a bear hug.

"Are you positive?" Washington asked as he held off the Frenchman.

"The exact translation reads, 'Fleet—three thousand troops—sail—attack British—Virginia Bay—Washington—All,'" the old soldier stated. "That would be the Chesapeake Bay at Yorktown, Virginia. The 'All' means the combined forces of the French and Continental Armies."

"When? Does he say when, my good man?" Rochambeau asked.

"According to this, it would be right about now."

"Dear God, George, this is it!" Rochambeau could barely contain his excitement. "This is the confirmation we need, this courier's word. The Watchman and Armistead. It all fits together. If Admiral de Grasse defeats the British fleet at Yorktown, we can trap and destroy Cornwallis. It would mean—"

"The end of the war. Yes." Washington stood stock-still as he absorbed the news. After a few seconds, he turned to the soldiers who held the courier's arms pinned in behind him. "Release this man."

"Yes, sir!" The two guards released the courier and took a step back.

Washington walked over to Captain Perrin at the desk and began barking orders enthusiastically.

"Assemble our fastest riders. I want them up and down the Hudson River spreading false information to the British in three hours' time," instructed Washington. "Contact the agents we have in Manhattan. Start rumors immediately of a planned attack by the Continental Army against the redcoats in New York."

"Yes, General!" Captain Perrin took his bottles of invisible ink and hurried from the tent.

General Washington then faced the other soldier who stood at attention by the desk. "Begin construction of ovens and have your men amass supplies and take them closer to the British camps. Deception is everything. We must convince General Clinton we are preparing to go against him!"

"Yes, sir!" The soldier saluted and ran from the tent.

He then grabbed Rochambeau into a bear hug and lifted him off his feet. "By heaven, we've got them!" Washington set the French general down, reached for his hand, and pumped it.

"By God, by George!" laughed Rochambeau.

"We march to Yorktown!" Washington strode to the open flap of the tent and gazed upon the thousands of soldiers under his command. "William."

"Yes, sir?" William went to the general's side.

Washington pressed the gold watch into William's hand and put a gentle hand on William's shoulder. "We must get you a drum."

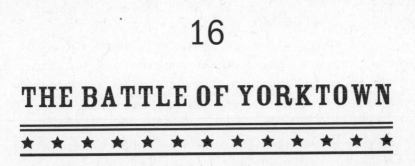

16

THE BATTLE OF YORKTOWN

★ ★ ★ ★ ★ ★ ★ ★ ★ ★ ★ ★ ★

A shell!" came the warning call. William looked up into the wet fog of the afternoon sky to see a fused bomb arch in the air and begin its deadly tumble. He held his breath as it came ever closer. Quickly, he threw down his shovel and dove behind a barrel of sand, covering his head as he pressed his body against the muddy ground. The bomb hit and stuck in the soft earth. The fuse spit and sputtered. Suddenly, the shell exploded and the earth shook. Shrapnel buzzed overhead and dirt rained all around him.

"All right, lads! Back to it now!" ordered Sergeant Joseph Martin as he paced along the American siege line. Instantly, William was on his feet along with hundreds of the sappers and miners, patriot soldiers who were charged with the task of building barriers of protection for the Continental Army. Under the direction of the French engineers, they braved the unrelenting barrage of British cannon fire as they dug into the damp earth to fill the wooden gabion baskets. Trees and branches fell under the ax as long, round fascines were constructed and dragged to build up the massive siege lines in preparation for the allied assault on Yorktown, Virginia.

William worked furiously alongside the others. Though he had been given a new drum, as well as boots, a shirt, and a blue tricorn hat, he was not content to sit safely with the other drummer boys back in his tent and wait for the call to arms. He dropped his shovel and grabbed a hatchet. Crouching behind the growing mound of the earthen siege line, he began hacking at the pile of long, thin branches used for the fascines, his muscles feeling stronger with every blow. The French labored on William's left. Behind him, several thousand patriot soldiers with muskets were hidden in the woods and ravines, ready to protect them as they strained to complete the nearly one-mile trench. Eight hundred yards ahead, the British fired salvo after salvo into the ranks of the allied soldiers.

William looked around at the grim, sweating faces and felt a growing kinship for his fellow patriots. He had gotten to know many of them in the fast three-week march south. General Washington had succeeded in his great deception. With British General Clinton expecting an assault in the north, the American and French forces had instead amassed nineteen thousand soldiers in Yorktown. Free black men as well as many slaves had been organized to fight. Admiral de Grasse, with three thousand troops, had sailed in and defeated the British fleet, sending most of their ships battered and limping back to New York. They had General Cornwallis trapped.

With the cry of "Huzzah!" General Weedon and the 3rd Virginia thundered past. One of the dragoons, adorned in a white-plumed helmet, pulled his horse to a stop and circled back. It was Rebecca.

"William!" She nudged Lady Blue to stand alongside him. "We're going after Bloody Ban!"

"General Weedon let you in?" William shouted above the din. It was well-known among the troops that Rebecca was a young woman. Try as she might, it had been difficult to convince many of the officers to let her fight. For the journey south, she had been offered cooking duties.

"The men don't mind! And, you know, I've met several other women and they don't care what anyone says. And they're as good as any of the men. Look! They've given me a saber." She touched the hilt of a small sword that dangled next to her musketoon. "This white cockade I don't much care for. General Weedon insisted. Wants to know my whereabouts at all times." She impatiently brushed the white plume on her helmet.

"I heard Tarleton was crossing the river."

"That's right. He's in Gloucester. Scroope is with him. If we can cross the river and defeat them, there'll be no way out for Cornwallis. Wish me luck. Be safe, William!" Rebecca launched Lady Blue after her fellow dragoons.

"Good luck!" He watched her gallop away. With her musketoon loaded and pistols at her side, she dashed into battle for her country.

★ ★ ★

It was three o'clock and French cannons exploded into action. Patriot soldiers were anxious to attack, but General Washington would not give the order until everything was in place. Wagons full of bombs, gunpowder, and cannonballs moved slowly through the woods along Wormley Creek. Men, horses, and oxen struggled to pull and push the cannon, mortars, and howitzers up the siege road. The British were sending everything they had. Solid cannonballs designed to bring down forts and buildings shrieked overhead, some pounding into the side of the siege line, while others bounced off the top and skipped across the field behind them. Explosions from the fuse bombs of the mortars shook the earth.

Once the cannon and ammunition wagons reached the edge of the woods, Colonel Alexander Hamilton directed them across the field and into position behind protection of the siege line. William dropped his shovel and started hefting cannonballs of solid cast iron, stacking them by the cannons. Patriot soldiers began dragging kegs of powder and placing them against the dirt hill of the siege line. Mortars were set into wooden brackets dug into the ground with their flat, round barrels pointed skyward. Men sat preparing fuses for bombs that were meant to explode in midair or lofted to wreak havoc behind the enemy perimeter. At five o'clock, the word came that General Washington would begin the American assault.

William ran to get his drum and then fell into formation with the other drummers, behind the siege line. He stood poised with his sticks, hands in position as Washington gave the signal to raise the American flag. William beat To Arms, his hands flying over his drum. General Washington struck a long match and held it to the touchhole of a huge cannon. The great siege gun answered with an earsplitting crash and sent the twenty-four-pound cannonball soaring over the British perimeter and onto the roofs of occupied Yorktown.

For five days, William beat his drum as the assault raged. Great tumbling shells from the mortar batteries were lofted over the British lines. The heavier eighteen and twenty-four pounders sent their loads far off onto the rooftops. Flashes of light were followed by the crash of wood and glass. But the British answered valiantly and General Washington could not move his army closer. He had to extend the trench and build a second siege line. If he succeeded in this, he would close to within two hundred yards of the British perimeter. Cornwallis would be crushed. British Redoubts Nine and Ten were the final obstacles standing between the patriots and victory. Hidden mortars behind these raised forts of earth were protected by a bristling abatis made of rows of sharpened stakes and fallen trees. The redoubts pounded the allies, costing them casualties with every foot of ground gained. General Washington had to take them out fast. The only question was, how?

William sat near General Lafayette among several hundred of the toughest and most battle-hardened men of the Continental Army as they drank rum and gnawed on hardtack. Mad Anthony Wayne, French drill master General

Frederick von Steuben, and Alexander Hamilton were in a heated tactical discussion.

"Bayonets!" a voice boomed.

They turned to see Peter Francisco limp into the circle lit by the campfire. The greatest soldier, barely able to walk from his old wounds, was ready for battle.

"You've heard of Forlorn Hope?" Peter Francisco said to the grim faces. "We captured the fort in minutes using this very tactic. Chop down the abatis and charge!"

"But most of your men were lost, I recall," countered French Colonel de Gimat.

"We had twenty. You have four hundred. What you must understand, my dear colonel, is that a rush of men coming at them with bayonets will panic the Brits," Francisco reasoned, nodding toward William. "William, my boy! Am I right?" Peter Francisco drew his sword and sliced the air with a loud *swoosh*. He limped over to William and put a massive hand on his shoulder. "Would you say our men running mad over the top of the redoubts like wolves might loosen the bowels of the best of King George's men?"

The soldiers turned to William. These ragged men, chosen from the best, were eager to go into battle. He wondered what he could possibly say that might satisfy the hardened looks and curious stares cast his way.

"It would put the fear of God into them," William said, swallowing his hardtack.

"I believe Mr. Francisco is correct. Bayonets!" agreed General Lafayette.

"Colonel Hamilton will lead!" General George Washington said as he emerged from the shadows into the circle. "Colonel de Gimat, I need you to stand ready with fifteen hundred of your men. Should the first wave fail, you will lead the second. Muskets loaded. Will that be satisfactory?" Washington turned to Lafayette.

"Most." Lafayette nodded in respect of his older friend. "Colonel?"

"As you say," replied de Gimat.

"Good. The French are ready and in place to advance on Redoubt Nine. We shall attack at precisely eight o'clock." Washington nodded to Alexander Hamilton. "Colonel Hamilton, prepare the men."

"Bayonets only!" cried Hamilton.

Instantly, the clang of metal rang out as the soldiers began to unload their muskets and fasten their bayonets to the barrels.

"Upon our charge, our watchword for this night will be…" Lafayette hesitated as another soldier entered the circle of fire. General Rochambeau, his round face full of admiration for the rugged American troops, went man to man, shaking hands and offering encouragement to the soldiers of the Continental Army.

"Rochambeau!" The soldiers cheered and stood for the French general. "Huzzah!"

"Yes!" cried Lafayette. "It will be Rochambeau!"

William waited breathlessly in the trench as the French mortars bombarded the two redoubts. The four hundred soldiers with bayonets and axes were crouched down, ready to sprint the deadly distance to Redoubt Ten. Suddenly the shelling stopped and everything went quiet. William clicked his drumsticks together and beat the signal to attack. Peter Francisco stood beside him and let out a great roar.

"Rochambeau!"

"Rochambeau!" went the call up and down the line. The four hundred charged Redoubt Ten. "Rush on, boys!" They scrambled up the slope, braving the barrage of lead as the British fired their muskets at the charging hoard. A mortar blasted from behind the redoubt. William threw himself into a muddy ditch as the bomb tumbled and exploded just feet away, sending shrapnel inches over his head. He struggled to his knees and grabbed his drum and continued to beat Advance. Several men went down under the redcoat muskets, but still the patriots attacked. The lead soldiers swung their axes, smashing the sharpened stakes as they broke through the deadly barrier. Bayonet-wielding Americans gained ground and began to spill over the top of the earthen redoubt into the ranks of the redcoats. Flashes from musket fire revealed the twisting fighting bodies of the soldiers as the British tried mightily to hold on to their fort. But the raging mission of the Continental soldiers was too much. Gradually, the clanging of bayonets and the battle cries of men diminished. Redcoats could be seen running for their lives back to the British perimeter defense line. In just minutes, Redoubt Ten was taken, and the British flag was hauled down and replaced by the American flag. William stopped drumming.

Thirty minutes later, the French claimed Redoubt Nine. Yorktown grew silent, but only for a while.

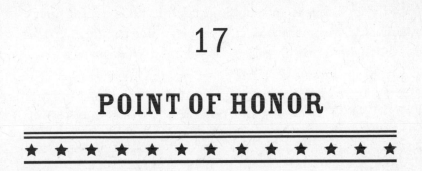

17

POINT OF HONOR

★ ★ ★ ★ ★ ★ ★ ★ ★ ★ ★ ★ ★ ★ ★

William struggled to carry the man's feet as he helped take him to the hospital tent. Blood poured from a gunshot in the soldier's leg. In the torch-lit hours before dawn, surgeons hurried from man to man, gauging the severity of each soldier's wounds before bringing them into the tent for surgery.

"Over here!" A surgeon in a bloodstained smock adjusted his wire glasses and motioned for William and the other soldier to set the man down. He then peered at the man's wound and stuck his fingers into the bullet hole. Quickly, he tied a leather strap around the leg and gestured to an area where a dozen wounded soldiers lay in a line. "Not too bad, the ball went right through. Hot tar for this one. Put him over there with the others and give him some rum." He pointed to a keg that stood near the opening of the tent.

William helped lay the wounded man at the end of the line, and then he ran to fill a cup with rum from the keg. He gave the soldier a long drink just as the surgeon came back carrying a bucket of bubbling tar. The poor man let out a moan of pain as the doctor slathered hot tar on the bullet hole with a brush, sealing the wound. "Well, that's it. He'll make it."

"There are more coming," said William.

"They'll have to lay them out here. We've got no free cots inside." The surgeon stood up and moved to the next soldier in line.

"They might have room in the other tents across the field. Shall I tell them to take the wounded there?" asked William.

"No," said the surgeon as he checked the head wound of another soldier. "That's where we keep the sick. We have to keep them separate. We just received a hundred off a prison boat and more are coming in by the hour. All smallpox and the fever."

"Prison boat!" exclaimed William, jumping to his feet.

"Poor souls have been ferried in all night." The doctor sighed.

William sprinted past the wounded soldiers toward the other end of the field. The thought that Rebecca's father might be alive filled his heart for his friend. He rushed into the largest of the hospital tents only to be stopped by the horrible stench. He knew it well. It was the same deathlike smell of human rot all too familiar from his time aboard the *Jersey*.

"You'll want to stay out of here, young man." A doctor, his face covered with a cloth, caught him by the elbow. "These men all have smallpox."

"It's all right, I've had it. I'm looking for Lord Townsend. Is it possible he came here?"

The doctor went to a small desk, picked up a ledger, and scanned the list of names in the light of a lantern. "What ship? There are three."

"I don't know."

"I know he's not in here. Check the other tents. Look through this. I've no time." He gestured to the pocked and blackened men who lay on cots and blankets along the tent floor. "Smallpox on the left. Fever on the right. The row and tent number is listed by the name." The doctor left William to fend for himself as he turned back to tend to the sick.

William went over to the desk and studied the list of names until he came to Henry Townsend. Row 7. Tent 3. He set down the ledger, grabbed the lantern, and ran outside. He darted to the left and went to the seventh row of tents. He pulled back the flap of the third one and stuck his head inside. He held up the lantern and saw four emaciated bodies lying in cots.

"Lord Townsend?" William whispered quietly as he entered the tent. One of the filthy men gestured to the cot in the far right corner. William crept to the cot. "Are you Henry Townsend?" The man did not answer. His breathing was ragged, his face ravaged by the horrible rash. It seemed only a matter of time before death would come. He had seen many cases of smallpox aboard the *Jersey*. His heart fell for Rebecca. William put his hand on the man's shoulder and said a silent prayer. Then he set the lantern by the cot, left the tent, and staggered, exhausted, to find sleep.

★ ★ ★

The thunder of the big guns echoed across the battlefield and spitting bombs lit up the night sky as men fought hand to hand. Groaning men lay writhing in pain, pierced through the chest against the bristling wooden spears of the abatis. Sabers and bayonets clashed as patriots and redcoats fell over the earthen mound of Redoubt Ten. The screaming of dying soldiers was interrupted by the loud whinny of a horse. Lady Blue appeared, crying, humanlike, for Rebecca. The familiar trumpet of Honor answered the blue-eyed horse. The lonely cries continued. Lady Blue called. Honor answered, again and again against the din of fighting men and cannon fire.

William bolted up in his cot, gasping for breath. Cold sweat dripped down his chest in the crisp October morning. He shook his head to rid himself of the nightmare. He looked around the tent at the young drummers who lay asleep on their cots. In the distance, he could hear the rumble of the big guns. Suddenly, a horse cut loose with a loud whinny. He knew that call. It was Lady Blue. William pulled on his boots and headed for the corral. Honor stood behind the fence line, bellowing like never before. Lady Blue, blood streaming down her flank, answered him, screaming for all her might as she galloped past Honor. A wounded soldier, hands grasping the reins and the pommel, clung desperately to her. The soldier raced toward William. William threw his hands in the air and Lady Blue reared up and pawed at the sky. The Virginia dragoon jerked Lady Blue in a tight circle. A saber had sliced through part of the saddle and a deep slash creased Lady Blue's flank. The dragoon gained control and spurred Lady Blue down the road toward the Maryland camp.

William knew something terrible had happened. Blood was all over Lady Blue. He raced to the tent to pick up his saddle and guns, and then sprinted outside to get Honor. After checking the rifle to make sure it was loaded, he shoved it into the scabbard. He then tucked the pistol into its holster, threw his shot bag over his shoulder, and mounted Honor. They galloped toward the fence, clearing it easily, and shot after Lady Blue.

William flew by a row of tents. Fifty yards ahead, a dozen soldiers of the Maryland Four Hundred were saddling their horses and checking their weapons. Several of the soldiers helped the wounded man off Lady Blue and laid him the ground. Just as he galloped into their midst, he heard Peter Francisco's deep bellow.

"I can't walk much, but I bloody well can ride!" The great man struggled to mount his huge horse.

William pulled Honor hard to a stop and dismounted. "Where is Rebecca?"

"She went down, William," Francisco said as he checked his musket.

"She gave her horse to me to go for help," said the wounded soldier, gasping for breath. He lay in the arms of none other than Captain John Rodgers of Rodger's Tavern. "We were in a fight with Bloody Ban. Had him penned in tight. Weedon ordered ten of us back across the river to scout and Scroope ambushed us. We're outnumbered three to one."

"Where are they now?" Captain Rodgers signaled to a soldier who then managed to corral Lady Blue and tie her to a post.

"Less than a mile on the other side of Yorktown. They won't hold out for long. Scroope and his dragoons will have them at swords in minutes!" The Virginia soldier staggered to his feet and several soldiers helped him aboard a wagon.

"Swords, then!" Peter Francisco said as he drew his great sword from its scabbard. It made a deadly hum as he sliced the air. "Time to pay Mr. Scroope a visit!"

"Four Hundred, mount!" Captain Rodgers ordered.

Instantly, the dozen veterans of the Maryland Four Hundred mounted their horses and fell into two lines.

"Good God!" cried Captain Rodgers, and he spurred his horse toward the siege road.

"What brave fellows I must this day lose!" answered the battle-hardened Marylanders as they galloped behind in formation.

"William, I know what you're thinking, lad," Francisco said as he sheathed his sword. "We'll find her. You stay here and keep yourself safe." The great soldier sped after the Four Hundred.

William ran over to inspect Lady Blue. The blood on the saddle and along her side dripped in the sand. While the gash in her flank was deep, she would be all right. He fought the pressure that built in his chest. The thought of

Rebecca wounded, lying helpless, awaiting a horrible fate, froze him with dread. He turned to see Francisco and the Four Hundred riding away.

William vaulted onto Honor's back. With the reins tight in his left hand, he gripped the black mane in his right.

"Honor! Go!"

William galloped up the siege road after the Maryland Four Hundred. Along the way, columns of militia marched toward the siege lines; companies from New York, Rhode Island, and New Jersey. From Virginia, Maryland, and Pennsylvania. He sped past shoeless men in torn breeches, hands gripping muskets, hats pulled down, all marching to the fife and drum. Honor flew up the road, closer and closer to the artillery batteries. They emerged from the canopy of the woods, William pushing Honor hard, oblivious to the cannon fire and the tumbling death from the sky. They leaped over mounds of dirt and great sunken holes created by the British guns. They soared over burned-out wagons, hooves flying over the field, past the booming American guns.

William closed the gap to fifty yards as they swept past the French line, veering closer to the edge of the burning, smoking ruins of Yorktown. The crash of cannonballs slamming onto rooftops mingled with the shouts of the British infantry as they ran through the streets, seeking cover from the allied bombardment. So fierce was the assault, the redcoats did not even notice as the Four Hundred stormed past the town. In just minutes, they had covered thousands of bloodied yards.

They raced to the far end of Yorktown and into the woods

near the river. Ahead, the crackle of musket fire and the clashing of metal urged them ever faster as they broke into a clearing. Several hundred yards ahead of them, nearly thirty redcoats on horseback swept down on seven members of the 3rd Virginia. Forced from their horses, the Americans were fighting for their lives behind a cluster of trees in the middle of the field, fending off sword blades with their muskets and sabers.

Captain Barrington Scroope, the black plume on his helmet streaking in the wind, pulled his gray horse to a stop. He barked an order and immediately his men began to reload, some drawing their sabers to prepare for a second wave of attack.

William pulled Honor into the rear of the column as Captain Rodgers signaled his men to stop.

"William!" Francisco swerved his horse close to Honor. "Stay out of this. You'll get yourself killed!"

"I can help!" William yelled back. Up ahead, he could just make out the white plume of Rebecca's helmet against the green of the pine trees. She was still alive, firing her musketoon.

"We're going in close, William. They'll cut you down in a minute! Stay here!"

"Muskets when we're in range!" ordered Captain Rodgers.

"Then pistols and sabers!" roared Peter Francisco.

"Once more, boys! Good God!" cried Captain Rodgers.

"What brave boys I must this day lose!" The Marylanders pulled their light muskets and galloped into battle just as Captain Barrington Scroope gave the order to charge with his sword.

The British dragoons swept toward the seven patriots; the muskets in front of their formation cracked as they drew near. Puffs of white exploded from the trees as the Americans answered back. The second wave of redcoats, sabers drawn, began to hack at the swords and guns of the patriots, giving them no time to reload. The battle would be over in seconds.

William watched as the Maryland Four Hundred streaked across the field, raking the ranks of the British dragoons with musket fire. Four redcoats fell instantly. Peter Francisco, his five-foot sword gleaming in the sun, slashed at the British dragoons over and over as he drove his horse into their midst. Men scattered in fear of the huge patriot. Pistols barked and two more redcoats went down under their horses. Scroope waved his saber and a dozen of his troops galloped to a safe distance to reload as others tried to keep the Americans engaged. Suddenly, the Virginia soldiers broke from the trees with their swords.

William realized Peter Francisco was right. Without a saber, he would be cut down in no time. He dismounted and tied Honor to a tree a hundred yards from the battle. Then he took his Virginia rifle and his shot bag and jogged low across the field as the blue-clad soldiers closed in on the redcoats. He knew, if pressed, having his feet on the ground would make him a better shot. Through the mass of men and horses, he could see the white plumed helmet of Rebecca. With only her empty musketoon in her hands, she swung and parried, limping badly into the fray. Her right side was streaked with blood.

Captain Scroope and his dragoons charged straight at the patriot soldiers, firing their pistols at close range. Two Marylanders went down with their horses. The redcoats holstered their pistols and drew their sabers, slashing and cutting. The fighting was hand-to-hand. Two of the 3rd Virginia fell to the ground. William's breath caught. One had a white-plumed helmet. Rebecca was down.

Scroope and his dragoons pulled away and circled their horses. This time they did not pause. With sabers drawn, they charged back to the fight. Rebecca tried to raise herself. She crawled on the ground, searching for her musketoon. Grasping it in her hands, she turned to meet the charge of Barrington Scroope.

William shoved the stock of the Virginia rifle to his shoulder as he saw Scroope charge straight at Rebecca. He struggled to hold his nerves in check and keep his hands steady as he followed Scroope's every move through the sights of the big gun. Scroope closed to within yards of Rebecca, his saber poised to take the life of his friend. As he spurred his horse and raised his sword to deliver the final blow, William fired.

Captain Barrington Scroope flew out of his saddle and crashed to the ground. At first he lay still, but then rose to his knees, blood streaming down his chest. Wounded badly, he grabbed his sword and began to crawl to the shelter of the trees. William reached into his shot bag for a cartridge and began to reload. His eyes searched for Scroope through the fighting, twisting men, through the stomping horse hooves. Rebecca tried to get to her feet but collapsed to the ground.

William ran to the edge of the battle and knelt beside his fallen friend.

"Put your arm around my neck and hold on."

"Oh God. William…" Rebecca looked at him in disbelief and clasped her arms around his neck. She pointed to her musketoon some feet away. "My musketoon."

William grabbed it and handed it to her. Then he stood up and put his free arm around her waist. Together they staggered toward the safety of the trees. A British dragoon veered his horse and sliced at William with his saber. William met the blow with his rifle and deflected the blade over his head. Peter Francisco yanked his horse close to them and brought the redcoat down with his long sword.

"Close ranks!" ordered Captain Rodgers and the members of the Maryland Four Hundred formed a circle of protection with their horses around William and Rebecca as they made their way to the trees. Without their captain, and now cut down to fifteen men still on horses, the redcoats rode some distance away to regroup.

"Had enough, boys?" Peter Francisco shook his sword at the redcoats.

"Reload!" ordered Captain Rodgers.

Immediately, the patriots loaded their guns.

William leaned Rebecca against some rocks, hidden from the battle. Her head lolled on her shoulders as she weakly reached for him.

"William. My shot bag…help me." She struggled to pull the strap over her head.

"Stay here," he said as he placed the bag by her side.

William picked up his Virginia rifle and headed to where he'd seen Scroope disappear into the trees. Creeping quietly, he came to a trail of blood that led deeper into the woods. His ears picked up the sound of metal. He held his breath as he followed the blood. Ten feet farther, he saw the broken body of Captain Scroope. Propped against a tall pine tree, the redcoat was trying desperately to load his pistol. His saber lay at his side. A stain of dark red blood was spreading across his chest.

"Do you remember me?" William asked quietly.

The British captain looked at William in disbelief as he tried to ram the ball down the pistol barrel.

William raised his rifle and pointed it at Scroope's head. "You once told me you never forget a face."

"The drummer boy." Scroope studied William in amazement. "William Tuck."

"That's right."

"You did this?" He touched his wound.

William nodded his head. Scroope stared at the blood seeping from his body. He shook his head and closed his eyes for a few long seconds.

"You have me." He replaced the short ramrod and held the pistol by his side. "I ask mercy."

"You were going to hang me. Why should I show you mercy?"

"Point of honor, boy. That was war." Scroope tried to smile, but the scar that ran down the side of his mouth forced his face into the familiar ghoulish sneer.

"You executed my brother, Asher. You could have shown him mercy, but you had him killed without a thought."

"Again. That was war." Scroope took a deep breath, wincing at the pain. "He shot my men."

"Raise your pistol. Over your head." William held the rifle rock steady as Scroope painfully raised his gun. "Pull the trigger."

Scroope pulled the trigger and the unloaded pistol clicked harmlessly in an act of surrender. His hand collapsed to his side. "My life is in your hands, William Tuck. Again, I ask. Mercy?"

William's finger rested on the trigger of Henry Townsend's Virginia rifle. A simple pull, a twitch, and the British captain would be dead. Every part of William's being wanted to kill the man. If shooting this captain could have taken away the pain, soothe the ache in his heart. If it could have healed the lonely sense of loss he held within him. And yet, William found no joy in holding the man's life in his hands. Killing him might bring some level of satisfaction, and yet it would never be enough. Scroope would be dead and the British captain would never be forced to suffer for his own terrible acts. But William knew that for a man like Scroope, there was something worse than death. If he spared him, Scroope would be forced to live it for the rest of his life. Defeat.

"Killing you now would be plain murder." William lowered his rifle an inch.

Peter Francisco limped through the trees and stood by William's side. His sword still dripped from the blood of

British dragoons. He put a hand on William's shoulder. Captain Scroope shifted uneasily as he took in the American soldier and the great sword he held in his fist.

"Point of honor, Captain Scroope," said William.

"Yes, Master Tuck?" answered the captain.

"I will let you live on one condition."

"You give me conditions?"

"Yes. You must consider yourself on parole from this moment on and never again raise your hand against my country. Return to England. Give me your word as a captain in the British Army."

"How dare you!" Scroope's face flushed with humiliation. "You're just a boy. You have no right!"

"I believe he does, Mr. Scroope." Francisco raised his sword and wiggled the blade slightly. Scroope's eyes widened at the idea of his head being struck from his shoulders.

"You asked me for mercy. These are my terms," said William. "Point of honor."

Captain Barrington Scroope seemed to fold inward. He could not bring himself to look at the twelve-year-old boy in front of him. He nodded his head. "You have my word. Point of honor."

William eased the firelock and lowered his rifle.

"Your sword, Mr. Scroope." Peter Francisco held out his hand. Scroope weakly handed his saber to Francisco by the hilt. Francisco took the sword and buried it into the tree trunk just inches over the redcoat's head. Then with a flick of his wrist, the Virginia Hercules snapped the blade and handed the broken hilt back to Scroope. "Now then, all your men have agreed that the day is ours. You and they have leave to return to your camp. Your horse awaits you. Up you go." He reached down to Scroope and yanked him to his feet. "Well done, William," said Francisco as he limped off half dragging, half marching Scroope through the trees.

William ran back to Rebecca. Her eyes were closed, but she was still breathing. He set down his rifle and bent to pick her up. Cradling her wounded body, he walked over to the patriot soldiers and horses in the field.

"Let me have her," said Captain Rodgers as he rode toward him. "We'll take her straight to the hospital tent, William."

Rodgers dismounted, took Rebecca gently from his arms, and placed her atop his own horse. He then mounted up, sitting behind her.

William turned back to get the musketoon and the rifle when he saw Peter Francisco toss Scroope onto his mount. With a slap on the horse's haunch, Francisco sent the British captain off to the waiting redcoats, who then rode back toward Yorktown in defeat. The surviving patriot soldiers placed the dead and wounded on their horses. William grabbed his rifle and musketoon and ran across the field to Honor. Mounting quickly, he galloped to Francisco's side and, together with the 3rd Virginia and the Maryland Four Hundred, headed back toward the thunder of the cannons.

18

SURRENDER FIELD

★ ★ ★ ★ ★ ★ ★ ★ ★ ★ ★ ★ ★ ★

William held back tears of relief. Holding the hand of his best friend, he had sat by Rebecca's side as the surgeon worked on her. The doctor labored through the night, managing to close the eight-inch gash with a needle and thread. True to her character, she bravely took it like a soldier. For thirty-six hours, William had tended to her every need. He had helped her drink and cleaned her face. He had fed her, whispered to her. Miraculously, she had lived. Upon receiving the news of her survival, the troops had given her a hearty, "Huzzah!" Stories would be told. In fact, she was already at it, whispering hoarsely to William how General Weedon and her fellow dragoons got the better of Colonel Banastre Tarleton.

William grabbed his drum and crouched among the thousands of French and Continental soldiers. The sound of bayonets rang up and down the line, and the men loaded their muskets and readied for the attack. The heavy cannons continued to pound the British forces. At any moment, the infantry would swarm across the field just a few hundred yards for the final assault.

The order was given. A great roar went up from thousands of troops as they prepared to storm the redcoat defenses. William clicked his drumsticks and he and the other drummers began to beat Advance but stopped when a lone British drummer suddenly appeared on a dirt mound in the center of the British defenses two hundred yards away. Small in stature and dressed in his red uniform, he stood facing them, beating his drum directly in front of the booming allied cannons. William strained to hear what the boy's signal might be, but the explosions made it impossible. Then, another British soldier, an officer, appeared next to the boy.

George Washington stalked along the siege line with his telescope. He signaled to the drummers for cease-fire. William and the other boys instantly began to beat the call and the explosions from the allied cannon stopped. An eerie silence descended on the battlefield. The only sound was from the British drummer as he beat the call to Parley.

General Washington walked over to William, touched him on the elbow, and motioned him to follow. "It seems they're asking for a conference. This may be it, my boy."

Together they climbed the dirt defenses of the American siege line and stood upon the mound as the British officer and drummer walked slowly across the battlefield and then stopped just one hundred yards away. William held his breath. In back of him, thousands of French and American soldiers, muskets lowered, stood in silence. The world seemed to stop and watch the brave young man with his drum. The redcoat officer then raised the piece of white paper.

"General Cornwallis has had enough," said General Washington as he peered through his telescope. "Answer the call, Master Tuck."

William raised his drumsticks and struck them together three times. Then, on this day of October 17, 1781, at nine o'clock in the morning, William beat the call for Parley. Yorktown had fallen.

★ ★ ★

William sat on his cot in his tent. His drum was at his side. All around him, the drummers talked excitedly about the great victory. They recounted the long procession of British soldiers marching past the ranks of patriot and French troops that lined Hampton Road. The faces of the redcoats were etched with the agonizing defeat they had suffered. Many of them had cried, humiliated, as they made their way past the Americans. Others had gone about smashing their muskets and breaking their own swords as they'd laid down their weapons at Surrender Field. Allied soldiers everywhere had sung songs of celebration.

William stared at his hand. General Washington had shaken it, thanked him for his service to his country, and given him leave to go home. It was time. William longed to see his mother, to feel her warm embrace. He had a powerful urge to help his father work the farm, dig into the earth, and plant the seeds that would yield their bounty.

A young drummer boy, his arm in a sling, lay on his cot in the corner of the tent, alone. His drum sat by him, dented and damaged from battle. William picked up his own drum and went over to him. Quietly, he set the drum next to the sleeping boy. He looked at it for a few seconds, running his hand over the skin. Then he turned to gather his saddle, guns, and belongings and headed out the tent to the corral, where Honor stood next to Lady Blue. He walked over to the valiant white horse, murmured affectionately in her ear, and softly touched her wound. Stiff thread had sewn the saber slash closed. William stroked her muzzle and looked into the deep blue eyes one final time. Lady Blue gave him one of her friendly whinnies and bent her head to the grass.

William saddled Honor, sheathed the rifle and pistol, and hung the shot bag and a canteen of water across the pommel. He stuffed a sack of hardtack and dried pork in the saddle-bag. As he rode toward the hospital, he was worried about what he might learn. He guided Honor to the end of the field until he found Lord Townsend's tent. He tied Honor to the post and took a deep breath. He had not told Rebecca about her father, fearing if her father died, the shock would set her own healing back. But now, he knew he must tell her whatever the news may be. He owed everything to his friend. He pulled back the tent flap and held it open to see inside. Only one cot was still occupied.

"Lord Townsend?" William said softly.

Slowly, the man shifted on his cot and turned to William. The disfiguring rash of smallpox covered him from his head to his chest. His tattered breeches were stained from waste, his once-expensive shirt reduced to rags.

"Don't look at me." Lord Townsend gestured weakly to William to turn away. "You had best get yourself out of here."

"It's all right, sir." William tried to reassure the man. "I've had smallpox."

"You?"

"Yes." William walked closer and pointed to the slight scarring on his own neck. "Look here."

Lord Townsend strained to look at William's neck.

"Good, then. Now let me die like the others." He shifted to face the tent wall.

"You must live, sir." William took a breath. He sorted through all the things he wanted to tell the man. "For your daughter."

Lord Townsend lay still for many seconds. Finally, his shoulders began to tremble and a soft, agonizing cry rose from his diseased body. "My daughter?"

"Rebecca, yes."

"How do you… What do you know of her?" Townsend struggled to prop himself up. He gestured to a cask of water that sat next to the cot. "Please."

"She's here, sir. In camp." William reached for a cup and dipped it. He held it while Townsend drank.

"What on earth is she doing in camp?" he asked, wiping his lips.

"She's been wounded."

"Wounded? How?"

"Fighting alongside General Weedon and the Virginia Light Dragoons," William explained. "They stopped Banastre Tarleton. She was cut by a saber, but the doctor said she'll be all right."

"A saber, you say? Dear God." Townsend stared in disbelief. "My crazy girl." His chin began to tremble as he tried to make sense of the information.

"Do you know if she has been inoculated?" asked William.

"What?"

"For smallpox, sir. Has she ever had the pox?"

"No."

"Then she must stay away from here until you are well."

"Until I am well. Yes." A new light began to pour from his blue eyes as he focused on William. "Boy? Who are you to my daughter?"

"Her friend. My name is William Tuck. I have something for you." William rose and headed out of the tent. He lifted the Virginia rifle from its scabbard and shoved the Kentucky pistol into his breeches. Grabbing the shot bag, he headed back inside. "I believe this rifle is yours."

"Where did you…?" His eyes lit up at the sight of his favorite gun. With shaking hands, he held it up and smiled. "You know, boy, Thomas Jefferson gave me this," he said proudly.

"I know, sir. I must tell you, it pulls a little to the right." He placed the pistol and shot bag on the cot.

"You don't say?" The poor man looked totally confused.

"It is a very long story, sir. Rebecca can explain things. I will tell her I found you. She needs you."

"Needs me. Yes." Townsend's hands shook as he raised the cup to his lips. "William, was she riding Lady Blue?"

"Yes, sir."

"And carrying that blasted musketoon?" A wry smile creased his pocked face.

"She always has it by her side." William smiled and headed outside.

"That's my Rebecca."

★ ★ ★

"He's alive?" Tears trickled down Rebecca's face as she clenched William's hand. Her color had improved and she was getting stronger. "Oh dear William, this is the best news."

"You won't be able to see him for a while according to the doctor."

"The smallpox, of course," she said, nodding her head. "Some of the men want to join up with Francis Marion and ride to South Carolina now that Bloody Ban has surrendered. They asked me to go with them. Isn't that grand?"

"Will you?" William had to smile. The old sparkle was returning to Rebecca's eyes.

"Dear me, no," she said through happy tears. "Father needs me now. I'll take him home. There is much to be done, repairs on the house." She reached out and touched William's arm. "Many of the militia are going home. What about you, William? Back to your farm?"

"Yes."

"When?"

"Now." He took her hand and held it. He looked at his friend. "Your hair is growing."

"Is it?" She touched the curls and laughed.

There was no sign of young Robert, William thought to himself. The farm boy was gone; the soldier of the 3rd Virginia was no more. She was the same pretty girl he'd met that morning some three months ago.

"We did something. For our country. Didn't we, William?" She searched his face with her eyes. "It's hard to believe."

"Yes, we did." William struggled with his thoughts. There was so much to say, but it was difficult to find the words.

"I will miss you so." Her emerald eyes shone as she smiled. "Will you come visit me?"

"I will. Yes," he said. "Maybe in the spring. After the planting."

"Good." She took his hand and kissed it. "Go on, then, William. Go home."

William left Rebecca's side and walked out the tent to Honor. Stepping into the stirrup, he settled into the saddle, gave the reins a gentle tug, and headed for the siege road He made his way along the battlefield; the heavy guns, still pointing at the smoking ruins of Yorktown, were silent now. Ragged men of the militia filled the road out of Yorktown. Released from service, they walked home to their farms and families, muskets and rifles on their shoulders or clutched in their hands.

For two hours, William rode under the canopy of trees and listened to the birds and the humming of the insects. The fall colors were beginning to creep into the rich green of the woods. The smell of wet bark entered his senses and the stench of gunpowder faded from memory. As he traveled through Williamsburg and turned onto Duke of Gloucester Street, he took his time, taking in the sights and the people. He passed the Governor's Palace, noting the hanging tree. The redcoats were gone. Songs of singing soldiers and the cheers of the townspeople filled the streets. A crowd of people waited in line in front of Raleigh Tavern. A man in a white wig, leaning on a cane, stood on a platform reading the Declaration of Independence. William listened for a while; then he led Honor around the side of the tavern and headed down the street. He came to the winding path near the creek and crossed the little wooden bridge to the barn where he first met James Armistead. Tristin, the gray mare, was in the stall. She greeted them with a high-pitched whinny. Honor answered with a throaty chortle of recognition. William took off the saddle, blanket, and bridle and set them in the corner near a pile of hay. The same chain that had bound his body that July night still dangled from the wall. He caught a glimpse of the little table where Armistead had sat with the Watchman's message. For several minutes, he waited, sitting on the wooden barrel. He felt as if all the things that had happened to him these last months were a dream.

Honor gave him a nudge with his nose. William felt the hot breath of the great horse on the back of his neck. He turned to him and ran his hands along the muscular body. The brown coat shivered with the touch. He led Honor into the stall by Tristin, checking that there was plenty of water and feed. Then he brought his face to Honor's nose and kissed him farewell.

William grabbed his canteen and picked up his sack of food, tossing it over his shoulder as he closed the barn door. He crossed the creek and made the turn past the Raleigh Tavern. Soldiers and civilians sang and celebrated, yet he felt he wanted no part in it. He felt distant from it all. An inner longing kept him moving as he walked slowly through the crowd and made his way down Duke of Gloucester Street, toward home.

EPILOGUE

William stood in the field and gazed upon his home. Things looked the same, and yet everything had changed. Or changed inside of him. Set against the woods, smoke trailing lazily from the chimney, the little farmhouse seemed much smaller than he remembered. His throat thickened as he thought of his parents inside. The old plow stood stuck in the earth, just where it was when he left that June day. There were no crops to be harvested. Blazes of red and gold painted the thick forest.

Slowly he made his way toward the house, his boots brushing against the tall grass. As he covered those last yards, he noticed all the work to be done, the things that needed mending. Resting his hands on the garden fence, he felt a pang of guilt, for it was clear the farm had suffered from neglect and the effects of war. Weeds appeared where vegetables once grew and the smokehouse stood empty and dark. No pork hung from the rafters. He walked as in a dream, past the henhouse where a few chickens scratched and pecked at the earth, when something made him turn his head. A tombstone stood on Asher's grave fifty feet away. It was a new marker. Carved in granite.

Here Lies
Asher Tuck
1762–1781
"He was a Hero at Cowpens"

William gazed at the stone for the longest time. Images of his hero brother drifted in and out of his mind. For a moment his eyes welled up and his chest swelled. He took a deep breath, closed his eyes, and listened to the silence. Suddenly, a wet tongue and the most powerful dog breath smeared his face. Then Bo sent up a great wail. William threw his arms around his friend and hugged him to his chest.

"William?" He heard his father's voice. "William! Martha, it's William!"

William stood and turned in the dimming light to see his father, a crutch under his right arm, stagger to the end of the porch. His mother flew from the house, hands to her face. With arms outstretched, she ran to William, nearly knocking her husband's crutch to the ground.

"Dear William!" she said again and again. He fell into her heaving chest, pressed his face to hers. Felt the tears on her cheeks.

"I'm home, Mother." As he held his mother, he noticed how frail she felt. How thin she was. He felt her heart pound with excitement. Pound with love.

"I prayed every day, every day, that you would return to

me." She held him at arm's length. "Dear me! I'm shrinking!" Then she hugged him tighter and smothered him with kisses.

"Lord, Martha, you'll crush the poor boy!" his father said, attempting to light the lantern that hung on the porch post. He stumbled and dropped his crutch. "Damn leg. Bring the lad over here!"

"All right, dear." She kissed her fingers and touched Asher's headstone. Then she led him toward the house. "My, William, you're a sight. Wash up. We'll have some supper. There isn't much. Some carrots and greens."

"That's fine, Mother." He struggled to find the words. His mind suddenly flashed back to the gruel served up on the HMS *Jersey*. Carrots and greens would indeed be just fine.

"I've left everything as it was in your room." She took his face in her hands and gently kissed his cheek. "You've still a change of clothes." Her eyes twinkled in the lantern light. They were much younger than the deeply lined face smiling before him.

"Yes. Thank you." He watched her disappear into the house.

William picked up the crutch and handed it to his father.

"Your leg. Is it from the bullet wound?" he asked as he steadied Mr. Tuck.

"It never did heal properly. I get around poorly." Mr. Tuck straightened to face him. "You've grown, William."

"Have I?" William studied the man in front of him. His father had aged in the months he'd been away. He seemed to be a shadow of himself.

"Come." He took the lantern off the hook and nodded toward William's room at the side of the house.

William opened the door to his room. The two beds were neatly made. Two sets of clothes hung on nails on the walls—one on William's side, the other on Asher's. Asher's shoes were polished and rested below.

"It's just as you left it," said Mr. Tuck. He put the lantern on the little table. "Your mother comes in here every day. She cleans and dusts. She talks to you and reads your letter." He held the parchment for William to see.

"My letter?" William asked. It seemed so long ago that he'd sat to write it. It saddened him knowing his mother suffered over him.

"It's been hard for her. To lose a son is a terrible thing. But two?" Suddenly his father sat on the edge of the table and began to weep.

"I'm sorry, Father. I'm sorry for leaving you and Mother this way." William went over and hugged his father to him. He could feel how the once-powerful broad shoulders had lost their strength.

"We've got nothing, William. I can't do much with this leg. We live off the kindness of the neighbors."

"Don't you and Mother worry." William felt the deep sobs of his father down to his very core. "I'll do the work. We'll get the farm going again."

"Thank God you're home." Mr. Tuck quickly gathered himself. He cuffed William's head playfully and looked at the letter. His lips began to move as he read it to himself. "I've read this a thousand times. Did you beat your drum?" Mr. Tuck asked.

"Yes." William closed his eyes and for a split second he was back in Yorktown, on top of the siege line with General Washington, beating Parley. There was so much to tell. In time.

Mr. Tuck placed the letter carefully on the desk, and then he grabbed his crutch and stood. As he walked out the door, he turned back.

"We'll want to hear all about it. Go ahead, wash up for supper, then."

As his father left the room, Bo sauntered in for a scratch. William sat on his bed and stroked his dog. He leaned back against the wooden wall of his room and watched the shadows on the rafters above. Closing his eyes, he could still hear the distant rumble of the cannons, the clashing of bayonets, the cries of war. Perhaps over time they would go away. Faces came to him. Faces of his friends and his enemies. Of the leaders of the country, of spies and dragoons. And Rebecca.

William gazed down at his feet, at the boots of some unknown soldier. His breeches were torn and full of holes. A patch of loose thread where the hidden message had been sewn now held nothing. The great secret had been told. The most important battle of the revolution had been won. His arms fell to his side in exhaustion. His left hand brushed the gold chain that spilled from his pocket. He brought out the Watchman's gold watch. Holding it up to the light, he gave it a gentle spin. It was a beautiful piece indeed. A new beginning.

It could be worth perhaps a horse and a cow. Maybe even a good Virginia rifle. He leaned over to put the watch on the wooden tree stump that served as a table between the two beds. As he did, he felt something against his right leg. Reaching into his pocket, he pulled out the ragged shard of his drum. He turned it over, to the painted side of the metal, and stared at the gold talon of the eagle. Clutched in the eagle's claw was the flag. The blue flag that held one word... FREEDOM.

THE HISTORY
BEHIND THE STORY

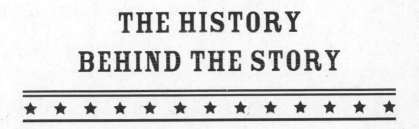

I've often wondered what it might be like for a boy, or girl, to find him or her self thrust into the middle of history, given a task so great and important as to turn the biggest events of the world. I thought about the American Revolution, about secret messages and spies, about Loyalists and Patriots. What must it have been like back then as our country was being formed? Imagine a boy finding one of those messages and having fate send him on the mission of a lifetime. I set the book a few months before the Battle of Yorktown, 1781, on a little farm by the Roanoke River in Virginia. Before I began to write the story, I wanted to take in the countryside, see the battlefields, and get a sense of the times. Ole' Joey, my dog and four-legged writing partner, had to stay home for trip, but he was there in spirit. So, I flew to Virginia, talked to historians, walked and studied the great battlefield in Yorktown, investigated Williamsburg, took pictures, and wrote notes. What a blast!

Reasons for the American Revolution

Just what were some **reasons** for the American Revolution? Over time, America's **thirteen colonies** grew tired of King George III's rule and taxes. In Great Britain's view, they needed to pass laws and tax the colonies to pay for the huge debt left over from the French and Indian War. Parliament's position was that they fought the war to protect the American subjects against the French. The colonists detested these laws and claimed that England fought the war for their own good and to expand their empire. Here are a number of acts and their descriptions, some mentioned in this book, that drove the colonists to fight for independence. The **Sugar Act** raised money from the colonists by increasing duties on sugar from the West Indies. The **Stamp Act** taxed many common items such as playing cards, dice, newspapers, and marriage licenses. The money from this was supposed to pay for America's defense. The **Currency Act** was imposed because the Parliament claimed colonial currency devalued British trade, so America was banned from issuing paper money and bills of credit. American colonists were also ordered to house and feed British soldiers when the **Quartering Act** was passed. The **Townshend Acts** taxed paper, tea, and glass. The **Intolerable Acts** outlawed town meetings, and the **Tea Act** gave the control of tea trade to the British East India Company.

People

There are lots of references to **redcoats**, **patriots**, **Whigs**, **Loyalists**, and **Tories** in *The Secret Mission of William Tuck*.

Redcoats are British soldiers. **Loyalist** is a term given to those living in the colonies who believed life was best under British rule, citizens should pay the taxes, and that the colonies would profit from trade with England. Lastly, because Parliament was so far away, there should be no colonial representation in British government. A **patriot** was someone who believed that they had rights that could not be taken away by the British government, that the taxes were taking away their property and money. They resented being ruled by a government so far away, and believed that there should be no taxation without representation. Many patriots fought in the French and Indian War and felt they had done their duty to England. A **Tory** was a term given to anyone who remained loyal to the British crown. A **Whig** stood on the side of the patriots.

Weapons of the American Revolutionary Period

The basic weapon of the war was a musket. The British soldiers, and many patriots, used the Brown Bess musket, which was a single shot, smooth bore gun, not terribly accurate, but it could also be used with a bayonet. Loading included the following steps. First pull back the firelock to half cock. Bite off the top of a paper cartridge and shake gunpowder into the pan. Shut the pan and charge the barrel with powder and a musket ball. Ram the ball down the barrel with a ramrod. Replace the ramrod; bring the musket to shoulder firelock, then poise firelock position and cock firelock. Take aim and fire. Soldiers were trained to repeat this as many as four times in one minute.

William Tuck used a Virginia **rifle**. This was also a single shot gun, but the inside of the long octagonal barrel was made so that the lead ball spun when fired, therefore making it effective from nearly three hundred yards. Back country patriots were known to be excellent shots and were often used as sharpshooters and scouts, supporting the main musket-bearing troops of the Continental Army. The redcoats greatly feared the accuracy of these rifles. The gun's main drawback was that it took one minute to load and fire a single time. Also, one could not use a bayonet with it. **Pistols** were also carried as a side arm, either in a soldier's belt, or in holsters attached to saddles of cavalrymen. Like the musket, they were single shot and loaded in a similar fashion. A soldier might carry a **sheathed knife**. William had Asher's **jackknife**, which had a blade that folded into the handle allowing the knife to be carried in a pocket. Different **cannons** were described in the book. Some **field cannons** were called twenty-four or eighteen pounders, for example, depending on the weight of the cannonball it fired. Sometimes smaller grapeshot was used against massed troops much like a giant shotgun. A **mortar** was a short, fat-barreled cannon that fired a fused **bomb** that would explode either in the air or on the ground. The bomb was lofted high in the air behind protected enemy forts or siege lines. The heavier cannons, some weighing over three thousand pounds, required a number of oxen or horses to transport it.

Siege lines were constructed at the Battle of Yorktown

by the French and Americans to protect themselves against the barrage of British cannon fire. **Miners and sappers** were men who built these dirt barricades by constructing baskets called **gabions** out of sticks. These were lined up, stacked, and filled with dirt or sand in preparation for the **fascines**, long bundled stakes that were laid out in front and back of these dirt mounds. Once the cracks and joints were filled with dirt, the mass of the siege line could withstand a cannonball attack and give the troops protection. In Yorktown, the French and patriots built the first siege line very quickly over a period of days. In order to advance closer to General Cornwallis's army, they had to build a second line. British earthen forts called **redoubts** stood in the way. These forts were circular mounds of earth and protected by rows of sharp pointed stakes called an **abatis**. Redcoats could loft mortar fire from behind them and prevent an enemy advance. In Yorktown, General George Washington ordered the redoubts to be destroyed. The American's attacked **Redoubt Ten** with four hundred men armed with only bayonets. They took the fort in just ten minutes. The French used bayonets and musket fire and won **Redoubt Nine** in about thirty minutes.

The HMS *Jersey*, nicknamed the Hell, was the most notorious British prison ship and was anchored in Wallabout Bay in New York. During the Revolutionary War, the patriots lost over 4,435 soldiers in battle. However, because of the terrible conditions over 11,000 lost their lives to disease or starvation aboard the prison ships. Green-coated **Refugee Guards** were particularly cruel toward patriot prisoners. The *Jersey* was truly hell on earth, many men dying each day. Prisoner exchange was rare, but there is a documented case of a young boy escaping in an officer's chest of belongings during one such exchange. In all, 8,000 prisoners had been confined over a period of years aboard the ship.

Medicine and Disease

There was little knowledge of germs and medical instruments were not kept very clean or sterile. **Smallpox** was rampant during the American Revolution, and many people, including Native Americans, died from it. Methods of dealing with the disease were **inoculation**, which was what George Washington ordered the Continental Army to do, or confinement of the ill. The southern colonies were the last to **vaccinate**. This process was simply to give a mild case of smallpox to a healthy person by scratching the arm with infected matter, which caused the disease, and then hope that person survived. If he did, then his chances of dying from it were greatly reduced. It was suspected that the British used smallpox as a sort of germ warfare by placing infected people into enemy camps. **Dysentery** was common, and soldiers, especially prisoners of war aboard ships, were often covered with **lice**. **Cholera** was caused by contaminated water. One method for dealing with this disease, as well as many other ailments ranging from headaches to dysentery, was **bloodletting**. The theory was that bad blood had to be let out of the body and replaced by new blood. Too much bloodletting and the patient would die. The **fever**, or **malaria** as we know it, was another common ailment that took many lives. During the colonial period, it was believed the fever was caused by bad air, not transmitted by mosquitoes. The solution was to cleanse the air with smoke. This was actually somewhat effective in that, in ignorance, the process drove the mosquitoes away. **Limb amputations and battlefield surgery** took place often. When a bullet wound was deemed to be too serious, the victim would be given rum and held down while the field surgeon sawed off the leg or arm. The stump would be clamped and arteries sewn shut. The cut was then sealed with hot tar or cauterized with a red-hot poker. The operation was done quickly, sometimes in as little as forty-five seconds. A method called **trephining**, drilling a hole in a bone or the skull with a corkscrew-like saw, was done to relieve blood clots and pressure. Another instrument vital to the field doctor was the **extractor** to remove musket balls. Because these procedures were incredibly painful, **bite sticks** made out of leather or wood were used by the patient so he would not cry out or bite his tongue.

Historical Figures

Historical figures mentioned in this book are many. **General George Washington**, named the father of our country, was a **Virginian** who fought during the **French and Indian War** and was chosen by the **Second Continental Congress** to head the **Continental Army** against the British. In spite of being out fought and outmanned by superior British forces, he was a good leader and held the patriots together. His two major victories at Saratoga and Yorktown were vital in winning the Revolutionary War. **French General Rochambeau** became a great ally to the **patriot** cause and ultimately a friend of Washington's. Though they differed in war strategy, Washington believing the war would be best won defeating British **General Clinton** in New York whereas Rochambeau believed the Chesapeake to be key, they banded together when it was learned **French Admiral de Grasse** and his fleet were sailing to **Yorktown, Virginia** to attack the British there commanded by redcoat **General Cornwallis**. **General Marquis de Lafayette**, a dashing young French aristocrat, became Washington's loyal friend and a most able soldier. He greatly admired General Washington and was given a command of American forces. Among his responsibilities was to try to control the fighting in the south where General Cornwallis and the notorious British **Colonel Banastre Tarleton** were wreaking havoc. **General "Mad" Anthony Wayne**, patriot commander of the Pennsylvania Line, was a seasoned leader who was known for his audacious war tactics. He had the reputation of ordering his troops to attack with only bayonets when confronted with superior numbers. He was instructed to fight alongside Lafayette in the southern colonies to combat Cornwallis and Tarleton. **General George Weedon,** leader of the **3rd Virginia**, was a patriot commander who resigned his commission in a dispute with Congress over his seniority. He opened up **Weedon's Tavern** in Fredericksburg, Virginia. Thomas Jefferson requested that he head up Virginia's **militia**. His contribution during the

Battle of Yorktown was vital in that he contained Colonel Tarleton in Gloucester across the bay and cut off any retreat by Cornwallis. The **Maryland Four Hundred** was the cream of the crop of the **Maryland Line**, thought to be among the best troops of the Continental Army. These brave soldiers were ordered by General Washington to remain behind to cover a bloody retreat during the **Battle of Long Island**. Barely a dozen of these soldiers survived the battle, but they were able to hold off the overwhelming British numbers and allow Washington to escape with his army intact. **Peter Francisco** was known as America's greatest soldier. Nicknamed the Virginia Hercules because of his massive physique, he participated in many battles and showed tremendous bravery. Legend has it he once picked up a cannon weighing over a thousand pounds and carried it off a battlefield on his shoulders. His most famous fight was at **Ward's Tavern** where he took on eleven of Bloody Ban Tarleton's soldiers by himself, killing several redcoats and driving off the others. Though present at Yorktown, his many injuries prevented him from fighting. Briefly mentioned in this book was **Captain Peter Harris**, an actual Catawba Indian. Though most **Native Americans** sided with the British who had promised them the colonies would not expand to the west, Harris fought with the patriots.

Taverns, Couriers, and Spies!

Sometimes called **ordinaries**, taverns were very much an essential part of colonial life. They were meeting places for social gatherings, political discussion, and sometimes a sanctuary for reading or writing. Letters could be posted, newspapers were read aloud, and crop prices and trade were discussed. Taverns had rooms available for lodging, linked the rural communities up and down the colonies, and were often a nest for spies. Patriots spied on loyalists. British agents infiltrated these ordinaries to spy on Americans. **The Raleigh**, **Ward's**, **Spencer's**, **Weedon's**, and **Rodger's**, all mentioned in this book were actual taverns of the times. General Washington needed to use every means possible to deal with the superior redcoat forces in New York and the colonies. The **Culper Spy Ring**, masterminded by **Benjamin Tallmadge**, was the most successful. An intricate book of secret codes and symbols was used to write information that was carried by **couriers** on horseback up and down the Post Road from South Carolina to Boston Harbor. Fast riders could make the trip from the Carolinas to New York in a matter of days. Many of these secret messages were written in **invisible ink**, which were then made visible with certain chemicals when they reached their destination. A less effective means was to write invisible messages in **lemon juice**, which could eventually be seen when the paper was held over a flame. **The 35 code** is a name given in this book for a hidden message that lies within the visible text of a letter. The secret was spelled out using the third letter of each word containing at least five letters. Some codes were simple, others more inventive. Communications were hidden in food, shoes, clothing, pens, or other common items. Troop movements were sometimes even signaled by women with different colored laundry, which they hung on a clothesline. British and American agents often planted false messages and dispatches. It was risky to spy for either side if caught. Punishment was often death by hanging, the fate met by **Nathan Hale**. The most famous patriot spy, a double agent and former slave named **James Armistead**, would manufacture information and give it to the British. He would include just enough real secrets to convince the redcoats of his loyalty to them, but he was most definitely on the American side of the war. Many historians have credited his service as one of the major reasons the Americans were victorious. Having won his freedom, he changed his last name to Lafayette out of his admiration for the French general.

The Continental Army

The Continental Army was established by America's governing body, the **Continental Congress**, in 1775, and commanded by George Washington. Initially a ragtag and underfunded army, they eventually received European type training in order to compete with the highly professional **redcoat** soldiers. The British army was the most powerful in the world and their warships dominated the seas. Without help from the **French** fleet and military it is most likely America would never have gained her freedom. The Continental Army's purpose was to consolidate the soldiers of all thirteen colonies in order to fight against the redcoats. Each colony had a **militia** that was made up of citizens who were able and at least sixteen years old. By and large they were unskilled, untrained soldiers who provided their own muskets or rifles. Often dressed in farm clothes or hunting shirts, they were used to add support to the Continental Army. Gradually, the army became increasingly effective by using different war tactics, hit and run attacks, and spies and was expanded to about 17,000 men at one time. About a quarter of the soldiers serving in the militia were **minutemen**. These younger, fit fighters could travel quickly and respond to more immediate war threats. Young boys not old enough to fight were used as **drummers**. A number of **women** disguised themselves as men to fight in the Continental Army. Some were later recognized and given pensions for their service. When a prisoner of war was returned to either side, he was usually forced to agree to being **paroled** and could not fight again. A **dragoon** was a light cavalry soldier and was armed with a musket, sword, and pistol. **German Hessians** made up about a quarter of all British forces that fought during the American Revolution. These soldiers were hired out as mercenaries by German princes to aid King George III against the patriots.

Slavery

Slavery was established long before the Revolutionary War and was thought crucial to the economy of the colonies, especially in the south. The slave population grew to over a half million. Their duties were to tend the crops, cook, clean, take care of their masters' children, and other chores. Some were treated very well and considered members of the family. Others were bought and sold like livestock, were horribly disciplined, tortured, and even killed. It was forbidden by many whites, especially in the south where there were more slaves, to allow them to learn to read and write. If caught doing this, a slave might be whipped. It is difficult to imagine that the founding fathers, who so believed in freedom, pronouncing that all men were created equal, would condone the institution and even own slaves. The main reason they skirted the issue while drawing up the **Declaration of Independence** was to bring the southern colonies into a solid central government. George Washington, Thomas Jefferson, Benjamin Franklin, and many more notables abhorred the concept of slavery, and yet they owned them, eventually setting them free. The British, fearing the patriots would organize the slaves to fight against them, proclaimed that any slave who fought on their side would be set free after the war. In fact, 10,000 slaves were indeed freed and moved to Canada, Britain, and Jamaica. Some of the colonies, like Virginia, granted freedom to about 5,000 black people that fought with the Continental Army. A significant number of slaves fought at Yorktown on both sides. Many returned to the plantations and their previous lives after the war.

The Siege of Yorktown

The Siege of Yorktown was the last significant battle of the American Revolutionary War. General Washington and Rochambeau, after receiving word that French Admiral de Grasse and his fleet were heading to fight the British navy in the Chesapeake Bay, planned an elaborate ruse to make

British General Clinton think an attack was coming in New York. In just three weeks, they moved 19,000 troops, made up of the Continental Army, French, militia, black free men, and slaves, south along the Chesapeake Bay and set up camp near Yorktown. On October 6, under heavy cannon fire from the British, they began to build siege lines in preparation for the attack against redcoat General Cornwallis. Admiral de Grasse had already defeated the British fleet and succeeded in cutting off Cornwallis and his army of 7,200 redcoats. On October 9, the French and Americans had their own cannons in place and began to return fire from behind the protection of the siege lines. After a relentless attack that lasted several days, Washington ordered the destruction of Redoubts Nine and Ten in order to advance closer to British defenses. Thoroughly beaten, Cornwallis surrendered on October 19, a major defeat that virtually ended the Revolutionary War.

The Route

The story of William Tuck begins in June of 1781 on a little farm near the **Roanoke River** in southern Virginia near the border of North Carolina. Many of these 100-acre farms grew **tobacco** as their main cash crop, along with fruits or vegetables for personal consumption. Pigs and chickens were commonly raised. Small wooden outbuildings used as **cookhouses** or **smokehouses** were usually built away from the main house. William's brother Asher is executed by British **procurement troops**. During the war, the redcoats raided farms to take livestock to supply their army, often destroying what they left behind. Not old enough to fight, William vows to avenge his brother's death by becoming a drummer in the **Continental Army**. He leaves the farm in the middle of the night in search of **French General Lafayette**'s army to join up, which had been sent by **General Washington** to fight against **British General Cornwallis** and the notorious **Colonel Banastre Tarleton** who were rampaging through the southern colonies. After searching for two weeks, William crosses the James River farther north in Virginia and takes a **pig trail** through a swamp and nearly drowns. **Patriot Light Dragoons**, cavalry soldiers, pick him up and take him to camp where he is patched up and given a post as a drummer boy. General Lafayette and **General "Mad" Anthony Wayne** receive information that General Cornwallis has left Williamsburg and is crossing the James River to the south. The patriot army marches to the **Green Spring Plantation**, which was located just miles from the first American settlement of **Jamestown**, in order to surprise the British with an attack. William finds himself drumming in the middle of the **Battle of Green Spring**, and is knocked unconscious and nearly killed when Cornwallis springs a trap and counterattacks.

A dying courier gives William a **gold watch** to prove the authenticity of a **secret message** that could change the outcome of the war. He is told to take the message to the Raleigh Tavern in **Williamsburg**. William makes his way through the woods and swamps fifteen miles to Williamsburg and finds the Raleigh Tavern. Williamsburg, the former capital of the colony of Virginia, was under control of the British governor **Lord Dunmore**. It was a center of political events that lead up to the revolution until the capital was moved to Richmond in 1780. The Raleigh Tavern served as an important meeting place during the revolution where the **House of Burgesses** once convened and was a frequent rendezvous of notables like **Thomas Jefferson** and **Patrick Henry**. William is taken to **James Armistead**, a former slave, who was also a double agent working for the patriots. The same British captain that executed his brother captures William. He escapes and is given a horse to take the secret message to Lord Townsend six miles north. He rides past **Spencer's Ordinary** and sees the horrible evidence of destruction from British procurement troops. William finds the burned-out Townsend plantation only to learn from his daughter Rebecca that Lord Townsend has been taken prisoner by redcoats. William and Rebecca decide to ride fifty miles to Richmond to find a courier to take the message to George Washington. Along the way, they witness a horrible scene of a slave that **overseers**, men in charge of slaves on plantations, are preparing to **hook**. Hooking was a form of execution, like hanging, where a man is hauled up on a rope by a large hook stuck through his belly. They manage to save the slave and escape pursuit through the swamps, cross the Chickahominy River. In two days, they make it to **Richmond**, which had been nearly destroyed by the patriot traitor **Benedict Arnold**. Richmond was the home of **St. John's Church** where **Patrick Henry** gave his famous **"Give me liberty or give me death!"** speech. This famous

speech was instrumental in convincing Virginia to partici-
pate in the Continental Congress. Using a map with coded
information, they discover the whereabouts of a patriot spy
only to find that he has been hung. During the revolution,
both sides hunted the spies and couriers of the other. William
and Rebecca are nearly captured and are chased by redcoats
up the Post Road north. Legendary soldier **Peter Francisco**
saves the day. Known as America's greatest soldier, he defeats
the British troops, and the three of them ride north over
fifty miles to **Fredericksburg**. In Fredericksburg they find
Weedon's Tavern, operated by **General George Weedon**, a
former patriot commander who opted out of the war and
opened a tavern. Though Fredericksburg had not been
destroyed to the extent of Richmond, the British were determined to level just about everything in their path in their
southern campaign. **Colonel Banastre Tarleton** attempted
to capture **Thomas Jefferson**. He blew up munitions facto-
ries, and raided and burned farms, businesses, and churches.
William and Rebecca continue north under the protection of
the 3rd Virginia toward Baltimore with the secret message.

Ninety miles and several days later they make it to
Baltimore, a harbor controlled by the patriots. There were
many rich tobacco plantations in Maryland, loyalist and
patriot alike. No major battles were fought in Maryland, but
it was home to some of the best patriot soldiers of the war
called the **Maryland Line**. Baltimore served as a temporary
capital during the early part of the war after the British had
captured Philadelphia. Its harbor was a depot for supplies

for the Continental Army. After another near capture by British agents who were tracking them, William and Rebecca rode toward Philadelphia, stopping first at **Rodger's Tavern**. **Colonel John Rodgers** was a very effective commander of the **5th Maryland**. His tavern near the **Chesapeake Bay** served also a depot for a ferry that moved supplies across the one-mile expanse of the Susquehanna River. At the tavern, William meets up with some surviving members of the **Maryland Four Hundred**, the company of brave soldiers who held off tremendous numbers of redcoats to enable George Washington's retreat at the **Battle of Long Island**.

Crossing the river, they ride to Philadelphia to find a patriot spy to help them in their journey. He instructs them to wait for word at the **State House**, or **Independence Hall**. There they witness a discussion about **prison ships** and **prisoner exchange** between members of the **Second Continental Congress**, **the governing body** that had **adopted the Declaration of Independence**, served the thirteen colonies, and managed the war effort. Two of the delegates at this meeting were **Samuel Adams** and **James Madison**. From **Philadelphia**, William and Rebecca ride for several days in the company of a guide through the forests and along the roads and deer trails, past **Valley Forge**, the campgrounds of the starving and diseased Continental Army in the winter of 1778. They continue toward New York and end up at the massive estate of loyalists who were supplying the British with arms and food. William is captured and taken aboard the **HMS** *Jersey*, the war's most horrendous **redcoat prison ship** that was docked in **New York's Wallabout Bay**. Thousands of patriot soldiers died aboard these ships from starvation, disease, and abuse. William manages to escape in a trunk with the help of Rebecca and they gallop the remaining distance along the Hudson River to General Washington's headquarters at **Dobbs Ferry**. In all, they traveled over four hundred miles in just over five weeks. In August of 1781, Washington and **French General Rochambeau**, planning to fight redcoat General Clinton in New York, received a message from a courier who galloped through the night with news that French Admiral de Grasse was sailing to the Chesapeake Bay with his fleet and 3,000 troops to fight Cornwallis at Yorktown. Historians tell us that Washington may have first believed that this was a **false message** sent to camp by the British to get him to abandon New York. It was debated that a ship from the West Indies delivering the message to Rhode Island could not possibly have made the voyage in one week. He needed some kind of confirmation. William and Rebecca deliver the secret message containing the admiral's original plans, and thus convince General Washington to take his army to Yorktown and trap the British there.

The French and Continental Armies quickly head south the four hundred miles through Philadelphia and down the Chesapeake Bay and, after a short stay to organize in Williamsburg, prepare to do battle against General Cornwallis in Yorktown. The patriot and French combined forces defeat Cornwallis and Tarleton in what was the last major battle of the American Revolution.

ACKNOWLEDGMENTS

I'd like to thank the following people and organizations that helped me along the way with this book.

The dedicated historians and all the folks who are so committed to their work in Williamsburg and Yorktown, Virginia. They made my visit there a spectacular learning experience.

The National Park Service rangers of Yorktown for their enthusiasm in answering so many of my questions.

My agent, Adriana Dominguez, for her skilled and caring guidance.

Steve Geck, and the entire Sourcebooks team for helping to hammer this book into shape.

My manager, Marilyn R. Atlas, for all her positive reinforcement through the years.

My family and friends for their unwavering support.

The Hornsby House Inn in Yorktown for providing a most special stay while I researched this book.

The MPIBA for gracing my first novel, The Last Ride of Caleb O'Toole, with their Reading The West Book Award.

Teachers, booksellers, and librarians everywhere for keeping the flame lit.

The organization Kids Need To Read, and all who contributed, for teaming up with me in a special project to provide books for children who so desperately need them.

ABOUT THE AUTHOR

Eric Pierpoint is a professional actor of stage, screen, and television. He has appeared in a great many of your favorite shows from the recent *Hart of Dixie* and *Parks and Recreation* to old nuggets like *Hill Street Blues*, *Fame*, *Star Trek*, *Alien Nation*, *Liar Liar*, *The World's Fastest Indian*, and *Holes*.

Photo by: Sue Ganz/Sue Ganz Photography

Born in Redlands, California, he was raised in Washington, DC, where he studied classical theater. After a stint in New York, he moved to Los Angeles in the mid-eighties and now lives in the rustic hills of nearby Topanga among the owls, crickets, coyotes, and rattlesnakes, a place he likes to just put his feet up, watch the hawks circling overhead, and write.

Visit him and learn more at www.ericpierpoint.nct.